ALSO BY NATALIE WRIGHT

EMILY'S TRIAL: BOOK 2 OF THE
AKASHA CHRONICLES

THE AKASHA CHRONICLES

BOOK 1

EMILY'S HOUSE

Natalie Wright

EMILY'S HOUSE
Copyright © 2011, 2013 by Natalie Wright
First Edition Published by Boadicea Press 2011.
For any questions about the novel or the author, please refer to contact details at:
http://www.NatalieWrightsYA.blogspot.com

Book Cover Art copyright © Phatpuppy Art
Book Cover Design © Cheryl Perez

Edition: October, 2013
ISBN: 0615560628
ISBN-13: 978-0615560625

For Sarah.

CONTENTS

PRONUNCIATION GUIDE

Readers may find this pronunciation guide useful for reference while reading *Emily's House*. Please note that for many of the ancient Celtic words (and a few of the modern ones as well), there may be more than one way to pronounce the word. These are the pronunciations that the writer referred to while writing *Emily's House*:

Characters:

Bian Sídhe	BAN shee
Brighid	BREE id
Cathaír	KA heer
Cian	KEE in
Cormac	KUR a mac
Dectire	deck TIR ra
Dughall	DU gal
Lianhan Sídhe	LAN an shee
Macha	MASH a
Ruaidrí	RU a ree
Saorla	SAYR la
Sídhe	Shay
Sorcha	SOR kha

Places:

Loughcrew	LOCK crew
Slieve na Caillaigh	sl-EE-ve na CAL-i
Umbra Nihili	UM bra NEE Lee

Other:

Anam Cara	uh -nam kar-uh

The most beautiful experience we can have is the mysterious. It is the fundamental emotion which stands at the cradle of true art and true science. Whosoever does not know it and can no longer wonder, no longer marvel, is as good as dead, and his eyes are dimmed.

– Albert Einstein

PART ONE

The Order of Brighid

"Possibility is the secret heart of time."

-<u>Anam Ċara: A Book of Celtic Wisdom</u>, by John O'Donohue

PROLOGUE

The whoosh, whoosh, whoosh of that infernal machine. Its bellows pump up and down as black, tarry sludge is sucked up the tube and into the holding tank.

She lies on the bed like a robot corpse, tubes and lines going in and out of her body. Her once rosy lips are pale, tinged slightly green. Her once vibrant emerald green eyes are closed, sunken into the eye sockets. Her once strong body lies still and shrunken. Only her hair looks the same, flowing like a red wave across the white shore of the pillow.

Whoosh, whoosh, whoosh.

I stand at the door and gingerly peek in. I don't want to be there. I don't want to see her like that. I don't want the putrid odor of dying people stuck in my nostrils.

I don't want to go in, but I'm sucked into the room anyway. My legs feel powerless against the invisible force that draws me in. I flail my arms and try to command my body to obey me and run from the horrid scene.

But I'm in the room anyway, drawing ever closer to the bed.

Whoosh, whoosh.

What is that tarry black stuff? Is it being sucked out of her body? Or put in?

I'm close enough to touch her, but I don't want to. The last time I touched her I saw a vision of her taking her last breath. The last time I touched her, I saw her die. I don't want that to come true. And I don't want to see her die again. The first time I saw her die I ran and ran, trying to escape the vision. I don't want to touch anyone ever again.

But my hand reaches anyway, a mind of its own. My mouth opens to scream, but nothing comes out. My lips are locked open in a soundless "O."

My hand quivers as it reaches in slow motion toward the sleeping body that bears a resemblance to my mother. *Is she still in there? Or has the cancer stolen the last of her?*

My fingertips shake as they touch her hand. The skin on her hand is as thin as an onionskin and shows the blue-red blood vessels beneath.

As soon as my fingers touch her hand, her eyes pop open in a look of terror. Her mouth is open in a scream. But it's not a human scream. It's the loud whoosh, whoosh, whoosh of that tar-sucking machine.

She sits up. The long, wavy red hair flying about her head is the same, but the face is no longer my mother. It looks at me with large, solid black eyes, devoid of light or emotion, staring out of a bare skull. Her hand is no longer covered in thin flesh but is instead the hand of a skeleton. The hand of bones grips me hard.

I pull and pull to get free of the monster, but it has me. I'm caught in its grip.

Whoosh, whoosh, whoosh.

I finally wake, dripping in sweat. My mouth is still open in an "O," the scream still caught in my throat.

I awake once again from the same ghastly dream I've had for the last seven years, only to find myself in a house of nightmares.

1 A RUN-IN WITH MURIEL THE MEAN

It sucks to see your mom die twice.

That's what I was thinking while I walked home that day. The second day in my life that everything changed.

The day started out normal enough. Getting a D on my math test. Trying not to trip over my own too-big-for-my-body flipper feet on my way to lunch. And getting handed a report card that felt like a bomb that was about to explode in my backpack.

"Muriel the Mean is going to kill me," I said to my best friends, Fanny and Jake. We ambled ever closer to my house of doom. My stomach knotted itself up, and the all-too-familiar feeling of dread took over as we got closer to my house.

My house. Once it was filled with my mom's laughter and singing. Her colorful paintings once decorated the walls.

My house.

It wasn't really mine anymore. It was Muriel's. And Aunt Muriel had filled the place with dove-grey walls and meanness and fear.

My mom died when I was seven, and she took her laughter and her singing and her colorful paintings with her.

She took something else too. Something that I'd kept secret, even from Fanny and Jake.

For as long as I can remember, I could read her thoughts. It was like a radio station playing in my head. All I had to do was tune in my receiver, and there she was. The 'Mom Station'. She could read my thoughts too. It seemed like the most normal thing ever. Mom let me know that it wasn't normal and that it was best to keep it between us, so I did.

The day she died, I held her hand as that horrible tar-sucking machine whooshed away. Then her station went off the air. I never heard it again.

Inside my head, it was so quiet and lonely. I was seven years old, and it was the first time in my life that the only thoughts rolling around in there were my own.

To make it all worse, my dad turned into a zombie and my Aunt Muriel came to live with us. Dad's work at the university takes most of his time, so he thought my old widowed aunt (fourteen years older than my dad) could come live with us. "It's a win-win," he had said.

Only it wasn't a win for me. Muriel is meaner than a dog chained in the hot sun with a choke collar on. I'm not sure why she's such a heinous person, but she is, so I call her 'Muriel the Mean'.

Seven years living with a zombie who used to be my father. Seven years of Muriel treating me like the bastard fourth cousin of a retarded rhino. I felt as if I was slipping away. I felt like if something didn't change, I was going to disappear completely.

"Maybe I should just keep walking," I said. We were a couple of houses away from the sidewalk leading up to my front door. "You know, run away."

"You can't do that," said Jake. His voice sounded panicked. "I'd miss you too much. Besides, where would you go?"

"Then tell me how I can deliver this to Muriel the Mean and not end up dead."

"Let me come in with you," offered Fanny. "If she lays a hand on you, I'll go banshee on her."

"Fanny, we've been over this before. I'd love to let you go gorilla on my Aunt Muriel, but I can't let you do that. *You* have too much to lose."

She shut up about it. She knew I was right. Even though we were only freshmen, Fanny was a shoe-in for at least one sport scholarship, and we all knew it. Spending time in juvenile detention for beating up my aunt would waste that dream for her.

"I don't know Em, maybe you should just go with the direct approach. That's usually best," said Jake.

"Best for what nub? Getting her butt kicked? No, I suggest the time proven method that has worked for generations of kids," said Fanny.

"What's that?" I asked.

"Lie."

Fanny's suggestion had considerable merit. Problem was we were at my house, and I had no lie in my head. I had planned no strategy for how to hide the incriminating paper in my backpack from Muriel.

"I'll see you guys later?" I asked.

"Yep, and I'll help you with your algebra homework," said Jake.

"And I'll be over to keep Jake from boring you to death," said Fanny. "We'll meet at your tree later."

"Wish me luck."

"Good luck, Em," said Jake.

"Hope you live to see me later," Fanny joked as they both walked away.

Fanny's joke, like most humor, had a core of truth. Aunt Muriel wouldn't actually kill me, but when displeased with me, which she was just about all of the time, she'd make my life miserable.

I walked lightly across the creaky wooden porch of my house, trying not to make a sound. My hand hesitated on the door handle. Once I would have bounded in with laughter to a kaleidoscope of color. That day I crept with dread into a house of monochrome.

I finally opened the door. Muriel waited for me just inside. *Not a good sign.*

"Okay, let's see it," she said.

"See what?"

"Don't be cute. You know what. Hand it over," she snarled back.

I dug in my backpack and brought out a wrinkled piece of paper. Muriel snatched it from my hand and pored over it. When she finally looked up, I thought for sure her eyes would incinerate me on the spot.

"If you were smart you wouldn't have come home with this. It appears that your grades do reflect the sum of your intelligence which, I'm sorry to say, is not a terribly large sum."

"Then I must get my intelligence from your side of the family," I replied. I know. Stupid, stupid, stupid. Sometimes it's like my mouth has its own brain and just shoots stuff out. Stuff likely to get me killed.

Crack!

I should have seen it coming. She hit me so hard I swear she made snot shoot out of my nose. My backpack fell, and stuff flew out all over the floor. Blood trickled from my nose over my upper lip. I didn't want to cry in front of Muriel, but tears welled up in my eyes anyway.

"Pick up this stuff," she hissed.

I bent down and shoved all my stuff back into my backpack. My nose bled so much that it dripped all over the wood floor in the entryway.

"Now look at what you did! You clean that up and go to your room. I don't want to see you until morning. And for God's sake, stop sniveling." Muriel turned and stomped out of the room.

I wanted to run away. I wanted to run and run like I had that day back when I was seven. Run and run until I was far away from that house and Aunt Muriel and Zombie Man. Run until I fell over.

But I didn't run. Instead, I pulled it together enough to clean up the blood, snot and tears off the floor. I ran upstairs to my room, shut the door, and shoved wads of toilet paper up my nostrils to stop up the blood. I flopped down on my bed and I kept crying.

It wasn't the wailing or hiccupping to catch your breath kind of crying. That's how it usually was for me. No, that day it was a long, slow, stream of hot tears kind of crying. And they weren't all tears of sad. A lot of those tears were mad tears. Really mad tears.

You probably think I was mad at Muriel. And I was a little. But mostly I was mad at my mom, Bridget.

It had been seven years since she died, and I was furious at her. The more I cried the more I thought about how she had up and left me. And the more I thought about how she cut out on me, the madder I got. And the madder I got at her, the more I cried. I was starting to hate my mom as much as I hated Muriel.

"Mom, why did you leave me?" I whispered to the emptiness around me.

The silence of my room was suddenly filled with a low hissing sound.

"Mom?"

No answer, just a low hiss that sounded like steam coming through an old radiator. *What the heck is that?* I opened my window and listened. The hiss came from my old tree house, still perched in the large oak outside my window.

I went to my bathroom and wiped the tear tracks from my face. My eyes were red and puffy and my face blotchy from crying. I pulled the wads of toilet paper out of my nose and put on a clean T-shirt. I went to my window, opened it up and eased out onto the large oak branch.

I didn't know it then, but scooting myself across that branch was the beginning of a long journey.

2 EMILY'S VISITOR

Before my dad became a zombie, he built a large tree house in an old oak in our backyard. Neither he nor Muriel bothered to tear it down so it remained wedged amongst the large branches of the old tree.

My legs were still a little wobbly from my run in with Muriel, but I stayed low and climbed across the branches until I got to the tree house. The closer I got the louder the hissing noise.

I sat on the limb at the opening to the tree house and looked in to see what was making the noise. The inside of the tiny house was dark and dusty. The only light came from the small opening that my body was blocking. I couldn't see anything in there. I crawled inside. My five feet six frame barely fit through the hole that had been made for a small child. Once inside, I couldn't stand up but had plenty of room to sit. I sat to the side and waited for my eyes adjust to the darkness.

The hissing grew louder, and after a few minutes, I saw a faint light appear in the middle of the tree house. The light hovered in front of me. It started small like the light from a mini flashlight. It grew to the size of a softball and as it grew, it became brighter.

I thought Aunt Muriel had knocked my head around good and that I had a concussion. *Great, now I'm losing my hearing and seeing weird lights.*

I blinked my eyes, rubbed them and tipped my head and tapped the other side, like you do when you're trying to get water out of your ears. *Nope, didn't work.* I still heard the hissing sound and the light ball continued to grow. Soon it was about the size of a large dog. Then the hissing changed. It became a low, slow hum. The light got so bright I had to shade my eyes from it.

Suddenly, POP! The bright light disappeared, and the humming became low and soft, more of a droning background noise. I squinted my eyes to see through a misty, silvery fog. *What's there?*

I saw the outline of something. As my eyes adjusted to the sudden darkness, the image became clearer. What I saw made me want to scream.

I wanted to scream, but I didn't. If I screamed Aunt Muriel would find me and I'd have more trouble. I thought about shimmying back across the tree branch and into my room. But something about the thing drew me in.

Before me stood a small furry creature. It was about four feet tall but seemed fully-grown. Its head was doglike, with a dog nose and whiskers, but its ears were more like a wild boar. His eyes were the oddest thing about him. They were large and dark brown, almost black, but seemed to be stuck in a perpetually sad look, with bags and wrinkles underneath.

The creature's body was hairy all over like a dog, but he had hands like a man and wore clothes. He wore a collared shirt with the sleeves rolled up to his elbows and a brown tweed vest topped his dark brown wool flannel pants.

I should have been scared. I mean an alien creature had just landed in my tree house. But I figured I was hallucinating. Aunt Muriel had whacked me hard. Anyway, his eyes were so warm and with his cute little tweed vest, he didn't frighten me.

"Can you see me, child of Brighid?" said the creature.

"Yes, I ... I see you, whatever you are," I said.

"I am Hindergog, Bard of the Order of Brighid, keeper of the tales of the High Priestess, servant to her majesty in the Netherworld," he said.

"Well, I guess that answers it." After I said it, I realized my sarcasm. I enjoyed being a smart aleck to my aunt, even though I'd pay for it. But I immediately regretted being so smirky to the strange creature.

"I'm sorry," I said. "I didn't mean to be sarcastic with you. My aunt always tells me that I have an awful mouth."

"There is nothing awful about you, daughter of Brighid. It is your lack of training that is awful," he said.

"Training?"

"You have reached the age of fourteen Beltane fires, have you not?"

"Well I don't know anything about Beltane, but I'm fourteen years old."

"Then you are four years late for the start of your preparation. But there is no time to waste. We must start now. You are the last in the lineage of the Order of Brighid. You are the only one with the powers to defeat Dughall the Dark One, but you require training," Hindergog said.

"I don't know what you're talking about. And that is truly strange because you are a figment of my imagination and you'd think I'd know what my own imagination is talking about."

"Daughter of Brighid, I am not of your imagination."

"Then you are real?"

"Real? What is real? In your world, you are all about this 'real'. That is quite the wrong question you know."

"Now I'm getting really confused. Well, whether you're real or not, you seem kind, and I could use a friend. So it's nice to meet you Hindergog." I reached my hand out to shake his.

But when I reached for his hand, my hand went right through him. He wasn't flesh and blood after all.

"So you are a figment. Too bad," I said.

"In my world, I am quite 'real' as you say. But I can only come to you in this form through the use of the Crystals of Alsted. I am, what in your world might be called a 'hologram'," said Hindergog. "A projection of sorts."

"Where is your body then?"

"My body resides in another realm called the Netherworld. In your world, it is called another dimension. My body cannot travel to your realm without damage so I must meet with you this way."

"Are you serious? So you're using some sort of cosmic telephone?"

"I do not know this 'telephone' of which you speak. Please listen child of Brighid, as I do not have much time. It took what in your world would be several hundred years to collect the amount of crystals needed to project myself to you. I should have about one hour of your time, but no more. And I have much to tell you as you have had no prior education in these things."

I heard Jake and Fanny talking to each other down below. They were at our meeting place, the tree, just like we'd planned.

"Wait a minute little dude," I told Hindergog. I crawled on my knees over to the opening of the house. "Hey guys – up here," I whispered to Jake and Fan. They both came over to the ladder that led up the tree.

"What 'ya doin' up there?" asked Fanny.

"You'll find out in a minute. Get up here. But listen, when you get up here, *don't scream*."

Jake and Fanny looked at each other and shrugged their shoulders but were totally silent as they climbed up. Jake came first. I could see his spiky blond hair and coke-bottle glasses when he reached the top. As soon as his eyes cleared the top rung, he gasped. He didn't say a word and he didn't scream, but it looked like he had stopped breathing.

Fanny was right behind Jake, her dark curly hair contained under a ball cap. When she got to the top, she let out a soft cry of surprise but quickly caught herself and covered her mouth with her hand. She climbed in too and Jake was on one side of me and Fanny was on the other. All three of us sat silently and stared at the creature. When Hindergog broke the silence, all three of us jumped a little.

"Daughter of Brighid, who are these others? This will not do. My message is for you alone."

"First of all, stop calling me Daughter of Brighid. My name is Emily, and if you want to talk to me, you can get my name right."

"Yes, as you wish, daughter of, I mean, Emily."

"Second, this is Jake, and this is Fanny. They are my two best friends and anything you want to say to me, you need to say to them, too."

"Oh, Mistress Emily, I do not have time to argue the point. This is likely to cause severe problems. But my time grows ever shorter and with so much to tell ... " His voice trailed off. He looked like he was thinking and he looked plenty worried.

"So be it, they can stay. But listen well, all of you, as I have much to tell you."

"What is this *thing* and why is it here?" asked Jake.

"His name is Hindergog," I said. "And I have no idea what he is or why he's here. He says he's a holographic projection from another dimension."

"Shut up!" said Fanny.

"*Please* hear me humans of fourteen Beltane fires," Hindergog pled. "I will tell you all that you are required to know. And when I am done, the one who calls herself Emily must prepare for her journey to the Sacred Grove."

"Emily, you're leaving?" asked Jake.

"I wasn't planning on it. I have no idea what the heck this little dude is talking about."

"I beg for your patience, Younglings," Hindergog pled. "It is most urgent for all of you, and all in your world, that Emily, descendant of my Saorla, last High Priestess of the Order of Brighid, learn of her heritage and of her destiny."

"This sounds heavy, Em," said Fanny.

"What are you talking about Hindergog? What destiny?" I asked.

"Miss Emily, you know of your unique abilities."

"What's he talking about?" asked Jake.

I felt squirmy. I didn't say a word. Jake and Fanny stared at me, waiting for me to explain what the little alien guy was talking about.

"Spill it, Adams," commanded Fanny.

"Look, it's nothing spectacular or anything. It's just that I have these visions. It's like seeing the future."

"GET OUT!" shouted Fanny.

"Shh, Muriel," I warned as I put a finger to my lips.

"But there is more to it than that young one, much more," Hindergog said.

"More? You can do more than see the future?" queried Jake.

"Crapballs! I *so* didn't want anyone to know this stuff." I'd tried to weasel out of talking about it. The three of them stared at me in silence, and it was clear that Jake and Fanny weren't going to let me off the hook without explaining about my strange abilities.

"Alright, here's the thing. When I was little I could hear what my mom was thinking, okay. It was like a radio station playing in my head. I only had that with her, and when she died, her radio station went off the air permanently. Now I don't even get static."

"And?" Fanny asked.

"And?"

"You said you could see the future. What's up with that?" asked Jake.

"I don't know. Look, I hate talking about this."

"Have you seen my future?" asked Fanny. "Am I like a famous sports figure?"

"No, Fanny, I haven't seen your future. I haven't seen anyone's future, not since ... "

"Since when, Em?" asked Jake.

"Since my mom died."

The crowded little house was silent. The only sound was the low drone of Hindergog's cosmic telephone. Sometimes it seemed like it was more painful retelling the story of my mom's death than it was going through it in the first place.

"You saw your mom die?" asked Jake.

"What do you think she saw nub, fluffy bunnies and flowers?" said Fanny.

"Yes Jake, I had a vision. I saw my mom die. I was holding her hand one day and there it was, just like a movie in my mind's eye. I saw her hooked up to machines and saw her eyes sunken into her drawn, pale face, and I saw her take her last breath. And when she died for real, it was exactly like the vision I'd seen."

"Good job Jake, making Emily go through that," said Fanny. She rubbed my back as she glared at Jake.

"It's okay Fanny, really."

"Sorry Em, I didn't mean to make you sad," said Jake. "I'm thick I guess. You saw that one vision, and then it just stopped?"

"Well, sort of. I started to have another vision. With Greta."

"Greta?" said Fanny. "What the heck?"

"Remember my first day back to school after my mom died?"

"Who could forget it? You ran out of the school like a maniac. I never did understand what that was about," said Fanny.

"Well it was about Greta. She came up to me and was saying she was sorry about my mom. Blah, blah, blah. She put her hand on my shoulder all sincere like. But that turned on my receptor, and I started to see a vision of the future. Greta's future. I screamed for her to get her hand off me and I ran. I didn't want to see what that movie was about. Bought myself a trip to the guidance counselor."

"That's when Greta started calling you 'Freak Girl' and being mean to you," said Fanny. The puzzle pieces were finally falling into place for her.

"Yep."

"I guess you don't rebuff Greta-the-Charming without consequences," said Jake. "Now I get why you don't play sports and try to avoid ... "

"Being touched. Yeah, I don't want to see anyone die."

"There is more Miss Emily, so much more," said Hindergog.

The little blabbermouth.

"More than seeing the future?" asked Jake.

I didn't want to say anymore. I'd already had to spill enough. But Fanny wasn't going to let it go.

"Out with it, Em," demanded Fanny.

"I can move things with my mind too," I said.

"You cannot!" said Jake.

"Yep, I can."

"I don't believe you," he said.

"Show us, Em," said Fanny excitedly.

"I'm not a show dog."

"Oh, come on. Show us," she whined.

I hadn't seen visions for a long time, but I continued to use my telekinesis, at least in the privacy of my room. I knew better than to let Muriel know about these 'special abilities' as

Hindergog called them. The cat was out of the bag with Fanny and Jake. *Why not show them so they stop bugging me about it?*

I stared at Jake's backpack that he'd flung down. I concentrated on wanting the backpack, and it slowly raised then floated through the air right to me.

Silence filled the space between us. My heart raced, and my palms started to sweat. *This is it, the moment I've dreaded.* Once Fanny and Jake knew my secret, they'd know for certain what a colossal freak I was. Their stunned silence and gaping mouths said it all.

Finally, Jake broke the silence. "THAT WAS ABSOLUTELY BRILLIANT! I wouldn't have believed it if I hadn't seen it with my own eyes."

"Coolest-thing-ever! Do it again." Fanny squealed like a little girl.

"Younglings, we do not have time for Miss Emily to perform more demonstrations. My time is short, and I have much to tell. There is much for Miss Emily to learn before she begins the journey to her destiny."

"Why do I have to go on a journey, and to where? What destiny are you talking about?" I asked.

"Miss Emily, there is an ancient evil set on a path that will lead to the destruction of your world. He lived in the time of your ancient ancestor, my mistress Saorla, the last High Priestess of the Order of Brighid. He is responsible for ... "

Hindergog paused. His face looked pinched, and a tear was in his eye.

"Go on, Hindergog. What was he responsible for?"

"This dark one, Dughall, was responsible for the end of the Order of Brighid. He is in human form once again and we fear that if he succeeds with his plan, it will likely destroy your world."

"Whoa, whoa, whoa. What are you talking about? Is he, like, reincarnated? And destroy our world? How?" asked Jake.

"I know you have many questions Younglings, and I will answer these questions by telling you a story. I am a bard and keeper of the sacred stories of the Order of Brighid. Please humans, rest easy as I tell you all that you need to know."

"I gotta' hear this," said Fanny.

"We'll listen Hindergog," I said.

"Yeah, we got nothin' better to do," said Fanny.

"Except algebra," said Jake.

"Shh," Fanny and I both said at once.

Hindergog took a deep breath, closed his eyes for a moment then opened them slowly.

"Listen well Younglings as the tale I have to tell is an important one. The tale is of my most beloved mistress and of Miss Emily's ancestor. Some of it will be difficult for me, as I must tell you of a terrific battle and of the tragedy that lead to the last days of the Order of Brighid. Please do not interrupt so that I may say all that must be said before my crystals run out."

The three of us settled in. Our eyes were on the hologram Hindergog as he began his story.

3 SAORLA

Like all Priestesses of the Order of Brighid before her, Saorla left her home when she was ten and entered the Sacred Grove. After much preparation, lessons and hard work, Saorla took her place as the High Priestess of the Order of Brighid.

But it was a difficult time for the Order. Much change came to ancient Ireland, known in those times as Érie. Because it was an island and well protected by its fearsome Celtic warriors, the ancient ways survived on the Emerald Isle far longer than in most of Europe. But in Saorla's time, powerful invaders came from the south with large armies and ships.

More powerful than the soldiers and their weapons were the ways of thinking the newcomers brought with them. The strangers prayed to one male god rather than to the many gods both male and female of Saorla's ancestors. The Druidic ways were being lost.

The raiders wiped out whole villages. Those that survived adapted to the new ways in order to avoid scrutiny, ridicule or worse – death to them or their family.

All over Ireland the old ways were forgotten. Priests replaced the Druids. Nuns replaced priestesses. Saorla's Samhein became 'All Hollow's Eve.' Alban Arthuan became the day of their god's birth, Christmas. Imolc became the day of their god's death and resurrection, Easter.

"I didn't know that those holidays existed before Christians," interrupted Fanny.

"Yes, most of what humans celebrate today existed in the ancient world. None of it is new. You just rename it from time to time. Now listen."

Saorla's most crucial task as High Priestess was to protect the golden torc, an object imbued with immense power. Faerie hands forged the torc in the first days of the Order, in the time of the Great Pyramids. From the start, it was blessed with magickal power and wrapped while still warm around the upper arm of the first High Priestess of the Order. It was passed from High Priestess to High Priestess, each time imbued with the powerful energy of the wearer. Over the millennia, it became a most powerful object indeed.

"Wait a minute. A 'torc'? What's that?" I asked Hindergog.

"Ah, that is right. Humans no longer wear them. A torc is a piece of jewelry, usually worn around the neck but sometimes worn by warriors around their upper arms. The craftsman would twist many thin wires of precious metal around each other to form a ring that could be worn. The Torc of Brighid, worn by the High Priestess of the Order for millennia, was made of the purest gold."

Saorla's other role as High Priestess was to be the highest-ranking advisor to the High King of Ireland. She used the sight to seek out visions that could alert the king to any plots against him or his lands.

But by Saorla's time, few knew that the Order of Brighid existed. The Order had been held secret by so many for so long in order to protect it that there were few to believe in it. In the minds of the common folk, the Order of Brighid and the Sacred Grove were considered myth.

While Saorla was the highest and most trusted advisor to the King, Saorla's most trusted advisor was Cathaír. Cathaír was the liaison between the High Priestess and the King.

Cathaír was also charged with the duty to protect the Sacred Grove and the Order of Brighid from outsiders. Cathaír was, in fact, the only living human man to know of the exact location of the Sacred Grove.

"You mean no men lived there at all?" asked Jake.

"That is correct. And once a young girl was inducted into the Order, she never left the Sacred Grove again."

"So they were like nuns," said Fanny.

"Are you saying that Emily has to become a nun?" asked Jake.

"Settle yourselves. Times, of course, are different now. The order no longer exists. Please listen as you learn what happened to my fair mistress Saorla."

One day, Saorla summoned Cathaír to her.

"Cathaír, you must ride to the King at once. I have foreseen an army, large in numbers, and with a most fierce leader. They plan to invade our fair land in the coming months."

"I trust your vision my Priestess, but we have survived many invaders in the past. I will tell the High King, and he will raise his armies to protect our fair land."

"This invader is different, Cathaír. He is fork-tongued and will promise much to those who follow him. And I have foreseen a terrible plot against the King."

"Then I will ride to the King at once and tell him what you have foreseen."

"Cathaír, there is more. But this you must not tell the King."

"What is it? What have you seen?"

"I have seen a dark invader here, Cathaír. At the Sacred Grove."

"No, that is impossible. The protections are too strong. An army of men would never see the walls. Even if they did, the enchantments that have protected it for thousands of years will hold. And of course there is Lianhan Sídhe. She will not let any man enter. And if anyone did manage to find the gate, let alone get past Lianhan Sídhe, Madame Wong would dice them to pieces."

"I know that it seems impossible, Cathaír. I do not know how it will happen. I wish that I did. I only know what I saw. A dark haired man with a large army will enter through the gates of our beloved Grove."

"Your gift of sight is most powerful, your Highness, but I hope for the sake of our fair land that your vision has failed you this time."

"I do too, Cathaír. I do too."

That night Saorla took her usual evening stroll to the Moon Well to meditate and speak with the Goddess. As she looked into the Moon Well, she saw a vivid and violent scene. She wished with all her heart that she had not seen it. The second vision, from the sacred Moon Well itself, confirmed the first. There was no doubt of it. Her remaining days in the Sacred Grove were few.

4 THE WEDDING

Cathaír rode through the night to the walled city of the High King of Érie. He advised King Ruaidrí of all that Saorla had said, all except for her prediction of invaders at the Sacred Well. Cathaír told the High King of Saorla's recommendation that the King raise his armies and arm all available men and women in the port cities to protect against the invaders.

Ruaidrí scoffed at Cathaír's news. "Lad, this land has lived in peace for many harvests. My lookouts know of no invaders on the shores of fair Érie. I'm afraid our Lady of the Well is replacing her vision with fear." Ruaidrí raised a mug of mead to his lips.

"Your Highness, the High Priestess's vision has never failed you before. She implores you to take action to fortify the port cities. She has seen a large and fearsome army overtaking our land," replied Cathaír.

Ruaidrí drank more mead and thought for a few minutes. *If the wise woman's vision is true, mayhaps it is a warning from the Goddess herself,* thought Ruaidrí. In order to appease the Christian bishops and local monks, Ruaidrí and his estate followed the Christian rites, eschewing the old ways. By decree, he had forbidden many of the ancient practices and approved of the renaming of others. Many of his people were devoted to the new religion. But many, like Ruaidrí himself, mouthed the words of the hymns and prayers, but in their heart, they longed for the Beltane fires.

As he reflected, he thought that perhaps the Goddess was upset with him. Maybe he needed to appease her. He felt certain that an offering to the Goddess and a festival to honor her would put him again in good favor with the gods and goddesses of his homeland. *Mayhaps the High Priestess's vision does not portend of what is to come but is only a warning*, Ruaidrí thought.

At last Ruaidrí spoke. "What is called for is a great ceremony to appease the Goddess. We will perform a *ban-feis*. Now go, Cathaír, and tell the High Priestess to ready herself for the ritual."

"My King, I mean no disrespect, but as you know the Lady of the Well has taken sacred vows. She cannot attend a festival outside the walls of the Sacred Grove. Another priestess, one of high rank, must perform the ceremony instead."

"Cathaír, return at once to the Sacred Grove and give this message to the High Priestess. Let her know that her vows are of no consequence when the very soul of our fair land is at stake. We shall have the *ban-feis* at the next full moon, and I expect the High Priestess to perform the role of Goddess." Ruaidrí dismissed Cathaír without another word.

"What is a ban-feis?*" asked Fanny.*

"The ban-feis is a ritual that had not been performed in many years. During the ban-feis, the kings, lords, ladies, knights and all of the people come together for bonfires and feasting, and the King is married to the Goddess," answered Hindergog.

"You mean a real Goddess existed, and the King married her?" asked Jake. "Okay this is starting to get too weird, even for me."

"There's no 'real' goddess Jake," I said.

"There is indeed a Goddess, fair Emily. But for the ban-feis the King ritualistically married a priestess or druidess disguised as the

Goddess, thus uniting the people with the forces of nature and the land," said Hindergog. "Listen as I continue my tale."

The announcement of the *ban-feis* spread across the land. Those that still followed the old ways were excited and pleased that the King was making peace with the Goddess. Many who did not outwardly follow the old ways out of fear of scorn were secretly happy within their hearts too. The people missed the joyous feasts of old when the High King, as well as all regional kings and lords opened their larders. High born and peasants alike would feast and celebrate.

The next full moon fell on Samhein itself, the New Year for those who followed the ancient ways. It was the end of October and the time when the veil between the worlds is at its thinnest. The time when spirits and beings from other worlds are more easily seen in your world.

Saorla had not left the Sacred Grove since she arrived all those years ago. While Cathaír was strongly against it, Saorla agreed with Ruaidrí that they were not in ordinary times.

In Saorla's heart, she also yearned to see the world outside the walls of the Sacred Grove. She had not attended festival since she was a child. Saorla was excited to see the famed festival fires, hear the thundering drums and feast on meat and game. As a Priestess, Saorla ate mainly fruits of the forest, bread, root vegetables and herbs and only occasional fish or fowl. She had not eaten game since she came to the Grove.

For the ceremony, Saorla and her attending priestesses traveled four days to the north and east until they reached the ancient, sacred site. For countless generations, her people had gathered there for ritual around the central stone cairn. It was all but abandoned. Most no longer remembered who was buried in the tombs on top of the hill or why the ancient peoples had made the intricate carvings of swirls and circles in the large stones placed there. But the site still had a sacred energy about it that made all who gathered at the top of the hill fall into reverent silence.

Saorla attended the *ban-feis* personifying the Goddess. To keep her identity secret, she wore a mask and an understated, long white tunic and cloak so that the torc around her arm was covered.

Saorla and King Ruaidrí gathered on top of the hill known as Loughcrew along with the regional kings, their ladies and other noblemen and high born. The ceremony began at dusk on Samhein. The highest-ranking Druid Priest in the High King's court performed the *ban-feis* ritual as the sun set over the Slieve na Caillaigh hills at Loughcrew.

Around the bottom of the great hill, common folk from all around gathered, ready to join in the revelry of the sacred union. As the Druid Priest spoke the ritual words, Saorla smelled the smoke from the large wood bonfires below and the scent of roasting meat and her attention wandered. Saorla wondered if all weddings seemed to last so long for a bride.

At last the Druid Priest announced the union was complete, and the High King, on behalf of all his people, was married to the Goddess and thus the land. The regional kings, lords, knights and their ladies cheered loudly. Their cheers were heard by the people gather below and led to a loud roar of hoots and hollers as all celebrated the union.

The last part of the ritual required the High King and the 'Goddess' to consummate their marriage in a wedding bed. Ruaidrí and Saorla, still wearing the mask of the Goddess, were taken to what looked like a stone alter bed, draped for the ceremony with linens for privacy. The crowd sent up a riotous cheer as first Saorla then Ruaidrí entered through the drapes to their wedding bed.

Once inside, the High King took Saorla's hand and kissed it gently. "It is my highest honor to meet you at last, High Priestess," he said. Saorla was frightened of what would come next as she had never been alone with a man in a bedchamber before. Ruaidrí was practiced in courtesies. But he was an old warrior, gruff and hardened by years of battle and war.

Ruaidrí must have sensed her fear. "You need not worry, my Priestess. I have no desire to offend the Christian gods by taking the sacred virginity of the Goddess's High Priestess of her most Sacred Grove. I would then offend all the gods while I'm trying to appease them."

Saorla was much relieved by Ruaidrí's statement but tried not to show the King her relief. She bowed to the king in thanks. "I thank you, your Highness, for honoring my sacred vows. I am sure the Goddess is pleased with your offering to her, and your diplomacy has saved you from offense to the one God of the Christians as well.

"But what should we do now, my king? The people expect the High King and Goddess to participate in the old rites and consecrate their marriage."

"We wait an appropriate amount of time. I will emerge from this bedchamber and look the part of the boastful stag. All will think that we have consummated our 'vows'," he replied. "You may remove your mask with me, High Priestess, if you would like. It is a warm evening and the mask is surely too warm on your fair face."

"No, my King, I must stay hidden, even with you."

"You are right, of course, of course. These are dangerous times, are they not?"

"Yes, your Highness. Cathaír told you of my visions?"

"Cathaír told me. Please forgive me, your Highness, but I cannot believe what you have seen. Your vision must surely be clouded or perhaps it was merely a warning from the Goddess. My men are the most loyal this fair land has ever seen. The people are more united now than in many harvests. I am not concerned of a plot against me, gentle woman."

"This makes me even more concerned my King. I know that your men are loyal and our land united. For now. But the invasion that is coming to Érie is different from those that came before. The leader of this army is dark, my King. He quests for power and his thirst is unquenchable. He will say and do anything to achieve his ends. He is without conscience my King. That makes him most dangerous."

"I am grateful for your fealty, High Priestess. And I will take your words to consideration. But this night, let us enjoy the feast and the fires of Samhein. Let us enjoy the beauty of our fair land and her people. I take my leave of you, your Highness. May the Goddess shine her light on you all of your days." He bowed low and backed out of the drapes and into the night.

Saorla, finally alone, removed her mask. The mask had made her hot and rivulets of sweat dripped from her temples. She knew that she should stay there and keep her identity secret. But the music was so enticing, the odor of roasted meat and smoke from the fires so delicious. She was practically salivating and her stomach growled with hunger. The low, thundering drums awakened in her desires that were animal and primeval. The night felt momentous and full of magickal power. It was a Samhein with a full moon, surely an omen of good fortune. The Goddess could not intend for her to sit alone and masked in a shrouded room rather than rejoice the life force of the Goddess.

She tore off the white cloak and tunic. Underneath she wore a rough spun and undyed linen tunic like the peasants wore. The long sleeves covered the torc. No one knew what she looked like. She could pass for a peasant.

I will. I will feast and dance.

Saorla snuck out of the linen curtains at the back of the makeshift marriage bedchamber. There was no one around to see her. Everyone else had ventured down the hill to join the feasts and merriment in the valley below. Most of the revelers had a few mugs of mead in their bellies and no longer paid attention to the 'wedding bed'.

Saorla stepped gingerly down the steep hill. It was difficult walking as she had only the full moon to light the way. Saorla blended into the crowd easily, and as soon as she could, she grabbed a mug of mead and a leg of rabbit. She ate the meat quickly and savored its musky flavor. Saorla drank down the mug of mead in one long draught. She had never had mead and was surprised by the slight tingling sensation it left in her lips. Her head began to feel swoony. Saorla decided that it was not an altogether unpleasant feeling.

She wandered away from the feasting tables toward the sound of the drums. Saorla watched the dancers for a few songs. When she felt confident that she knew the steps of the dance, she joined in. Between the mead, the power of the drums, and the spinning and twirling of the dance, she felt positively intoxicated.

After she had danced a few songs, Saorla looked up to see that her dance partner was Cathaír. He swung her around and danced with her for the rest of the song. They both laughed, and Saorla felt light and free as they danced together. After several more dances, Saorla looked as if she would fall over from exhaustion. Cathaír steered her by her elbow away from the crowd.

"What do you think you are doing, your Highness?" he whispered playfully into her ear.

Saorla hiccupped and said, "Enjoying my wedding night, good sir."

Cathaír could not help but smile. He felt a warmth toward Saorla he had never felt before. There, in the glow of feast fires and away from the serious business of the Sacred Grove, he noticed for the first time how truly beautiful Saorla was. Her green eyes were two brilliant emeralds. Her lips were rosy pink and full. Her cheeks were flushed from the dance and the ale. Her hair, usually tightly plaited, was loose and flowing, full cascades of soft red flowing over her milky white shoulders.

"Are you going to stand here and continue to scold me, or are you going to dance with me, Cathaír?" Saorla asked.

He thought he should pick her up, carry her to her horse and escort her right back to the Sacred Grove. As her sworn protector and one of the holders of the secret of the Fires of Brighid, that was what he should do.

But he was a man too, and would be a fool not to enjoy a night of dancing and laughter with Saorla. So he put out his arm for her and said, "May I have this dance?"

She smiled mischievously and took his arm as they joined the others in a raucous dance. After a few more hours, Saorla said, "Ach, my feet! My poor soles are not used to all this dancing."

"Come then and let us rest," Cathaír said. He took Saorla by the hand and they hiked the steep climb to the top of the sacred hill. It was late into the evening and they walked alone and unseen by the drunken crowd below. Saorla and Cathaír tucked back into the shrouded 'wedding bed'.

Inside, Saorla threw herself down on the large flat stone bed to rest. She was exhilarated and tired all at the same time. Cathaír stood nearby awkwardly, not knowing what to do next.

"Come rest with me, Cathaír," Saorla said. She motioned for him to lie next to her.

Cathaír hesitated. He knew it was most improper for him to lie on a bed with Saorla. She was, after all, the High Priestess. But he was tired, and as there was no place to sit, he did as she suggested. As Cathaír lay next to Saorla, their hands gently touched.

Although Saorla was tired, the mead had worn off, and her mind was clear, not foggy. She focused herself and knew in an instant that Cathaír was thinking of how much he loved Saorla. And how much he wanted to kiss her. Saorla's cheeks flushed scarlet.

Instead of speaking, she rolled over to look at Cathaír. Before he knew what was happening, Saorla gently kissed his lips. Cathaír's brain told him that he should push her away, but the love pouring from her was too powerful a magnet. He kissed her back and gently wrapped his arms around her. Her body softened in his arms. She felt as if she would melt from the inside out. Her insides had turned to jelly.

As their lips parted, Cathaír looked deeply into Saorla's eyes. "I love you, Saorla," he said.

"I love you too, Cathaír." They kissed again but more deeply. Their passion was ignited, and neither of them could stop the long embrace even if they wanted to. Catháir and Saorla stayed together, wound tightly in each other's arms until just before dawn.

When they awoke, Saorla once again dressed as the Goddess, complete with mask. Catháir slipped out without being seen but brought her horse around for her and escorted her back to the Sacred Grove.

"You mean that they stayed the whole night together?" broke in Fanny.

"Yes," replied Hindergog.

"Wait. If you know this you were spying on them," I said.

"Yeah, that's gross man. You were spying on them while they were making out," added Jake.

"I cannot expect you human children to understand, but Saorla knew that I saw all of her life. There was nothing she hid from me. She wanted me to see her fall in love."

"So she and Catháir were in love?" I asked.

"Yes, very much in love," replied Hindergog.

"Hindergog, did they make love that night?" asked Fanny.

"Yes, they did," answered Hindergog.

"Wow, that was totally against the rules, wasn't it?" asked Jake.

"Yes, young sir, it was. But for my fair Saorla, it was the loveliest night she knew in the whole of her life."

"You never told anyone, did you Hindergog?" I asked.

"No, I did not," replied Hindergog. "My dear mistress deserved to have that one secret. And I have never told anyone until now."

"But why tell us? I mean, it's a beautiful story and all, but what does it have to do with danger to their world or with me?" I asked.

"That is a fair question child so listen well as I continue. You will see why I chose to reveal this to you now," Hindergog answered.

5 CATHAÍR'S BAD NEWS

A full twelve moons after the ban-feis, Cathaír rode hard and fast to the Sacred Grove to meet with my mistress. In those months, Saorla's vision had proven true. Invaders entered upon the Emerald Isle. The army was large and their fighting tactics fierce. The King's own armies and even the fearsome rogue bands of mercenaries had been unable to protect Ireland's borders. Soon an army had surrounded the High King himself.

Cathaír rode through the night from the Hill of Tara to the Sacred Grove and brought with him unwelcome news. As was custom, Saorla met with Cathaír in the Great Hall.

"Saorla, it is with a heavy heart that I bring you news of a march coming toward your Sacred Grove as we speak. Their numbers are many, Saorla."

"I know, Cathaír, I know."

"You have seen the army coming?" asked Cathaír.

"Yes, dear friend, remember I foresaw this over twelve moons ago."

"That is right. I tried to forget it."

"The visions are strong and keep me awake at night."

"Your priestesses are well trained and well armed. You have Madame Wong, an army in her own right. And of course there are the Fair Sídhe and Lianhan Sídhe to assist you. Your women warriors are fierce, Saorla, but I fear that even the famed women warriors of the Order of Brighid will not be able to fend off so many a number."

Saorla said nothing to this. Instead, she poured herself more tea. She so loved hot tea. *I will miss tea and the company of my friends*, Saorla thought.

"Saorla, you look so sad suddenly."

"A moment of weakness."

"It is not weakness to feel. To be human. You know what is coming. Much blood will be shed. Many lives will be lost."

"Yes, Cathaír, and that is why I have no time for the human frailty of my emotions. My Order must be able to rely on my steady leadership."

"You are a strong leader, Saorla."

Saorla poured Cathaír a cup of tea as well.

"There is more news too. This you may not know. There has been a great betrayal."

"A betrayal? Of whom?" asked Saorla.

"Of High King Ruaidrí," replied Cathaír.

"Ah yes, the plot against him that I saw so many moons ago. But I have not seen a vision of this happening recently. How have I not seen this?" wondered Saorla aloud.

"I suspect that magick is involved. It is Cormac, son of King Brion."

"Cormac. Yes, he has an axe to grind. He has always blamed Ruaidrí for his father's death. So he is after revenge, is he?"

"There is more. As you told me many months ago, the leader of this invasion is different from the ones before. He calls himself Dughall, and he is after more than just the typical spoils of war."

Saorla suddenly felt as though she would vomit. All at once a terrible vision came into her sight. It was a vision of a dark haired man with blazing brown eyes riding hard and fast right to the Sacred Grove.

"He is on his way," was all that she could whisper.

"Then we do not have much time," replied Catháir.

"But how does he know? How did he learn of our order and of the portal?"

"That is what I was telling you. Cormac has betrayed King Ruaidrí and the Order. He saw his opportunity and sold us out to Dughall."

It was just as Catháir said. Cormac's father had lost the crown to Ruaidrí in a fierce battle. To assuage Cormac and his district, Ruaidrí had given Cormac a post as his second in command. Being so high placed within the kingdom, Cormac knew much – or had the opportunity to spy on much – of what happened in the King's court, both public and private.

Cormac, always intent on revenge, saw opportunity. He arranged a meeting with Dughall, as sadistic and power hungry of a human as ever there was. Cormac offered his services to Dughall.

"I have no need of a spy," replied Dughall in a low growl.

"Then perhaps you require an assassin. I am extremely close to the High King," offered Cormac in desperation.

"What makes you think that I need you to take out Ruaidrí?"

"There must be some assistance I can offer my liege."

"What do you know of the secret order of women guarding a well?"

"Ah, it is women you are after sire," laughed Cormac.

When he looked at Dughall though he stopped laughing. Dughall's jaw was set hard, and his dark eyes were unsmiling.

"If you have no information about this secret order, I have no use for you," Dughall said. He motioned for his guards to take Cormac.

Cormac saw the writing on the wall. He thought fast.

"I have information about the women of the well. I have information. I thought that you were in jest, my liege," he stammered.

"I do not jest," Dughall replied.

Dughall motioned his guards to halt. "You will tell me what you know and if you provide anything useful, I will spare your sorry life. For now."

Cormac told Dughall all that he knew. He told a tale of a secret order of all women, Priestesses, who lived in a walled compound surrounded by a grove of thick ash, thorn and oak. He told of how once a girl entered, she never left and inside learned the arts of magick and of war. Cormac told of the legend of a fierce woman warrior from China who taught the women in the Grove the ancient arts of eastern warfare but who was rumored to be over a thousand years old. Cormac told Dughall that legend had it that these Women of the Well were formidable warriors and much feared.

"What of the Well?" hissed Dughall.

"Yes, well, it is said that they guard a sacred well. It is said that the spring there has healing waters in it, maybe even the secret to everlasting life. Legend says that it is because of these waters that the old Chinese woman lives to this day."

"Healing waters? I have no need of elixirs or potions. Nothing else?" asked Dughall.

Cormac remained silent as he searched his mind for any other legends he knew about the witches of the grove. Dughall let out a tired yawn. At last, Cormac blurted out, "Some say that inside the grove is a door to another world, a place some call Anwaan, the Netherworld. And it is said that the High Priestess wears a magickal torc and that with it, she alone can open the door between worlds. But this is all legend my liege. No one believes in magick or sacred groves anymore," Cormac said.

Dughall sat back in his chair and smiled. Cormac could see a twinkle in Dughall's eyes. Cormac was relieved that he said something that appeared to please Dughall. He may live to see another day.

6 SORCHA

Saorla knew that she had one day, perhaps two, before Dughall and his army attacked her beloved Grove. A thick copse of wood and brambles surrounded the grove on all sides making it inhospitable to most who traipsed around the wood. The grove was protected by a high, stone wall. But thorns and stone would not deter men like Dughall.

For centuries, a powerful spell had hidden the wall from the view of all who passed. The spell could only be lifted by one who knew the proper incantation. Saorla lifted the spell briefly every time that Cathaír visited.

Saorla and the Order of Brighid could also count on their allies. The spirits of the wood, known as the Fair Sídhe, would use their trickery and cunning to slow the progress of Dughall's host. If the men got close to the wall, the powerful spirit that lived in the woods surrounding the grove, Lianhan Sídhe, would entrance and befuddle Dughall and his men. And if Dughall's army somehow managed to make it into the grove itself, the ancient spirit warrior Madame Wong would protect the priestesses. Madame Wong was practically an army in her own right.

But Saorla knew that an army of men determined to break down the walls could do so. No spell or the magick of forest folk could prevent it. She also knew that while the Priestesses of the order, the Fair Sídhe and Madame Wong would put up a fierce battle, twenty adult women, a handful of young girls, some faeries and a spirit warrior were no match for a whole army of men and horses.

The largest threat was that Dughall knew of the torc and he believed in the portal. Saorla's vision was clear. Dughall was after the torc and he wanted to enter the Netherworld. Saorla knew it was not for a good purpose.

She summoned Catháir to her chambers. *I know what I must do. Propriety be damned, I must see him alone*, thought Saorla.

Saorla had her back to the door when Catháir entered her small but warm and inviting cottage. Catháir knew her so well, he felt Saorla's worry and fear before she even turned to face him. Being alone, he did what he would never have done at any other time. Catháir turned her to him and gathered her in his embrace. Tears welled in Saorla's eyes as she returned Catháir's kiss.

Catháir wiped Saorla's tears and held her hands in his. "My dearest love, do not cry."

"Catháir, there is so much that I wanted to say to you, my Anam Ċara, my soul friend. But we do not have the luxury of time. There is something that you must do for me."

"Anything my love. You know I am your servant."

"You will protest this task and say that you cannot. But you must not argue with me. Remember that first and foremost I am High Priestess of the Order of Brighid. My duty is to protect the torc and the portal at all cost."

"Yes and my first duty is to protect you, your Highness."

"But you protect me in order to protect the torc, Catháir. Remember that now as I ask this task of you."

"What task, dearest? You know I will give my life for you if you ask it."

"Not your life, Catháir. You must live. You must survive and protect Sorcha. She is the most valuable life for you to protect now. You must complete this task for me then leave this grove, ride in stealth, cover your tracks well, and go to Sorcha."

"I cannot leave you, Saorla. Not now. You will need a strong warrior here."

"You must leave. Sorcha's life is what you must protect. She needs you."

"Yes, Sorcha needs me. She needs *us*. We will both fight and defeat Dughall. Then we will retrieve Sorcha and live together as a family."

Saorla gently touched Catháir's face. "My dearest. My love," she murmured as she kissed him again. Catháir did not need the sight to see the resolve and sadness in Saorla's eyes.

"There are secrets of this place that even you do not know, Catháir. Secrets that have been passed from the lips of one High Priestess to another. Secrets that now I and only I know. Secrets that must die with me."

"What are you saying?"

"Catháir, see this golden torc around my arm?" Saorla held out her arm and the light glinted off of the shiny gold. "This is what Dughall is after. If he gets his hands on it, he will eventually figure out a way to decipher its magick and enter the portal."

Catháir softly chuckled. "Is that what worries you, my love?" Catháir pulled Saorla to him, and kissed her brow. "You need not worry of that love. I have seen men like this Dughall before. They are nothing more than a brute soldiers and killers. If he is like other leaders of armies from the south, he is too dense to understand how to use the old magick."

Saorla pushed herself out of Catháir's arms. "That is what I am telling you. Dughall is not like others. And he has help."

"Who besides you or a Priestess of the Sacred Grove could interpret the spells?" asked Catháir.

"The Moon Well has shown me the truth. Dughall has one of the Dark Sídhe with him, and he will soon meet Cian, an old druid who was once on his way to being High Druid but who is now a Dark Wizard."

"A Sídhe? Who? A pixie I bet. Those rotten little ... "

"So you see, I must take drastic measures. With the help of Cian and a Dark Sídhe, Dughall may be able to find a way to enter the portal."

"What do you plan to do, Saorla?"

"This you must help me with. I cannot do this alone. You must help me break the Triad of Brighid."

"I have never heard of the Triad of Brighid."

"I know, love. Only the High Priestess knows of the Triad of Brighid. I am breaking my most sacred vow by speaking of it out loud to you now. But the times require that some vows be broken."

Saorla turned her back to Cathaír and walked the few steps needed to stand at her window. It was a warm, spring day. She gazed out at the yellow jasmine that climbed the walls of her cottage and breathed deeply of its sweet scent. *Is there anything more wonderful than the scent of the Earth?* Saorla wondered.

"Tell me, my love. Tell me of this triad."

Saorla did not leave the window but turned to face Cathaír. The morning sun illuminated her pale skin and the rays played upon her golden-red hair so that it looked as if it was touched by fire.

"The torc is not the only magickal object that must be kept from Dughall. The Triad of Brighid creates the magick that has allowed this grove to stay hidden and that has kept the portal open all these centuries, even when the magick at Newgrange and at the great Glastonbury Tor has been lost."

"What is the Triad Saorla?"

"The Triad of Brighid is as old as our people. The torc is one piece. The other is the Sacred Grove itself."

"What is the third piece?" he asked.

"The High Priestess of the Order of Brighid," replied Saorla.

Cathaír's face turned ashen.

"What do you mean?"

"The life force of the High Priestess forms the third and final link of the Triad. Once Dectire ordained me High Priestess, my life force was fused to the torc and to the Sacred Well to form the Triad. It is a great circle, Cathaír. All three must exist together to keep the magick of the Sacred Grove of Brighid alive. That is why a new High Priestess is always ordained prior to the death of the former High Priestess. The life force is constant and eternal, just as the water springs from the well and the fires of the sun burn, the triad keeps the Sacred Grove protected and the portal open."

"If you die, the spell is broken because there is no other High Priestess."

"Yes. Sorcha would likely have been the next High Priestess and when ordained, her life force would fuse with this place, and the Triad would be unbroken."

"But now we cannot wait for Sorcha, can we?" Tears welled in Cathaír's eyes.

"No, Cathaír, we cannot. I must depart this place and time. With my death and the removal of the torc to a place well hidden, the Triad will be broken. The portal will close and the Sacred Grove will become simply an ordinary grove of old trees. But the Netherworld will be protected from Dughall. He must not be allowed to enter the portal, Cathaír."

Cathaír dropped his head and cried openly. Fat tears flowed down his cheeks and wet his beard.

"You said you had a task for me. Please do not ask me to take your life, my love. That is something I cannot do for you."

"I would not ask that of you, dearest. Besides, the torc will not release from me if another takes my life. I must summon the courage to drain my own life force." Tears streamed down Saorla's face as well.

"But you must protect the torc, Catháir. You must ensure that the torc will never be found by Dughall or anyone else except a Priestess of the Order of Brighid."

Catháir's body was wracked with grief. Through his tears, Catháir said, "I will perform that task for you Saorla. I will do everything in my power to ensure no one finds it."

With a sigh of relief, Saorla replied, "Good. And once you complete that mission, you must go to Sorcha. Promise me, Catháir. Promise me that you will protect Sorcha."

"I will my love. I pledge that to you. I am in service to you, Saorla, my High Priestess."

Catháir spent the rest of the day and the night with Saorla. Neither cared that it was forbidden for a Priestess to be alone with a man. They no longer worried of what anyone would say or do. Saorla cherished her last night to love Catháir and share a quiet reverence for life.

7 THE ORDER OF BRIGHID

Dawn had not yet broken when the bell at the Great Hall rang again and again. The bell usually rang only for noon and evening meals. It was the signal that all should gather at the Great Hall. The air of the Sacred Grove was filled with tension as all in the Grove knew that the ringing of the bells meant trouble.

The Younglings nervously whispered to each other "What's going on?" and "Do you know what's happening?" They did not know why they had been summoned to the Great Hall before sunrise.

Saorla stood serenely in front of her chair at the head of the Great Hall and waited for all to filter in. She was dressed in her best white linen tunic and had a purple cape fastened about her shoulders with a large jeweled brooch. Her hair was tightly plaited and woven with small jewels. When they saw Saorla standing straight and solemn, bedecked in her best ritual finery, they fell quiet and took their seats. After a long silence, Saorla spoke.

"My sisters, you know that significant change is upon us. Since the beginning of the Order many moons ago, armies have come to our fair land to take what is not theirs. Our people have fought off these invaders time and again." Saorla paused and sat in her chair.

"Many of you have had visions and know that this time, it is different."

Saorla looked out and saw many of the priestesses nodding their heads. Their look of worry and fear meant that they too had seen the foretelling of the end of their world.

"Our High King is dead, and as I speak to you, there is an army advancing on this very Grove." Several novices and even a few priestesses let out audible gasps.

The priestess Coventina said, "But we are protected here. The spells and enchantments are strong. And we have powerful allies in the Lianhan Sídhe and Madame Wong."

"True, Coventina. These protections have served us well for centuries. But as we speak, a dark one comes to our Grove. He intends to gain use of the magick of Brighid for his own evil purpose. And he is being helped by a traitor of the High King, by one of our former brothers and by at least one of the Dark Sídhe."

The women whispered in disbelief. Saorla continued.

"We have not much time my sisters so listen well to my words. We are the last of our kind and all that stands between this dark force and the Sacred Well. All of your preparation and training have been for a day such as this. You will need to draw on your skills of war as well as your magick craft." Saorla paused and breathed deeply. *I must inspire them and help them move past their fear.*

"Each of you has a singular gift, something that you do better than anyone else. Use your gift in service to your sisters, in service to our noble land, and in service to the Goddess herself." Saorla could see the priestesses sit a taller and felt their fear dissipate, replaced by pride and determination.

"Within one more rotation, you will fight the greatest battle this Grove has ever seen. You will fight for your life and for the soul of Ireland. These invaders have never seen women warriors before. They will underestimate you. Use that to your advantage.

"I will hold council with our allies the Fair Sídhe and request their aid in our time of need. The elder Priestesses and Madame Wong have instructions from me for your preparations and battle strategy. Do exactly as they ask of you."

Saorla looked out on the faces of the Priestesses of the Order of Brighid and knew that it may be the last time she would see many of them. As she glanced down at the younglings in the first row, she felt a tear come to her eye. *Am I doing the right thing? Shouldn't I be by their side and fight with them?* The thought of her sisters shedding their blood in battle made her shiver despite the warmth of the dawning day.

She took a deep breath and suppressed her tears. She knew sure of what she had to do. *This is no time to question the deep knowing within.*

"My sisters, I love you all. Remember, you are the embodiment of the Goddess herself. Let the Goddess flow through you. May your sword be true, your shield strong, your breath steady and may the Light of the Goddess be with you always." With that, she put her hands in prayer position by her heart and bowed to her sisters. They bowed to her as well as she walked forward to bestow on each the blessing of the Moon. After she had blessed the last priestess, she walked out of the Great Hall for the last time, her purple cloak billowing behind her.

8 THE DARK ONE COMES

Hours after Cormac betrayed the most sacred secrets of Ireland, Dughall ordered his men to assassinate Ruaidrí, the last High King of Ireland. Dughall's official mission given to him by the Emperor was complete. Dughall had absolute control of the Emerald Isle.

But for Dughall, control over an island overrun with barbarians was not enough. He had his sights on something far greater. The next morning, Dughall put his highest commander in charge of Érie, and he set off with his best army to the south and west to search for the Sacred Grove of Brighid. At nightfall, Dughall ordered camp and went to his tent to eat alone.

As Dughall chewed his bread, he heard a slight rustling sound behind him. Within seconds, he was on his feet, turned around and had pulled his sword from its sheath. His men knew better than to enter his tent without permission.

In the darkness he saw a small figure appear. *Is this a child in my camp? Child or no, I will kill anyone who dare enter my private tent.*

But it was not a child. Standing before Dughall was a creature that had been relegated to legend. Dughall stood aghast and stared at a pixie.

Dughall could not believe in his own sight. He had heard the Celt peasants talk of forest folk and faeries, but he did not believe in it. Dughall thought it was just the talk of imbecile pagans.

Here it was though, standing no more than two feet high and extremely slight of build. Her ears came to a point, and her skin was as white and luminous as marble. Her wings were like those of a dragonfly. They were thin as onionskin, shiny, and iridescent. They changed colors depending on the light and her mood. The pixie's eyes were overly large for her small face and dark as coal with no color visible at all. The overall impression was frightening despite her diminutive stature.

The sprite said nothing but bowed slightly. In a small voice that Dughall had to strain a bit to hear, she said, "I am Macha, of the Dark Sídhe. I come to offer my assistance to the one who has slain the last High King of Érie."

Dughall was speechless. At last he said, "Why would you offer to help me? You are a faerie, and I seek to take over your country. Why help me in this plot?"

"There are many Sídhe in this fair land. Some are what the humans call 'Fair Sídhe'. Others are 'Dark Sídhe', like myself. Before humans came, we were in all corners of this isle. We of the Dark Sídhe have never forgiven the humans for taking our lands from us and driving us to the knolls, mounds, trees, and underground."

"Why do you think I would be different? I can tell you that I detest most humans, and I am not inclined to enjoy the company of bestial creatures any better. Your high pitched voice is already grating me." Dughall eyed his sword as he considered wielding it.

"We believe that you will treat us differently because we have something that you need." Macha's voice was steady and without a hint of fear.

Dughall stopped eyeing his sword for the moment. "Tell me why I should not swat you down here and now."

"We know why you are here and that your task is not yet complete," Macha said.

Dughall raised his dark eyebrows. "What task is that?"

"You seek the golden ring, the torc of the Order of Brighid."

She had his complete attention. Dughall's sword dropped to his side. "Continue."

"You seek the power that lies within the Grove. But there are potent spells and enchantments that protect the Grove. Despite these, you may break through. You have men to spare. But the Order also has allies such as the Fair Sídhe. Their magick is formidable, and they are loyal to the High Priestess and the goddess. You will need our assistance to even find the Grove, and once there, you will need our help to get inside."

"Let us assume that you are correct and that I, Dughall, High King of Érie, needs you. What do you and your kind want in return?"

"The Dark Sídhe will be your allies and protect you and your lands from your enemies. In exchange, we will be equal to the humans that live here and have our own lands."

Dughall thought for a moment and again eyed his sword. He did not know if he could trust the creature. *Perhaps it has been sent by the High Priestess as a decoy.*

On the other hand, Macha confirmed what Cormac had told him. And if it was true, the force of his armies may not be enough to obtain the object of his desire. *I may need the magick of this detestable creature if I am to succeed in my mission.*

"You may join me in this quest," he said finally. "But know this Macha. If you or any of your kind betrays me, you will not need to bother with running to the mounds or forests. Your faerie blood will trickle into the roots of your beloved trees, and it will be the end of your kind."

Macha simply nodded her head in understanding and took leave of Dughall as quickly as she came. Where she went he did not know and truly did not care. *I may keep my word to her or I may not.* It would depend on his mood.

Dughall lay on his bed of blankets and lamb's wool and grinned widely. He could scarcely believe his unexpected luck. *This is going better than I had planned. It is a sign of approval from the divine that my purpose is noble indeed. It will not be long now and I will hold in my hands the key to my deepest desire.*

9 MARCH TO THE SACRED GROVE

Despite the fact that Saorla redoubled all of the spells and enchantments protecting the location of the Sacred Grove, with the help of Macha and the other Dark Sídhe, Dughall was able to find it.

There were several skirmishes along the way between the Fair Sídhe and the Dark Sídhe. Dughall and his men stood almost speechless as small, brightly dressed faeries flew out of trees, mounds and woods, their wings glistening in the sun, and attacked the Dark Sídhe that were traveling with Dughall and his men. The Dark Sídhe, full of pent up venom and anger, dispatched their attackers quickly and with ease. After a few hours, there were no more surprise attacks by the Fair Sídhe, who apparently decided to give up rather than be exterminated.

At the suggestion of Macha, Dughall ordered two of his men to go forward as scouts as the rest pulled back. After two hours, one of the soldiers stumbled back to camp while the other soldier was nowhere to be found.

"What happened?" Dughall asked the hapless man.

The soldier stared vacantly and said over and over, "I am your servant, my love."

Dughall quickly lost patience with the man who had clearly lost his mind. He paced the floor and tired of hearing the soldier prattle on and on, he pulled his sword and in one swift stroke, cut off the man's head.

"Now he will stop with his incessant, mindless chatter," he said. The soldier's head rolled a few yards and came to a stop just a few feet in front of Dughall.

"Sire," Macha said in her soft but brittle voice. "He has been kissed by the Lianhan Sídhe, Sire," she said.

"Explain, creature," Dughall barked.

"She is a powerful spirit. Lianhan Sídhe is quite beautiful to human men and irresistible. She lures men to her then kisses them. But her kiss removes most of their life essence, and they become addle brained or kill themselves."

"So this hapless soul was already dead," Dughall said flatly as he nudged the lifeless head lying on the ground with his toe. "This is all very interesting, Macha, but how can we defeat this creature?"

"I do not know, Sire," replied Macha.

Dughall spun toward her, his eyes ablaze with fury. "You drag me all the way out into this wood claiming you can gain entry to the Grove, and now you tell me that you do not know how to defeat the creature that stands in my way?" Dughall bellowed.

"Sire, no one that has ever seen the Lianhan Sídhe has been able to say what they saw. No one knows exactly how she holds sway over men. We must send another scout, but this time, be close enough to see what happens," offered Macha.

Dughall's face softened ever so slightly. "You mean send another of my men as bait, is that what you are suggesting?" asked Dughall.

"Well, yes, Sire. I think it is the only way," answered Macha.

"Yes, Macha, I think you are right. You are a detestable little creature. So devoid of feelings for human life. I do believe I am starting to like you."

Dughall's compliment made Macha's skin brighten and her wings became an iridescent coral color. Together, Macha and Dughall made a plan to find at last the secret of the power of the Lianhan Sídhe.

10 LIANHAN SÍDHE

Dughall and Macha were in position. They followed a safe distance behind the soldier who they tapped to be the scout then scampered to the top of a small hill where they would have a view. The poor soldier had seen his mate come back from the last scouting trip addle minded and knew that the other had not been seen again. His legs quaked as he entered the area around the Sacred Grove.

If a person was observant, they could notice that when one got close to the entry of the Grove, all was still. There was no breeze and no birds chirped. The winds were calm. There was no movement at all. As the soldier approached, the stillness made him quake even more. The preternatural quiet made the area around the Grove eerie. The eerie quiet made most who experienced it flee in fright.

As the scout wandered the perimeter of the wall, he felt a slight breeze and a chill come over him. He turned and saw before him the most beautiful woman he had ever seen.

Her hair fell around her shoulders in waves of gold. Her eyes were the brightest blue, like two radiant sapphires. Her full, rosy lips were parted slightly. But it was perhaps her skin that was the most striking. Pale and luminescent, it almost glowed. The soldier was so immediately enthralled with her beauty that he did not notice that she was, in fact, hovering before him, held aloft by her large faerie wings.

Dughall and Macha watched the whole scene from afar. They saw the soldier immediately enraptured by the beautiful creature. They watched as the scout moved closer, a wide smile on his lips. He held out his hands to her, and she held out her hands to him. They heard music. It was faint at first, but grew louder. It was singing. The Lianhan Sídhe sang to the soldier, and it was the song that lured him ever closer to her.

Macha turned her small head to Dughall and said, "Do not listen to her song. Muffle the sound so you cannot hear her."

Dughall did as she said and wrapped a cloth from his saddlebag around his ears. He could see the Lianhan Sídhe but could not hear her beautiful song.

What he saw was totally unexpected. The Lianhan Sídhe smiled in a most beguiling way and continued to sing her song and lure the man closer. At last, their hands touched. She bent to kiss him, and he offered his lips to her. As soon as their lips touched, Dughall saw the man's body go rigid, and for a split second, he opened his eyes wide in terror.

The Lianhan Sídhe was no longer the beauty that had lured him to her. Her eyes had gone from beautiful sapphires to red as flame. Her fingers ended in sharp talons rather than neatly trimmed nails. Her wings, seconds ago light and glittery, were the scaly wings of a dragon. Her body and face, previously all light and luminous, were covered in reptilian scales. Her lovely blue billowy dress was replaced with rags.

As she drained the life force from the man, his eyes became vacant. The Lianhan Sídhe's beautiful song was replaced with a loud cackling. The life force of the man seemed to have made her even larger and more powerful. As quickly as she had appeared she disappeared with a loud crack as she flapped her large dragon wings and disappeared into the waning light of day.

Dughall and Macha stared in wonder at the spot where the Lianhan Sídhe had just been. It was Macha who broke the silence.

"You know Sire, legend says that if a man can resist her kiss, that she is defeated and doomed to wander the earth as a ghost for a thousand years, unable to take any more victims."

"You mean, if I can resist her ... "

"If you can resist her, you will defeat her. She will be powerless," Macha replied.

Dughall's lips curled into a sneer. He had discovered the secret of the Lianhan Sídhe, a secret unknown to any man in history until now. *I will defeat he and rob her of her power. No faerie harlot will stand between me and that which I most desire.*

"You know Sire, that ordinary cloth will not be enough when you get close to her. Her song will pierce right through it," said Macha.

Dughall had not thought of that. He would need something stronger.

"Do you have magick that will protect me?" he asked.

"No Sire, but I know of one who does," Macha answered.

Macha summoned Cian, a Dark Wizard. She told Cian that Dughall needed a potion that would render his ears useless for a time.

Cian eyed both Macha and Dughall warily. "I owe you nothing, Macha. Why should I do this for you or for this one?" he said as he gestured toward Dughall.

At that Dughall quickly grabbed the old wizard and put his sword to the man's throat. "This, my dear man, is why you should help me," Dughall hissed.

"Ah, you are all about might then. You fighting men. You think that piece of metal makes you superior," the wizard replied.

"Who is in a position to die now, old man? You will help me, or I'll run you through."

The wizard had been caught off guard and was not in a position to use his magick to defend himself. He found himself with no choice but to give in to Dughall's demands.

"It appears I have no choice but to aid you, oh dark one," Cian croaked. Dughall released Cian and the old wizard stumbled. "I will need time to gather the proper ingredients." Cian rubbed his throat where Dughall's sword had been.

"It grows dark. You shall have the evening, but no more. I want your potion at first dawn old man."

Cian went into the thick woods that surrounded their camp and worked feverishly through the night with only the light of a torch to help him find the forest herbs and fungus that he needed for his potion. By dawn, the potion was ready for Dughall.

"Here it is, as you demanded." Cian handed the tankard to Dughall. "Drink all of this and you will not have use of your hearing."

"I will not be able to hear anything, old man?" asked Dughall.

"You will not be able to hear the loudest thunder," replied Cian.

"And it is only temporary?"

"It will wear off after a few hours," said Cian.

Dughall took the cup and drank the potion down quickly. Midway through he gagged from the vile taste, but he forced himself to choke down the viscous draught. No sooner than he had swallowed the last of it, he was overcome with excruciating pain in his ears. His heart pumped faster and he heard the sound of his blood rushing through his veins. Dughall held his ears, fell to the ground and writhed in pain.

"I will kill you, old man." Dughall's voice was choked by his pain as he held his ears. He would have surely cut the dark wizard down if he had been able to get to his sword. But soon the agony began to subside, and as it did, he realized that he could not hear. He clapped, he spoke and let out a loud yell but could hear nothing. He smiled wide, a most unsettling sight.

"My hearing will return?" asked Dughall. The old wizard nodded.

Macha accompanied Dughall to their spot within sight of the Grove. Cian stayed behind at camp as being a human man, he was susceptible to the Lianhan Sídhe's song.

As Dughall approached, he felt the same stillness that the soldier had felt followed by the same slight breeze and sudden chill in the air. Then she appeared. *Even more beautiful up close.* He felt drawn to her even though he could not hear her song. For a brief moment, Dughall was worried. It was an uncommon emotion for Dughall. *Though I hear not, I am drawn to her. Macha, you imbecile! I have been tricked.*

But as Dughall drew closer, he saw that her while the faerie's lips moved, he could not hear her song. Her beauty drew him to her, and he wanted to kiss her lips, but he kept his wits about him. He knew that giving into one desire would doom his quest so he resisted her. Just as she bent closer with the softest rose petal lips to kiss him, Dughall shouted at the Lianhan Sídhe, "I rebuke thee! You do not charm me, devil woman. Be off with you."

Just as her lips were about to meet his, she heard Dughall's words and her beautiful visage changed instantly. Her eyes were again as red as flame, her hands talons, and her wings like a dragon's. She screeched loud and piercing for just a moment then fell silent. She was still visible but became as a ghost, there but barely. Her ghostlike image wandered off into the wood, her face sallow and her mouth open as if in a scream.

Dughall still could not hear so he did not know that no sound came from her horrible open mouth. But he knew that he had defeated Lianhan Sídhe and that she would no longer stand between him and the torc.

11 BATTLE FOR THE SACRED GROVE

"Now what, Macha?" asked Dughall.

"We must find the gate," she replied.

"There is nothing here but vines and trees," replied one of the soldiers.

"It is an enchantment, you imbecile," sneered Dughall. "All of you, earn your keep and hack away these plants," he barked.

"I would not do that if I were you," interrupted Macha.

"And pray tell, why not dear Macha?" asked Dughall.

"Because those vines and trees are not ordinary."

"Yes, yes, they are under a spell. I know. So we will break that spell," said Dughall.

"It is not just a spell. The vines and trees are enchanted and in service to the Sacred Grove. They will defend themselves. You cannot break the spell by cutting them," said Macha.

"Macha, I have over one hundred men here with axes, maces, swords and hatchets. The magick of the sisters of this grove is no match for the magick of steel. You heard me. CUT!"

The soldiers hesitated. After seeing one of their own come back from the Lianhan Sídhe addle minded, most of them had become believers of the magick of the Sacred Grove. But their fear of Dughall was greater than their fear of the magick, so they began to hack away at the vines and trees thickly covering all of the walls and gate to the Sacred Grove.

At first it seemed to work. The vines were dispatched and fell to the ground. But within seconds, the vines not only regrew themselves but also became even thicker. The trees, too, seemed to grow larger. Before they saw it coming, vines wrapped themselves around the men, axes and hatchets and all. Within minutes, all of the soldiers near the thicket were totally engulfed, swallowed alive by the living thicket. Their screams were loud and agonizing, all sounding at the same time. Even Macha covered her ears.

As their screams faded, the vines and trees returned to normal. The remaining soldiers stood still in their tracks, dumbfounded by what had just happened.

Dughall was beyond angry.

"Okay Macha, we will do it your way. What magick do you suggest we use to get through these evil branches?" asked Dughall.

"We need a spell to break the spell," she said.

"And so say it. Say the spell," Dughall hissed.

"I do not know the spell," Macha replied.

Dughall's hand moved to his sword, and he was just about to slice the little faerie in half when the Dark Wizard stepped forward. "I can recite the spell," he said. "But it will take time to gather the information needed to determine the right spell."

"You have five minutes," snarled Dughall.

Cian walked the perimeter of the thicket. He picked up leaves that had fallen and rubbed them between his fingers and tasted them. He held them to his ears. He stood quietly along the perimeter with his eyes closed for several minutes.

Dughall's patience was at its end. "Your time is up old man. Say a spell now or so help me, I will run you through."

"If you live a thousand lifetimes, it will not be long enough for you to learn patience, Dughall," Cian replied. The old man closed his eyes, circled his arms wide and held them above him as he cited the incantation.

"Holy Hawthorne, oak and ash,
twisted and gnarled, wound tight.
Pray let these servants of Brighid pass,
through this gate to the Sacred Grove,
there to do her bidding.
In honor always to the Goddess,
blessed be the keepers of her Flame."

At first there was no change. The air remained still. There was no sound of bird or bee, just the occasional snort of the horses.

Then a subtle change. The vines thinned. The trees moved farther apart. The thicket weakened.

There. Just a peek at first. Stones. Large stone walls came into view. Finally, a large wooden gate. The Sacred Grove of the Order of Brighid, visible for the first time to outsiders.

Dughall's face curled into a sneer, the closest his face ever got to happiness. Even Dughall was impressed with the magick that had protected the Grove for over a thousand years. *The so-called magick of these women is no match for my superior intelligence and desire to have what lay inside these walls.*

Dughall gave the order. "Tear down that gate!" he bellowed.

The men at once took their axes and hatchets and hacked away at the gate. In a matter of minutes, they had torn down the gate and funneled into the Grove on foot and horseback.

Dughall mounted his horse and sauntered into the Grove. Even he had to stop for a moment and admire its beauty. The light was softer inside, especially as compared to the dark and harsh light of the thicket outside the walls. Inside the Grove, it was peaceful. There was only the sound of the wind through the trees, a distant babbling brook and the occasional cricket or birdsong.

But most lovely was the smell. The wind wafted the most delicious odor of fruit blossoms through the air. For Dughall, it called to mind happy memories from the homeland of his childhood. He was momentarily lost in his thoughts when Cormac interrupted.

"Sire, we are inside the gate."

"I know that you idiot," Dughall growled back.

"What is your next order, Sire?" Cormac asked.

Dughall gathered himself. "Tell your soldiers to round up every person in this place, but ensure that they do not kill anyone. I need them all alive. For now. Go!"

The soldiers spread out and ransacked every building they found as they searched for the inhabitants of the lovely Grove. They searched the entire front half of the Grove and found not a single person. Dughall was frustrated and considered ordering them to torch the place when he heard a call.

"Sire, over here!"

The call came from the large building at the back and center of the Grove. As he entered he saw the priestesses in a tight circle in the center of the building. They were dressed in ordinary linen tunics tied around the waist with a thin cord.

"Do not kill any of them," Dughall ordered. "Find the one with the gold torc around her upper arm. Bring that one to me. After you find her, kill the rest."

At that moment, the women untied their sashes and ripped off their tunics. Underneath all were dressed in their battle clothes. Leather breeches with a dagger strapped to each thigh. A strong leather harness slung around their shoulders armed with hatches, maces, swords and Chinese blades. The priestesses quickly put on the helmets that they had hidden behind their backs. They armed themselves and readied for battle so quickly the soldiers were frozen in fear.

Dughall was incensed at the sight. Each woman wore the same item around her right arm. All of them wore a torc. How would he tell which one was the magickal torc? He was ready to order the soldiers to kill them all, but Macha flew close to his ear and interrupted his thoughts.

"It is a ruse, Sire," she whispered.

"Ruse? What do you mean?"

"She is not here. The true Torc of Brighid is with her somewhere else."

It took a few seconds for Macha's words to sink in. *Look for her somewhere else.*

"Yes. Macha, Cormac, and the old man. You three are with me." Dughall turned to leave the Great Hall with Macha flitting lightly on the air beside him.

"Sire," a soldier called. "What do we do here?"

"Kill them all," he replied.

As soon as Dughall left the Great Hall, the women warriors spread out and Madame Wong flew from the center. She was a jumping, bouncing, flying ball of sword and dagger. She slashed and thrust her sword so quickly that any soldier in her path fell to his death before he could be sure of what had hit him.

The most trained and skilled women warriors flanked the outside of their circle, wielding their arms with grace and power. Intermixed with the Priestesses were many faeries, armed with bow and arrow and slingshots. And in the center of the circle were the younglings, well protected by their older sisters, the Fair Sídhe and Madame Wong. The younglings did their part by chanting their most powerful protective spells.

As soldiers began to fall in heaps, the remaining men got over their initial shock at the sight of the women warriors appearing out of what looked like a throng of devout priestesses. They had to contend not only with four foot tall Madame Wong slicing and dicing, but also the keen aim of the faeries' bow and arrows.

They squared off, each soldier battling a woman warrior. More soldiers fell than women warriors but still, as the battle waged on, the Order of Brighid too shed much blood.

In the midst of the fighting, the sound of their groans and shouts of pain came a loud and horrible screeching. For a moment, the battle stopped as all heard what sounded like metal scraping on metal while an injured cat howls.

Those fighting for the Order of Brighid knew instantly what made the awful noise. Bian Sídhe. And in an instant they also knew the reason for the Bian Sídhe's cry. One of the ancient blood of Ireland had fallen.

12 SAORLA AT THE WELL

After Saorla had given her last blessing in the Great Hall, she met with the Fair Sídhe to confer on battle strategy. She reinforced the incantations and spells that protected the Grove. After she had strengthened all protection spells, she went to the Sacred Well and spent the rest of the morning in silent prayer and meditation.

At the appointed time, Cathaír silently appeared at the Well. They looked into each other's eyes and without words spoke to each other all of the love they felt for each other.

As they heard the soldiers breaking down the gate of the Sacred Grove, they knew the time had come. They could wait no longer.

Saorla pulled her small, jeweled dagger from her cloak and without a single word, plunged it deep into her belly. Crimson liquid bloomed on the front of her white linen tunic as blood poured from the self-inflicted wound. Within a few minutes, all color had drained from her face. Cathaír caught her in his arms as her body began to fall. He gently lowered her to the ground and rested her head on his thigh.

They said not a word. Cathaír simply stroked her lovely red locks and forced a wan smile to his lips as he looked into the emerald pools of her eyes. He pulled Saorla to him, bent his head, and touched his warm lips to her cool ones.

As the life drained from Saorla's body, the spells and enchantments that protected the Grove faded too. Even the light began to change. It lost its soft quality and matched the harshness of the woods that surrounded the Sacred Grove. The air became cooler and the sun faded behind the gathering clouds.

The silence of the moment was broken as Saorla whispered her last word. "Sorcha."

As the last breath passed from her lips, the golden torc loosened its grip around her arm and fell gently to the ground. Catháir wanted to stay, to hold her and continue to stroke her hair. He wanted to plunge her dagger into his own chest to stop the ache that weighed heavy in his heart.

But he had made a sacred vow to his beloved. He knew what he must do.

He picked up the torc, still warm from her body, wrapped it in a linen cloth and hid it deep in the pocket inside his cloak. Catháir gently lowered Saorla's head to the ground, kissed her cold lips one last time then ran.

He ran as fast as he could run. He ran to the edge of the Grove, away from the Great Hall and the soldiers and Dughall. He ran and ran until he reached the edge of the Grove. He stopped to recite the spell required to lift the enchantment so he could get out of the tangle of vines and branches. But before he could recite the spell, he realized he didn't need it anymore. After Saorla had departed, enchantments no longer protected the Grove.

Catháir stepped out of the Grove and into a new world. It was a frightening world to Catháir where there was no longer a link between his human world and the world of magick. The light was harsher, the air more acidic. Maybe it was, or maybe it was just his sorrow and anger that made the air he breathed taste like a bitter poison. He pulled his cloak over his head and tread out of that grove, never to return.

He slipped easily through the tangle of vines. He found his horse where he had left it. Cathaír rode as fast as his steed could take him. The wind whipped his hair and vines and branches cut his hands and face as he rode through the tangle.

As Cathaír rode, he heard the mournful cry of the Bian Sídhe. Her hideous screech cut through the air surrounding the Grove. Her cries only made him ride faster, away from the dead body of his love. Away from the woman that was the embodiment of the goddess on Earth. Away from the fallen Sacred Grove of Brighid.

He rode with a single-minded purpose. He must go to Sorcha.

13 THE END OF THE ORDER OF BRIGHID

"Saorla killed herself?" I asked.

"Yes," Hindergog said.

"But she should have fought," said Fanny. "She gave up. If she and Cathaír had fought too, they could have whipped Dughall's butt."

"My mistress was a formidable warrior, and she might have 'whipped his butt' as you say, lass, but she could not take the chance. If there was any possibility that Dughall could lay his hands on the torc in the Sacred Grove ... well, it was just too dangerous to risk."

"Why?" asked Jake. "What would happen if Dughall had been successful?"

"Mysteries are revealed in the Netherworld. Some things are best kept a mystery."

"But you want me to go there. If some things are best left to mystery, why send me there?"

"You must go, my young mistress, so that you can prevent Dughall from learning the secrets of the Netherworld."

"Are you saying Dughall would use the information for evil, not good?" Fanny asked.

"Evil is all that Dughall knows," replied Hindergog. "Now young ones, my story is almost complete. Stay quiet while I finish the tale of Saorla and the Order of Brighid."

*   *   *

As Bian Sídhe wailed, Dughall, Cormac, Macha and Cian ran through the Grove on the old, hidden path to the Well. The wood was thick and cut into their ankles and wrists as they ran.

In time, the copse began to clear, and it opened to reveal a circle of stones around a well. Dughall burst into the clearing and there, lying beside the stones was Saorla, her body lifeless, her skin pale alabaster. Saorla's fingers were still curled around her dagger, wet with her own blood.

Dughall barked orders to Macha. "Remove her cloak so I may take my prize," he hollered.

"It is not here, you fool," Macha replied.

"What do you mean?" he yelled back.

"Do you not remember a thing that I speak to you? She killed herself so the torc would release. She probably had someone take it. If she did, they are long gone by now." As she spoke, Macha pulled Saorla's cloak aside to reveal her right arm, bare now that the torc was gone.

Dughall was silent for a moment then began a low, guttural scream that soon rose higher and higher until it vied with Bian Sídhe's own wailing. Dughall's fury encompassed him. He pulled his sword and in one quick movement, swung his sharply honed blade at Cormac and cut his head clean off his body. Cormac's body fell with a thud, blood gushing from the gaping wound where his head used to be.

"Feel better now?" Macha taunted.

"Watch your tone, pixie, or you will be next. I grow weary of the sight of you," he replied.

"You will not kill me," she said.

"Give me one good reason why I should not lay waste to you, the old man there, and everyone in my path?"

"Because this old man and I are the only ones that can help you achieve your greatest desire."

"I have listened to you and tolerated this insipid old fool. Look what it has brought me. This young girl has outwitted us all." Dughall punctuated his statement with a kick to Saorla's limp body.

The ground began to rumble and shake. The sky blackened further and thunder bellowed. All around Saorla's body the ground began to crack. Up through the cracks came grass and vines that wound around Saorla's corpse. Within a matter of seconds, the ground swallowed her and her jeweled dagger whole.

As quickly as the rumbling and shaking had begun it stopped. The cracks disappeared. The sky returned to its overcast grey. The thunder ceased. There was no trace of Saorla. Even the bloodstains on the ground were gone. It was as if she had never existed.

Even after seeing the pixie and Dark Wizard magick; even after his run-in with the Lianhan Sídhe; after seeing the vines and trees come to life to protect the Grove; even after all the magick he had seen, Dughall still had a hard time believing what he had just seen. For a moment, he questioned whether any of it was real.

"Ah, ashes to ashes," broke in Cian. With that statement, he turned to leave.

"Where do you think you are going?" asked Dughall.

"It is done here," he replied. "You have failed, oh angry one. Time for you to go on to your next conquest."

"I do not accept failure," Dughall hissed. "Someone took that torc, and whoever has it cannot be far away from here," he said.

With that, he turned on his heal and ordered Macha and the Dark Wizard to come with him. *I will find that torc if it is the last thing that I do.*

14 SEARCH FOR THE TORC

Dughall tromped through the thicket and back to the Great Hall. When he got there, he expected to see his men finishing off the last of the women he had ordered them to kill. Instead, he saw his soldiers fleeing. Grown men ran from the hall and screamed like little girls.

"What is the meaning of this insubordination?" Dughall charged up the steps of the Great Hall and opened its doors. Inside, he saw piles of bodies, mostly his own soldiers, lying in heaps. And there, at the center of it all was Bian Sídhe. Like her sister Lianhan Sídhe in her fearsome aspect, Bian Sídhe had large red wings covered in scales like a dragon. Her long, dark hair whipped wildly about her head and shoulders. Full of anger and fury, her red eyes shot flames at all that stood in her path.

The women warriors and faeries stood behind her, guarding the younglings, their weapons still drawn. And fighting at Bian Sídhe's side was Madame Wong. The ancient spirit warrior hurled her little body about and wielded a sword in each hand. Any ill-fated man who happened to get close would either be incinerated by Bian Sídhe or sliced and diced by Madame Wong.

Upon seeing the scene, Dughall understood why the men fled. There was no point in fighting. As he left the Great Hall, Dughall barked out the order for his soldiers to torch the place. "Burn it all down," he yelled.

"I would not do that if I were you," Macha curtly said.

"Again you tell me what I must not do, Macha. You excel in speaking of do nots yet you seem fresh out of dos," said Dughall. "I may well regret asking this question but I shall ask it all the same. Why should I spare this pathetic group of shacks?"

"Because there may be clues here. Clues about the torc and where it has gone. Clues about the portal and how to get in," she coolly replied.

In his anger, Dughall had not thought of the possibility that he could still find anything of use inside the grove. *Yes, search for clues and find the torc. Its power would be mine.*

Dughall, Macha, and Cian split up and searched the sleeping huts and other buildings for clues. Macha happened upon Saorla's own small thatch-roofed cottage. As she rifled through her belongings, at the very back of a high shelf Macha came upon a small leather-bound book with vellum pages. As she opened the book, she knew she had found exactly what they looked for.

She quickly flew to Dughall with her prize. Macha's wings were a shimmery luminescent orange. "Here," she said as she flung it at Dughall.

"What is this?" he asked.

"Open it and see. That is, if a brute like you can read."

"Of course I can read, you impudent insect," he snarled.

As Dughall opened the book, his eyes grew wide. He could not believe what he had. *All that I hoped for and more. This is a written guide for the secrets of the Sacred Well. In my hands I hold immortality.*

"Macha, you endearing little gnat," he beamed. "I shall spare your life after all."

"How kind of you," Macha retorted.

"What does it say?" asked Cian.

"What does it say? It holds the key to the whole thing, old man. According to this, it was not the torc at all. That sly minx. Putting all off the trail." Dughall's eyes flitted frantically over the pages.

"What is the key, then?" asked Cian.

"A chalice," replied Dughall.

"A chalice?" asked Cian.

"Yes, old fool. Is there an echo in here? A chalice. A cup," replied Dughall.

"That does not sound right. It may be a trick," said Cian. "I do not recall ever hearing about a sacred chalice in all my Druid days. The torc yes, but not a chalice."

"It was a well kept secret then, was it not?" replied Dughall. "These deceitful women hid their secrets even from you Druids." Dughall laughed.

"But if the key to the portal is a chalice, why did she hide the torc?" asked Cian.

"Who knows, maybe it has some magick to it too. But I am not interested in charming little spells. I will find this chalice. I will find it and when I do, I will open the portal once again and I will have all that I desire."

*   *   *

"A chalice? What is he talking about?" asked Jake.

"Yeah, you never mentioned a chalice, whatever that is," said Fanny.

"A chalice is a large cup. But, ah my dear mistress, how clever she was," Hindergog chortled. "She made this up, dear ones. There was no chalice."

"Oh my god, she lied," I said.

"Yes, she lied and what a beautiful lie it was. Dughall began a quest to find this 'sacred' cup, a quest that would last a lifetime," said Hindergog.

"Hmm, chalice. It wasn't the same chalice as they tried to find in the Crusades, was it?" asked Jake.

"That, young lad, I do not know. I wish I could answer all of your questions younglings, but sadly I cannot. Here is where my story comes to a close. All that I saw I could see because I am the keeper of the story of the High Priestess. When Saorla died and the torc was hidden, my ability to see into your world faded."

"But I have so many questions, Hindergog. Like how is it that this dude from over a thousand years ago is a threat to us now? And where is the torc? And when I find it, where is the portal and how do I get in?"

"I do not know the answers to all of your questions, Miss Emily. I wish that I did." Hindergog's voice sounded sad.

"But you must have some idea," said Jake. "Any clues you can give us."

"'Us'," I said.

"Look, we've got to find this guy," said Jake.

"I don't really see why 'we' need to do anything," I said. "Look Hindergog, this is a gripping story and all. But I'm just a fourteen-year-old girl who's flunking at least three subjects. I'm not really up for a quest to save the world and all," I said.

"Miss Emily, you may not have a choice," replied Hindergog.

"What do you mean, munchkin?" asked Fanny.

"Dughall may be a killer, devoid of human emotion, but he is exceptionally smart. He may track you down, Miss Emily. He will not take a chance that Saorla's descendant will outwit him this time," Hindergog said.

"What do you mean, 'Saorla's descendant?'" I asked.

"Yeah, you never did explain exactly how Emily relates to all this," said Jake.

"You are Saorla's descendant, of course. You have Priestess blood running through your veins," answered Hindergog.

"But Saorla died," I said.

"Jeez Em, weren't you paying attention?" asked Fanny. "Sorcha. She's your ancestor. She lived."

We were all quiet for a moment as we reflected on all that Hindergog had said. Of course. Sorcha was the daughter of Saorla and Cathaír.

I hurled questions at Hindergog. "Tell us more about Sorcha. What happened to Cathaír when he left the Grove? Did he go to Sorcha? Did he hide the torc?"

"I know youngling, so many questions. But I do not have time for additional tales. I must spend my last seconds telling you valuable information," said Hindergog.

"Where did Cathaír hide the torc?" asked Jake.

Hindergog was beginning to fade.

"Hurry," I said. "Before you disappear, you've got to tell us where the torc is and what to do with it when we find it."

"I do not know where the torc is my young mistress," said Hindergog.

"What? You don't know where it is? You start us on a wild goose chase, and you don't even know where to look for the stupid thing," I snapped. I was so mad at that little guy, if he were in the flesh, I probably would have tried to strangle him.

"Please, calm yourself Miss Emily. I do not know exactly where the torc is, but I do have some clues."

"Great, a madman is trying to screw up the whole world, and we have to go on a scavenger hunt," said Fanny.

"The torc's residual energy from Saorla allowed me to 'see' what it saw for a brief time after Saorla's body died. Cathaír went north and east for three days, past the Slieve na Caillaigh hills and Loughcrew. He thought to bury the torc in a place no Christian man would search. He buried it underground at a Christian church on the sacred land of fair Érie. I saw a cross of the kind that came to be known as a 'Celtic cross'," said Hindergog.

Hindergog was but a wisp, hardly there at all.

"Hindergog, wait. You can't fade yet. Tell us where to find Dughall and how to defeat him. And what do I do with the torc and where is the Sacred Grove and how do I ... "

"Fair Emily, in my last seconds, let me tell you more about the dark one. His soul has spent over a thousand years in the land of *Umbra Nihili*, waiting for this opportunity."

"Umbra-what?" asked Fanny.

"Opportunity for what?" asked Jake.

"To achieve finally all that he desires. He wants to come to the Netherworld and thinks he can achieve his goals here," said Hindergog.

"But how will he do this?" asked Fanny.

"He'll be coming after the torc too, won't he?" I asked.

"He spent his life searching for the chalice in the belief that it was the key to opening the portal to the Netherworld. He has given up on the ancient key to open the portal. His eyes are set on a modern key."

"Modern key? What is this key?" asked Jake.

"There is a machine under the ground of the old world. Very large. Trying to turn mysteries and magick into formulas ... "

Hindergog was breaking up and fading in and out. We still needed him desperately. He was speaking in riddles. I needed straight answers.

"What machine, Hindergog? Where is he?" I pled.

"Follow your heart, Miss Emily. Remember, you have the blood of my beloved mistress in your veins. You will know what to do. Listen to the hawk ... "

That was the last thing he said. He disappeared just as quickly as he had come. We stared stupefied at the place where the image of Hindergog had been. We sat quietly, alone with only riddles to keep us company.

15 PUZZLES

I was never good at puzzles. It infuriated me that the freaky little creature left me with so many unanswered questions.

"What the ... " said Fanny.

"I know," I said. "'Listen to the hawk'. What the heck is that supposed to mean?"

"That little nub left us without a clue as to where to go or what to do," grumped Fanny.

"Actually, he gave us quite a few clues," said Jake.

Fanny and I both glared hard at him. Fanny looked like she was going to throttle him.

"Okay, tell us where we're going," said Fanny.

"Well, obviously we have to go to Ireland. 'Fair Érie'," retorted Jake.

"Yeah, sure, we'll just whisk ourselves off to Ireland. Assuming we somehow find a way to get there, it's not like Ireland is a tiny country. We have no idea where to go or what to do once there," I said.

"I know all that, but Hindergog did leave us some clues. We can figure this out. He told us to go past the Slieve na something-or-other hills. And he said a Christian church. It has to be one that was there during Saorla's time, so one that goes back at least a thousand years. There can only be so many of those, right?" Jake asked.

I started to perk up a little bit. Thank goodness for Jake. He's always so clear headed like that.

"So we could come up with a list anyway, huh, to get started," Fanny said.

"Yeah, and it may take a few days," said Jake.

"Or a few months!" I groaned.

"But traveling by bus or train, it won't be too bad. And we're sure to find other clues if we keep our eyes open," said Jake.

"Okay, but first things first. I've got to get past Muriel, and we have to find a way out of here without money, or plane tickets. And the passport situation," I said.

"Well we've got money covered," offered Fanny.

"How's that?" asked Jake. "You know I'm broke."

Jake was right. His dad had cut out on his mom, Jake and his two younger siblings. His mom worked extra shifts at her nursing job to make ends meet while Jake helped take care of his sibs, but it was really tight for his family.

"Two words. Bat Mitzvah," said Fanny.

"You still have all your Bat Mit cash?" I asked.

"Yep, about eight large, rolled up and hidden in my secret money place," said Fanny.

"You have eight thousand dollars just hanging around your house?" asked Jake.

"Yeah, well I don't trust my money in banks."

"I can't believe your mom and dad let you keep your money at your house," I said.

"They don't know."

"Okay, well eight grand should be enough to at least get us to Ireland. What about passports?" I asked.

"Fanny, you've been to Europe before. You still have your passport?" asked Jake.

"Yeah, my picture was from when I was like ten, but it's still good," she answered.

"And Emily, your dad got you a passport to go to Canada last year, didn't he?" asked Jake.

"That's right. I almost forgot because we ended up not going," I said. Zombie Man couldn't tear himself away from work long enough to go on a vacation with his only daughter.

"But Jake, what about you? You've never been ... well, never been out of the country," said Fan.

"Yeah, that's true. But Fanny, your whole family went on that trip, right?" asked Jake.

"Yeah."

"Well, with hair dye and some luck, I should be able to use your brother Rob's passport, see? Problem solved," Jake answered. He was practically beaming.

"Holy crap, Jake," said Fanny. "Squeaky clean little Jake. I can't believe you're going to do that. Faking a passport is like a federal crime you know. Probably a felony even."

"Yeah, I know. But desperate times call for desperate measure. Besides, Emily needs us," he said.

"Okay," I said. "We'll go in, grab my passport and some clothes and junk. I'll grab my small stash of cash and then we have to get past Muriel."

We all crawled back across that tree branch and shimmied into my room through the window. It was getting dark, and we still had to get past Muriel. I rummaged through my junk in a small box under my bed for my passport.

"Man, I look like such a goob," I said. My hair had been particularly frizzy that day and it was a messy halo of orangey-red around my face. I had a big, red zit on the end of my nose and a sheen of grease on my forehead.

Jake looked over my shoulder at the picture. "Nah, you don't," he said.

"Who cares now anyway," said Fan. "Just grab some junk and let's get going."

I stuffed the passport into my back pocket, grabbed my backpack and jammed it full of clothes. I was just about to turn out of there and face Muriel when Jake said, "Hey, you should write a note to your dad."

"Are you crazy? I can't let him know what we're doing," I said.

"Em, he'll be worried about you. You don't have to tell him where we're going or what we're doing, but just let him know you're not running away," Jake replied.

The thing was, I couldn't say I wasn't running away because maybe I was. That's exactly what I thought I was doing. *I Finally have a chance to escape.* I may have been a nerd, a loser, and a smart-mouth. I may have been failing math. But I wasn't a liar and I couldn't bring myself to lie to my dad, even if he was a zombie.

Jake was right though. Just in case my dad got pulled out of zombie mode long enough to notice that I was missing, I needed to tell him something. I sat down and wrote a quick note. Even though my dad was a zombie, I still loved him. That love forced a tear to my eye as I wrote my note. *This may be the last thing I ever get to say to him.*

As I finished the letter, I looked up and saw the picture of my dad, my mom and me together. In the picture, we were at the lake, laughing and having a good time. It was probably taken a few months before she died. I quickly grabbed it and threw it into my bag. I turned the note over and finished it on the backside.

"Let's go," I said. I turned and left my room, maybe forever.

16 ESCAPE FROM MURIEL THE MEAN

We tiptoed into the hall. The house was still and quiet. *Maybe Muriel is asleep in her room watching stupid history channel shows?* We tiptoed down the stairs, trying our best not to make the stairs squeak or groan. *We might get out of here without a fight.*

Yeah right. It's never that easy, is it?

Just as I made it to the door, I heard Muriel's high-pitched screech. "Where do you think you're going? And how did these fools get in?"

I didn't want my voice to tremble or squeak, but it did both as I said, "I'm leaving."

Muriel laughed. "I don't think so. You idiots get home before I call your parents and tell them that you're stealing from me. And you," she said pointing her bony finger at me. "You get back to your room now."

Fanny and Jake stood frozen like two people blasted with a comic book freeze gun. They looked back and forth between Muriel and me. Her eyes were wild with anger and she looked determined.

But I felt something welling up inside me. It was like all the times she hit me, deprived me of food, or put me down flashed before my eyes. It was like at that moment, every cell in me hated her. I turned and faced her full on.

"I'm leaving. If you try to stop me, you'll be sorry."

"You little brat." Muriel lunged toward me.

I'm not sure exactly what happened next. All I know is that I thought about getting Muriel away from me, and the next thing I knew, she flew backward through the air like some giant had picked her up and thrown her. She landed with a thud on the wood floor in the hallway looking stunned and confused.

In a flash, the stunned look became anger like I'd never seen before. I think she was determined to strangle me. Like a half-crazed little bull, she charged at me again.

In that moment, I saw Muriel as she truly was. I'd never realized before how much taller than her I was. It's like the picture I had of Muriel was from when I was seven, not fourteen. I towered over her. As I looked at her then, she seemed so small and almost comical.

I felt a calm come over me as my fear dissipated. I focused my thought on throwing Muriel far and hard. Again, without anyone touching her, it was like an invisible force picked her up and threw her against the wall. She hit hard, and as she did, a large picture framed in glass fell down on top of her head. She was knocked out.

Jake and Fanny were still like statues and their mouths hung open. None of us moved.

"How? How did you do that?" Fanny asked.

"I'm not sure," I said. "But it felt really good."

Jake peered at me through his thick glasses. "You're smiling," he said.

I was smiling. I felt happy. It had been a long time since I'd felt happy. *Maybe I do have Saorla's blood coursing through my veins.*

"Let's go before that wretched beast wakes up," I said.

We got out of there and ran as fast as we could to Fanny's house. We knew we didn't have much time. Muriel would be unconscious only so long, and when she came to, she'd search for me. We knew she'd start with Jake and Fanny's houses.

We snuck into Fan's house and got her things. Her parents were out to dinner and her brothers were at the football game so it was easy.

Money, passport, clothes, cell phone and MP3 player ('I don't travel anywhere without my tunes' Fan had said). We used her mom's hair dye (Nice-n-Easy #2) to dye Jake's hair black. He looked freaky but without his glasses on he almost looked a little bit like Fanny's brother Rob.

Jake took one look in the mirror after Fanny finished his hair and said, "We're doomed."

"Chillax nub, it'll be fine. Just let me do the talking," Fanny said.

She snuck into her oldest brother's room and grabbed his passport. Fanny wrote a quick note to her parents and we left.

It was off to Jake's house to do the same. We didn't bother to sneak in and out. His mom was working, and his brother and sister didn't pay him much attention. He left a note for his mom in his room though just like we had done.

We were on our way. We took the train to the airport. Along the way, I had other opportunities to work on my skills. I tried a sort of 'Jedi mind trick' on the guy at the ticket counter (didn't work), but mainly it was Jake's fast thinking and Fanny's fast talking that got us on that plane. Somehow Fanny was able to convince the folks at British Airways that Jake was her 18-year-old brother Rob. How she got them to believe that a boy who stood only five feet tall with a terrible hair-dye job was her adult brother I'll never know.

We were finally on our way. I sank down into my seat on the plane. O'Hare to Dublin. I knew it would be a long night. Jake and Fanny quickly fell asleep. They looked almost cute all curled up in their seats, leaning on each other. Suddenly they looked small to me. *Still kids.*

What are we doing? We're just three fourteen-year-old kids. I felt guilty that I'd pulled Jake and Fanny into my wild goose chase. We were sure to get into ginormous trouble. They'd probably have the cops out looking for us three runaways. If they did respectable detective work, they'd figure out that we were the three fast-talking kids that got on the plane at O'Hare. Then they'd know where we were going. We might have the whole of Ireland looking for us before we even got there.

While Fanny and Jake slept, my mind became increasingly filled with doubts. *Maybe we should call our parents when we get there and apologize.* Jake and Fanny could blame me. That'd be okay. I'd take the heat. I owed them.

I was tired. More tired than I'd been my whole life, but I couldn't sleep. In a way, if they rounded us up in Dublin and sent us home, it would be the best thing that could happen. The end of running. No responsibility for saving anything. I'd have to face Muriel the Mean but hey, I'd just whipped her butt without touching her. I thought she'd probably steer clear of me after that. Maybe even pack up her stuff and hit the road.

But it occurred to me that maybe they wouldn't even look for me. Muriel might just decide to let me go. *Why would she care?* If she couldn't torture me at will, what would be the point? And Zombie Man? I wasn't sure he'd notice I was gone. It might take weeks for him to find my note. And when he did, would he care? Really, would he even care?

That thought made me cry. *It sucks to have no parents.*

I silently cried for a while but then found that I had no more tears to cry. If they didn't come after us, it would make our job a lot easier. *I'm on my own now. I'm free.*

I leaned back, closed my eyes and finally slept. I saw beautiful hills of green. An old cemetery with large stone crosses. *This is a weird dream.* Then I saw the torc – beautiful and golden. In my dream, I stood in a landscape with rolling green hills and the torc hovered in front of me and glowed. That was my dream as I flew to an unknown future.

PART TWO

Training the Modern-Day Priestess

You never can tell what a thought will do
    In bringing you hate or love –
For thoughts are things, and their airy wings
    Are swifter than carrier doves.
They follow the law of the universe –
    Each thing creates its kind,
And they speed o'er the track to bring you back
    Whatever went out from your mind.

    From "You Never Can Tell," by Ella Wheeler Wilcox,
    1850-1919

17 TO FAIR TARA

Amazingly we all slept well that night. Maybe we were just exhausted and didn't have a choice. Before we knew it, we touched down in Dublin.

Weary from the seven-hour plane ride, we practically stumbled down the steps and walkway to the custom's agents. I sailed through without a problem, lying and telling the Irish customs guy that I was there on vacation.

"For how long then love?" he asked.

I hesitated because the truth was I didn't know how long I'd be there. For all I knew, the Irish Garda would be waiting for us on the other side of customs and put us right back on a plane to the States. Or if we were successful we could be there indefinitely. Suddenly the words 'two weeks' popped into my head, and I realized that I was reading Jake's mind.

"Two weeks," I finally stammered out.

"'Ave a good holiday then," the agent said. He stamped a 30-day visa into my passport and handed it back.

I stood on the other side of the wooden customs booth and waited for Jake and Fanny. They were taking a long time and I began to get worried that they weren't being allowed through. But finally I saw them come out of the walkway together.

"I told you to let me do the talking," Fanny said.

"I'm supposed to be your older brother. It doesn't make sense that you would be the one talking for us."

"It does if my older brother is a moron," Fanny said. She smacked Jake lightly in the back of the head.

"Ow, stop hitting me."

"Stop being a nub."

I interrupted their gripping conversation. "You made it through. That's all that matters. Come on. Let's find a place to regroup."

We found a free table near the baggage claim area where they had a few places to get food. We grabbed some coffee and bagels and promptly inhaled them like we'd never eaten before.

"What now?" Fanny asked.

"I don't know about you guys, but I'm tired. We need to find a place to stay," I said.

Jake pulled his laptop from his backpack, tapped into the Wi-Fi connection and began typing away. With the help of the Internet and some questions to a bored-looking but friendly currency exchange agent, we came up with a plan. We found an inexpensive youth hostel in Dublin, a short trip by Airbus from the airport. In the heart of the city, we'd be able to find some maps, rest a bit and come up with a plan.

Once we'd settled into our room, we all crashed for a while before heading out to find maps of Ireland. After our naps, we grabbed coffee in the self-catered kitchen and discussed our situation.

"What is it that Hindergog said?" Fanny asked.

"About what?" asked Jake.

"You know, about where to go. Didn't he give us a clue," Fan replied.

"I don't know," I said. "It seems so long ago that we talked to him. In fact, I'm not even sure we did. Doesn't this all seem sort of like a dream to you guys?"

They both just stared at me. Could they see that I was losing my steam? Could they see, even without the 'sight' that I was close to bagging out?

"You're not chickening out, are you?" asked Fanny.

"No, I'm not chickening. It's just, you know, we don't even know where we're going. I mean, this is just stupid. We could end up sitting here in this frickin' hostel for weeks without knowing where we're supposed to go. We could run out of money before we find anything."

"Calm down, Em," said Jake. Other folks in the eating area were starting to look at us. "Hindergog was real. Well, at least as real as any hologram is. That little dude was there. We all saw him. We all heard him. You gotta' get a grip so we can figure this out. We have to use our brains and our technology to figure out these clues," said Jake.

We talked out the things that Hindergog had said. Jake wrote down our clues in his notebook but before long, he ignored our chatter and typed on his laptop.

"What are you looking for?" I asked.

"I'm searching for old churches and monasteries. That's the best clue Hindergog gave us. Remember, he said that the torc was buried near a church."

"Yeah, but there have to be tons of old churches here. It could take months to search them all," said Fanny.

"I don't think so. He also told us that Cathaír rode past the Slieve na Calleigh hills on his way to bury the torc. I found those on a map, so that narrows the list.

Jake read the list out loud and talked about the area where each was located. He pointed them out on the maps we had spread out on the table in front of us. I was only half listening, bored with Jake's lesson in Irish geography and history. Yawn. And I couldn't get what he was saying anyway because he was trying to pronounce the old Gaelic names and botched it badly.

Suddenly I had goose bumps going up and down my whole body. It was like something had jolted me out of my bored stupor.

"Wait," I practically shouted.

"What?" said Jake.

"Read back what you just said. What was the name of the last one?" I asked.

"Monasterboice," said Jake.

I got a chill down my spine when he said it. "That's it!"

"How do you know?" asked Fan.

"I don't know exactly, but when he said that, I got all goose bumpy and tingly. I've got chills going up and down my spine."

Jake and Fanny looked at each other like maybe they weren't sure whether I was off my nut or they should listen to me. But Jake turned his attention to his maps again and before we knew it, he figured out how to get there.

"We need to go north. County Louth," he said at last. Jake examined the online bus schedule for a few minutes, then said, "Really not too far and won't take long. We can hop on a bus here and be at a little town south of Monasterboice before you know it. There are small inns and a few hostels up there. We can find a place to stay when we get there."

With that, he closed his laptop, packed up his maps and stood to leave. "Let's get going," he said. "There's a bus in 45 minutes. Let's be on it."

I felt like I couldn't move. I had complained about how long it could take to find answers, but the truth was I didn't care if it took forever. It was moving too fast.

"Shouldn't we spend the night here, you know, and start fresh tomorrow?"

Jake shot me a look that I swear felt like he knew exactly how scared I felt inside. *Sometimes it feels like he's the mind reader.* But Fanny agreed with me. "I need my sleep," she said. If Jake had known what was ahead, he would have thanked me for being chicken.

18 THE INN

Jake had been right. The train ride was fairly short. We got to Drogheda and called around for lodgings and found an inn to stay in. We decided it was best to go to Monasterboice at night seeing as how we might have to dig in the ground and all. The locals would likely frown on grave robbing.

The innkeeper was a friendly little guy who went by the name Paddy. He wore a tweed cap and he had red, round cheeks and beefy hands. He didn't seem to question that there were three American kids wanting a room for the night. He did ask what we were about.

Jake thought quick and blurted out sightseeing. "We're planning to go to Monasterboice first, you know, to take a look at those crosses."

Like all the Irish we had met so far, Paddy was quick to offer his help along with a few stories and suggestions for other places to visit.

"You didn't come all the way to Ireland just to see a few Celtic crosses, now did you lad?" he asked with a chuckle.

"No sir," Jake replied. "But that's first on our agenda anyway. Could you suggest how we might get there seeing as how we don't have a car?"

"Oh, not a problem. It's about eight to nine kilometers from here. My mate Mack O'Donohugh, he has a cab. He can take you there."

"Eight kilometers? How many miles is that Jake?" I asked.

"It's about five to six miles lass," Paddy offered.

"Okay, thanks Paddy," I said as Paddy walked us to our room. "If we need that ride, we'll let you know."

"Here you go youngsters," Paddy said. He opened the door for us and showed us into a tidy room with one double bed and one twin bed. It had old red wallpaper and cream-colored carpet and walls. Paddy looked like he was going to stay and chat with us some more until Fanny faked a big yawn.

"Oh, you're tired from your long journey. Some jet lag, huh? Well, you let me know if you need anything." Paddy walked out and the door slammed shut behind him.

Fanny and I plopped ourselves onto the little beds to rest. I think we were both almost asleep when Jake yelled at us. "You can't sleep. We have to get out there," he whined.

"Sleep first," Fanny said. She rolled over with her back to us.

"You don't have time for sleep now," said Jake. "Come on, we have to make a plan for how we're going to get that torc."

"Calm down nub," said Fanny. "We've got time. Plan later. I need sleep."

"Come on Fan, Jake's right," I said. I wanted to sleep too, but Jake had a point. We needed to plan first, sleep later.

"You two plan without me. You haven't needed me so far. You don't need me now," Fan replied.

We'd been a trio since pre-school, and there's usually an odd man out. As the only sister to four older brothers, Fanny was pretty used to being the center of attention when she wanted to be.

"Fan, you know we need you," I said.

"No you don't. Jake's enormous melon brain will come up with all the plans you need and now that you're like a warrior goddess or whatever ... well, you don't need my talents anymore."

Ah, that was it. Fanny was used to being the muscle. She may be small, but Fanny is one of the strongest people I've ever seen. Ever since second grade when she kicked the crap out of this huge third-grader, Tommy, when he tried to take her lunch box from her. Well no one messed with Fanny again. The teachers had to come pull her off his chest, and she was still wailing on him. She was half his size and not a scratch on her but Tommy got led to the office with his nose bleeding buckets.

Between that fight and the fact that Fanny is the star player of every sport there is, everyone pretty much steers clear of her. She's been like my bodyguard ever since the Greta incident that started it all for me. It doesn't make her popular, but she stands by me to make sure no one messes with me.

I went and sat next to her. "Fanny, I need you. I'll always need you," I said.

"Em, you're strong too. You can take care of yourself," she said without turning over.

"Yeah, I've got some power building in me. But Fanny, you know I'm a big coward. I don't have your courage. Your bravery makes me stronger. I can't do this without you," I said.

There was quiet for a while. I heard a few sniffles but didn't say anything about it.

After a few minutes, Fan turned over, her eyes rimmed with red. "You know I'll do anything to help you, don't you?"

"Yeah, I know that," I said as I hugged her. "And I'll do anything for you. For both of you. We're in this together."

Drill sergeant Jake interrupted our beautiful moment.

"Are you two done with your Lifetime TV moment? We've got to make a plan, then get some sleep, then head out to find this thing ... "

Fanny and I both grabbed pillows and threw them at Jake, stopping him midsentence. Fanny threw hers so hard it knocked him over.

"See," I said. "You're still the biggest muscle here."

We laughed and promised Jake we'd listen. He didn't actually need us to come up with a plan. We mainly nodded as Jake outlined his strategy for the evening. Finally, we all decided to get a few hours of sleep before we set out. Soon we were going to be runaways and grave robbers. *I doubt any of us will ever get into college.* Good-bye scholarships.

19 THINGS GO BUMP IN THE NIGHT

We woke up around 10:00 that night, packed just the stuff we needed for our nighttime journey into one bag, and crept down the stairs. People were eating and drinking in the pub below. They didn't seem to notice us as we left.

"Okay, we're ready except for one thing," Jake said.

"What's that nub? A blankie," joked Fanny.

"Cut it out Fan, I've had enough of your crap," said Jake. He was tired and testy. "We need a shovel, okay? Unless you want to dig with your hands."

"Where are we going to get a shovel?" I asked.

"They have to have a shovel here somewhere," offered Jake. "Maybe there's a shed or something out back. We can lift their shovel and return it when we get back."

"Sounds like a plan," said Fanny as we left the room.

We had one flashlight between the three of us so we pretty much had to stay clumped together to see anything in the pitch black. We crept around to the back of the large brick inn and found a small building. It looked promising until we noticed that it was locked with a padlock.

"Crap, it's locked," I said.

"You give up too easy," said Fanny. "Padlocks are no problem. Jake, hand me the pack."

Jake flung the pack off his back and onto the ground. Fanny took the flashlight and rummaged through the bag until she found what she was looking for.

"What 'ya got?" asked Jake.

"A pair of tweezers."

"What are you doing with a pair of tweezers in the pack?"

"You're a guy. You wouldn't understand."

"Understand what? What use could you possibly have for those on this mission?"

"You never know when you're going to need to tweeze, Jake," Fanny said matter-of-factly. She got down on her knees and started working the lock. In a couple of minutes, we heard a click as the lock opened up.

"How do you know how to do that?" I asked.

"You don't wanna' know." She flung open the door and began to walk into the shed with Jake and I on her heels.

It was black as the blackest night in there. There wasn't a speck of light except for what was put out by the small flashlight. We were huddled together so tight if one of us tripped we were all going down.

"See anything?" I asked.

"So far all I'm seeing are old cans of paint and some crates of unknown origin," said Jake.

We stood still in the center of the room as Fanny swept the flashlight from one side of the room to the other. After a few minutes of slowly sweeping the room, we saw something metal glint in the light.

"There," said Jake. "Go back a bit. Back there, in the corner."

Fanny did what Jake asked and as our eyes adjusted to the light we saw it. A garden shovel caked with dirt and grass. Perfect.

"Go get it," Fanny said. She shoved the flashlight into Jake's hand.

"What? No, we're all going to get it. All for one, remember?"

"Come on Jake, you're the guy here. Man up."

"Oh, for Christ's sake, give me the flashlight then." Jake grabbed the flashlight from Fanny and left us in the dark as he slowly walked toward the back corner of the shed.

"Got it," he said. Fanny and I were in complete darkness now so I hoped he'd walk fast so we could get out of there.

"Come on Jake, let's get out of here," I said. I heard Jake's feet slowly shuffle then a sudden loud crash.

"What happened?" Fanny asked.

"I tripped," said Jake. A few seconds later, Jake let out a loud scream. The small beam of light cast by the flashlight moved erratically.

"What's going on Jake?" I screamed.

"Something just had my leg," he said as he came bounding toward us. "Come on – move – there's something in here!"

We all ran with Jake to the door of the shed and escaped outside. When we got out, Fanny grabbed the flashlight from Jake.

"What are you doing? Come on, let's just get out of here."

"Calm your panties, nub," said Fanny. She shined the flashlight back into the shed from just outside the door. She moved it back and forth until it caught the glow of eyes looking back at us.

"There. That's what attacked Jake," she said.

Jake and I both cowered on either side of Fanny as she shined the flashlight onto Jake's attacker. There were two beady eyes looking right at us, reflecting the light in that creepy way animals' eyes do. And in the light of the small electric torch you could see the eyes were surrounded by black fur.

"It's a cat," I said.

Fanny laughed so much I thought she'd have a seizure.

As soon as Fanny stopped laughing enough to talk, she said, "Okay, I concede Jake. We no longer send you to do 'man's' work."

"Shut it," Jake said. He grabbed the flashlight from her and stomped away.

We ran to catch up with Jake, neither of us wanting to be left in the dark Irish night without a flashlight. When we got to the sidewalk in front of the inn we followed Jake up the street. He looked like he knew where he was going.

20 MONASTERBOICE

"Jake, you know how to get there?" I asked.

"Sure. We take this street about four miles then we go left. We should be there in another mile or so. Easy."

We walked on the sidewalk until we ran out of sidewalk then we walked single file along the narrow road. We soon found ourselves in the Irish countryside, the houses thinning out and giving way to fields. We were three young teens alone on an open road. Though we were cloaked in the robe of darkness, I felt exposed.

"Hey guys, maybe we should get off the road," I said.

"Why?" asked Jake.

"So no one will see us. Three kids out this late carrying a shovel may be a bit out of place, don't you think? And what if they're looking for us? I mean, we don't know, but if our parents called the cops back home and they started looking for us, they may have tracked us to Ireland and so if we get stopped by the town fuzz ... "

"Yeah, Em's right," said Fanny. "We should get off the roads." Jake nodded his agreement and pointed us in the direction that he thought we should go.

Along the road, there was a low fence made of grey stone that we jumped over pretty easily. After that, it all started going to crap pretty quickly. I mean that literally. We soon found ourselves tripping over small bumps in the grass and trying to dodge cow pies.

"We're in a frickin' field of cows, Em," said Fanny. She quickly sidestepped what appeared to be fairly fresh cow poop. The dark of the night may have helped shield us from any onlookers, but it made the travel much more difficult. The only light came from a small sliver of moon that was just starting to creep above the horizon and a single, small flashlight.

After about a half hour of slow going through the cow field, we came to another fence. As we approached it, the reality of our situation began to dawn.

From the road, the stone fences looked about four feet high at most and easy to scale and jump over. But when you get up close to them, they're not only taller than that, but grown up all around the stone are bramble bushes. What was once an ordinary stone fence became a stone fence with a natural razor wire barrier.

We stood in front of the impenetrable fortress of rock and brambles for a few minutes, speechless. It was getting late. We had spent more time in the shed getting a shovel than we had expected. And with the slow going through the field, it was now after 11:00.

"What now?" asked Jake.

"I'm sorry guys," I said. "I'm not much good at this whole quest thing. Every idea I have turns to dog poop." I felt defeated and we'd only just begun.

"No need to apologize, Em," Jake said. "It was a good idea. How were you supposed to know the Irish protect their cow pie fields with natural razor wire?"

"Okay Jake, stop kissing Emily's butt long enough to navigate us back to the road."

We walked along the fence toward the road, climbed over the lower fence then started walking single-file again up the road. After about an hour of walking, I sensed that we weren't going the right direction.

"Hey Jake, you sure we're going the right way?" I asked.

"Pretty sure," he said. "Why do you ask?"

"Well, back there when we were first started out, the moon was coming up in front of us."

"Yeah."

"Now it's behind us," I said.

We all stopped. Jake looked back and up into the sky. "You're right," he said. "Crap, we must be going the wrong way."

"Oh that's great Jake! We've been walking for an hour in the wrong direction," Fanny said. She flicked Jake in the head.

"Ow! Don't flick me. You didn't figure it out either, Einstein," he said.

"Okay guys, stop bickering. Jake, pull out that map," I said.

Jake shone the flashlight on the map. "Problem is, I'm not really sure where we are. There are so many little roads that intersect. I'm not sure what road we got onto when we went back over the fence."

"Well, we know we're going the wrong way now, so we have to turn around and go back down this road," I said.

"Yeah, but then what?"

Fanny cut in. "Wait! I've got it." Fanny rummaged through the backpack.

"What now? More tweezers?" Jake asked.

"No Jakester, something way better for this situation." Fanny pulled something small and rectangular from the pack. "My phone," she said with a smile.

"You're not thinking of calling a cab, are you?" I asked.

"No silly, something better. I got GPS on this thing. I totally forgot about it."

"You've got GPS on your phone, and you're just now telling us?" Jake said through gritted teeth.

"Don't get your boxers in a knot Jake. I forgot, okay? Besides, I didn't think you'd get us lost, nub."

"Let's not waste more time bickering. Fanny, get that thing fired up," I said.

According to Fanny's GPS, after an hour and a half on the road, we were now six miles from Monasterboice instead of five when we started out.

"Let's get going. We gotta' hustle before we run out of time."

We walked as fast as we could along the edge of the narrow roads. We didn't see a single car so I guess my worry about being caught out there wasn't much of a problem. After almost two hours of walking and navigating the roads – tricky even with a GPS in rural Ireland - we saw a large stone tower in silhouette on the horizon to the east.

Monasterboice. The tower looked just like the pictures we'd seen of it on the Internet. It looked ominous in silhouette against the large October moon. Even at that late hour there were crows circling around it calling out.

We were exhausted, but we ran the rest of the way to Monasterboice. We finally got to the gate a little before 2:00 a.m. The air was chilly and filled with the smell of wet fall leaves, grass, and the lingering odor of cow dung.

Our elation at finally finding the tower soon turned to despair. Just like the cow and sheep fields, Monasterboice was surrounded by a grey stone fence all the way around. But the Monasterboice fence was even more menacing than the fences around the fields. It had jagged stones turned on their sides all around the top. You couldn't shimmy over it without ripping a huge gash in your stomach.

"Very effective security fences they have here," Jake said as we approached.

"What now?" asked Fanny.

Neither Jake nor I had an answer. Lit by the large, nearly full October moon, the cemetery with the large stone tower looked like an impenetrable fortress.

"I think we should walk around the outside of the fence. We can look for a place where the top stones have come off or something," I offered.

"As good a plan as any," Jake said as we headed out.

We trudged through a field on the south side of the site first. It wasn't long before we saw what we were looking for. There was a place about two feet wide where the jagged capstones were missing.

"Bingo," Fanny said. She wasted no time and scrambled up the wall. Fanny's a strong climber. It didn't take her long to scale the wall and slide through the narrow gap between capstones. After she got up and over the wall, she leaned over it from the inside and put her hands out to help me up.

I'm not a strong climber and not nearly as small as Fanny. It wasn't so easy for me to scale the wall and pop over. Fanny pulled me and I pushed against the bumpy stones with my feet as I tried to push my bottom half up the wall.

"Come on girl," Fanny grunted. "Use your muscles."

"I don't have any muscles." I huffed and puffed from the exertion.

"Jake, make yourself useful. Push Emily's butt up the wall," Fanny said.

"I'm not ... I can't do that!"

"Why not?" asked Fanny.

"I can't touch her butt," said Jake. "That wouldn't be ... a proper thing to do."

"Jake," I huffed. "It's okay. Desperate times, desperate measures, remember? Push my butt over this wall before Fanny rips my arms out of their sockets."

After a few seconds, I felt Jake's small hands shoving on my posterior. He had them just kind of resting there, not pushing at all.

"Come on Jake! This isn't the time to cop a feel. Push!" With that Jake gave a mighty shove and I was up and over the rock wall. Fanny let go of my hands, and I fell over and landed on top of her. "I'm over," I said.

"Really? Hadn't noticed." Fanny quickly scrambled out from under me.

"Okay, Jake. Your turn," I said.

"Not happening," Jake said back.

"What do you mean? You gotta' come over too."

"I can't. There's no one over here to shove my butt over," he said. "Here, I'll toss over the backpack and hand you guys the shovel. You can take it from here."

"No, Jake, we're all in this together, remember? We'll get you over."

The backpack came flying over the wall and landed with a thud.

"Here's the shovel." Jake handed it over the wall and Fanny leaned over and grabbed it.

"You guys go on in and try to find it. I'll wait here for you. Now get going. We're running out of time."

He had a point. It was getting late, and we didn't know how to find the torc. We were in a huge graveyard. It was full of large headstones, Celtic crosses and low gravestones. We could search for days and not find what we were looking for, and that's if we actually knew what we were looking for.

"Okay, Jake. You're right. But don't go anywhere. I don't want to lose you out here," I said.

"You won't lose me."

"Make yourself useful, Jake," Fanny said. "Be a lookout. If you hear or see anyone coming, hoot like an owl or something so we know to hide."

We heard Jake mutter something under his breath as we walked away from the wall. "What's the plan, Em?" Fanny asked.

"I'm not sure. I guess we need to walk up and down the rows and look at the markers. Look for clues, like a symbol or letters that seem to go with Hindergog's story."

Easier said than done, especially in the dark. From the wall, the ground sloped slightly. At the top of the small rise, we saw gravestones packed tightly together as far as our eye could see. The stones were in fairly even rows, but every now and then there would be a large rectangle of stone placed around a grave, only about two inches off the ground. The perfect height to cause someone to trip. Fanny and I must have each tripped and fallen face first into a gravel-filled grave about three or four times. Our shins and legs were scraped and bruised.

Row after row of old stone grave markers and large and small Celtic crosses. Fanny and I used the flashlight to illuminate each grave marker we could see, but even the light wasn't much help.

"I can't make out any letters on most of these," I said.

"I can't either," said Fanny.

Feeling with our hands didn't help. We knew we were looking for a marker or grave from over a thousand years ago so we could ignore the modern ones with words etched in marble. All the older ones had been worn down by weather and were covered with lichens and moss.

We had walked through probably half of the cemetery when we heard a scuffling in the leaves behind us. Fanny and I both jumped and turned around, moving together almost as one unit. Fanny shone the flashlight directly in front of us. We didn't see anything but again heard the leaves rustle.

We held our breath and didn't move a muscle. Here we were in an old graveyard in the middle of the Irish countryside during a full moon with crows calling out overhead. It doesn't get much creepier than that. We heard something come toward us. It sounded too large to be a cat.

"Who's there?" I called out into the dark.

"It's me." Jake appeared in the small pool of light made by the flashlight.

Fanny and I both released our grip on each other and began to breathe again.

"Jake, you major pain, what the heck are you doing? You scared the crap out of us," Fanny said.

"Oh, good to see you too."

"You shouldn't sneak up like that. You should have called out or something," Fanny replied. Her voice was filled with annoyance. Fanny didn't like to show weakness, especially around Jake.

"What? And miss the opportunity to see your face just now?"

Fanny lightly punched Jake's arm for good measure. He rubbed his arm where she hit him, but he continued to smile, enjoying the rare moment when he got the better of Fanny.

"How'd you get in?" I asked.

"Oh that. Well I sat there for a while but got bored. So I started walking the fence to see if I could find a way in. If you guys had gone a little ways further along the fence, you would have found a wrought iron gate. They forgot to lock it. All I had to do was pull it open and voila! Jake's in."

"I'm glad. We need your help. We've gone through row after row of graves – watch your step, by the way – some of them are raised. But most of the old ones don't have any visible writing left. We could be here for days and not see a single clue," I said.

Jake looked thoughtful for a minute. Sometimes, when he's thinking hard, you can practically hear wheels spinning in his brain.

"I've got an idea," he said at last. "Em, remember when I was saying names of burial sites, and you got that chill up your spine when you heard Monasterboice?" he asked.

"Yeah, I remember."

"Well, maybe you can use your second sight – or whatever you call it – you know, to sense when we're in the right place."

"I don't know. I don't have control over that stuff. It seems to come and go as it pleases. I can't just turn it on when I want to."

"But maybe you could try," said Fanny. "We don't have a lot of options."

We didn't have time to look at each grave in that place with our little flashlight. There had to be hundreds of stones in that place. Besides, even if we looked at each one, our eyes were no use. Any information that might have been a clue for us had long since worn away.

"Okay, I'll try it," I finally said. "I'm not sure what to do though to turn on my receiver."

"What did you do when you were younger?" Jake asked.

"I don't know. I mean, when I was little, it was like always on. I didn't have to turn it on."

"Well, try to meditate or breathe or something," said Fanny.

"Yeah Em, that's a good idea. Maybe if you quiet your mind and think about the torc, maybe it will lead you to it," Jake said.

"But we've walked through about half of this place already. And there wasn't any hair raising going on. I think we're at a dead end."

"We still have about half to go. Besides, what do we have to lose?" Jake asked.

He had a point so I did what Jake suggested. I sat on the ground, closed my eyes and tried to get quiet. It seemed so silly. Fan started giggling and that got me laughing. Jake looked stern and serious, which made us laugh more. But after a few minutes and Jake pleading with us, we stopped and I tried again.

With Fanny quiet, after a couple of minutes I was able to quiet my mind a bit. At first I felt sleepy. I could have laid down there and taken a nap on the hard ground between all these gravestones. But then a peace came over me. I daydreamed, just like on the airplane.

I saw the same green hills and a circle of stones. I saw the face of a beautiful woman with long wavy red hair. At first I thought it was my mom, but it wasn't. Then I saw it. The torc. Just as in my dream before. Shiny and golden and glowing. It hovered right in front of me. I felt like I could reach out for it. I saw the initials 'SCS' in my mind then the dream was gone.

I opened my eyes and half expected myself surrounded by lush green hills with the torc hovering before me. But I was still in the graveyard. Fanny was lying down, maybe asleep. Jake still sat across from me, his eyes droopy but awake.

"Well?" Jake asked.

"I don't know exactly, but I think we should look some more," I said.

I got up and began walking, not sure why I was going where I was going. My feet seemed to steer me to the west corner of the graveyard. Fanny and Jake followed behind. My feet led me to a small grave marker almost at the very edge of the cemetery.

It was different from all the others. It wasn't shaped like the usual tombstone but instead was a small obelisk shape. It stood only two feet or so above the ground, and it looked like it used to have a point on top but it had worn down. It was covered in lichens and moss and had turned a yellowy green rather than grey stone.

It was such a small, plain stone, most would probably walk by it and not notice it at all. It had no carvings or writing. But as soon as I approached it, I got that tingly feeling again all up and down my spine and my arms. The hairs all over my body stood on end.

I bent down and gingerly put my hands on the stone. I felt for a mark of some kind. I didn't feel any markings with my fingers, but as I touched it, I saw the letters 'SCS' appear in my mind, just like in my dream. As in my dream, I saw verdant hills and a circle of stones in my mind's eye. And there it was. The torc glowed gold and hovered before my eyes. The vision was so powerful it made me dizzy. I began to wobble.

"Em, are you okay?" asked Jake. He bent down to steady me.

"This is it," I said in a low voice. "Here. We dig here."

Fanny and Jake looked at each other and at me. Their mouths hung open like when I'd thrown Muriel against the wall. It was like they were in a daze.

"Jake, Fanny," I said. "We're running out of night. Come on, let's dig."

Jake came out of his stupor, grabbed the shovel and dug. It wasn't long until Fanny had had enough of Jake's slow and methodical digging. She snatched the shovel from him and hacked at the ground.

"Be careful," said Jake. "You don't want to break it."

For close to an hour, Fanny dug and found nothing but worms and slugs. As the first light of dawn peaked over the hills to the east behind us, Fanny hit something hard.

"Hey, I think we've got something," she said.

I shined the flashlight into the hole. I saw something glint in the hole as I shined the light. All three of us used our hands and the shovel to uncover the object Fanny had hit upon.

"Do you think this is really a grave?" Fanny asked.

"I don't know, but this is creeping me out," I said. "I don't want to find a corpse."

But our fears were soon alleviated. There was no coffin. Our digging revealed the shape of the object in the hole. It was a small box, no more than six inches all the way around. In no time, we had it out of the ground completely and began wiping it off.

"It's metal," Jake said. "And look, it has something carved on the top."

"What is that?" asked Fanny.

I shined the flashlight on the top of the box. "It's a tree," I said. The carved tree took up most of the top of the box. It was a magnificent tree with many branches. It looked like an oak tree. But the weird thing was that all its branches ended in a flame. "It's a flaming tree."

"Open it Emily," Jake said. He's been holding the box and he pushed it into my hands.

"No, you open it." I tried to shove it back to Jake.

"No, you should open it," he said.

He was right of course, but I was afraid. *What will happen when I open it? Will that torc thing crawl up my arm and wrap itself around me? Will I become someone – or something – else? Will the ground open up and swallow me into it like it did with Saorla?*

Even though questions of worry swirled in my brain, I decided to open the box like Jake suggested. I tried to pry it open with my fingers, but it was stuck shut, the clasp caked with dirt and age. I handed the box to Jake and he tried but it was no use.

"Oh, give me that," Fanny said. She took the box, knocked it on the ground a few times, and with one mighty pull opened it. As she held it open, I shined the flashlight into the box.

The light caught the golden metal. The torc lay inside.

It didn't move on its own or crawl its way onto me. It just lay there, a beautiful arm bracelet made of many strands of twisted gold that all came together in an oval. Each end was capped with a carved finial. One finial was in the shape of a bird. It looked like a hawk or maybe an eagle. On the other end was the head of a woman. Her hair streamed back from her face and ended in flame. *A chick with her hair on fire! What's with all the fire?*

The torc didn't glow or look in any way magickal. It looked like an old, hung of metal.

"I can't believe we found it," Fanny said.

"Yeah, I hoped we'd find it. But I had my doubts," Jake said.

I couldn't say anything. It was great that we'd found it of course. And yeah, it made me believe again in Hindergog, that weird little guy. But the truth is, I was kind of disappointed. I guess I expected it to glow like in my visions and for something magickal to happen when I found it.

"What's the matter, Em?" asked Fanny.

"Oh, nothing," I said. "It's just that it looks sort of looks, you know, ordinary."

All three of us stood peering into the box and stared at it for a few minutes. Jake finally broke the silence. "Put it on Em."

"Oh, I don't think I should," I said. "Look, the sun is coming up. We need to cover this hole and get the heck out of here."

Jake didn't argue with me, but he eyed me cautiously. I think he could see that I was scared of the thing, but he didn't push me. At least not then.

21 ON THE RUN

We hoofed it back to the inn and arrived as the town was coming fully alive for the day. We put the shovel back inside the shed and looked forward to falling into bed for a long sleep. As we walked inside the inn, there were already a few people gathered around the dining table eating breakfast. When we walked by the front desk, Paddy looked at us with raised eyebrows.

"Bit early, huh," he said.

"We wanted to see the sunrise," I said as we walked up the stairs to our room.

When we got to our room, Fanny and Jake both flopped down on their beds to get some well-deserved sleep. "I think Paddy was a little suspicious of us, don't you think?" I asked.

"Ugh-huh," was all Fanny said in reply. I think Jake was already asleep.

"I gotta go hit the head guys," I said. I tiptoed out into the hall and closed the door behind me. As I turned to go down the hall to the toilet, I heard Paddy talking to another man down the stairs in the reception area.

"Imagine that, some German tourist lady falling into a hole out there in that old graveyard," the man said.

I heard Paddy chuckle loudly. "I'd have liked to seen that mate! Old bird was she? Falling right in a hole."

"It 'taint funny Paddy. That's some serious stuff now," said the man.

"Well the ladies out there at Monasterboice said the German gal wasn't harmed. So what 'taint funny about that then, Officer Kelly?" Paddy asked.

"Oh the old bird going down, that's funny mate. But the hole being there? Now that's another story. The volunteer ladies who run the place, they said that half to nine a German tourist came to them and complained that his wife just twisted her ankle in that hole back there. They ran to where the old bird was down and when she got up, they got to lookin' at it, and it was a right proper hole someone dug up. Fresh too. Wasn't there yesterday when they locked up. In the night, someone dug a hole at one of those old grave markers."

"Can you believe it, some heathen defiling an ancient grave that way!" said Paddy. "Do you think they're after treasure or something?" he asked.

"Probably some teenagers, you know, pulling some kind of prank. Or maybe it's random vandalism like kids do these days," said the other man.

"Did they take anything, you knows, out of it?" asked Paddy.

"They don't rightly know seeing as how it's so old, no one knows if there was anything in there still. But the hole was pretty small, so who's ta say."

There was a pause for a minute then Paddy said, "Hey wait a minute. There are some youngsters staying here. American kids, teenagers."

"Yeah, so?" queried the other man.

"Well, my groundskeeper was out early this morning, and he couldn't find his shovel in the shed," said the innkeeper.

"Oh yeah? Tell me more."

"Well, those kids, they came in early this morning. They said they was out for sunrise, but I reckon they was out all night," said the innkeeper.

Then there was another silence. I didn't wait to hear what they'd say next. I ran back to the room and opened the door.

"Guys, wake up. Get up man, we gotta' go." I madly threw my stuff into my bag.

"What are you doin'?" Fanny asked. "I wanna sleep for a few hours."

"No time, Fan. We gotta' leave now. A local cop is down there and he's real curious about our shovel pinching. They've already found the grave that we dug up, and he doesn't sound too thrilled about it."

Jake and Fanny were up like a shot. I'm not sure I've ever seen Jake move that fast. He and Fanny stuffed their junk into their bags and shoved their feet into their shoes. We heard the loud steps of the portly Paddy and Officer Kelly coming up the stairs.

"What do we do?" asked Jake. "We can't go out the door. They'll see us."

I looked around the room. There was only one window in the room and it was small and fairly high off of the ground. It would be a squeeze, but it was our only way out. "There," I pointed. "Let's go."

Fanny was the first out. She fit easily through the window, stood outside on the small ledge, and jumped to the gable roof below us. Jake and I poked our heads out of the window and watched as she walked along the roof to the small shed at the back of the inn. Jake turned to me and said, "I can't do that, Em. I'll fall."

"You've got to. Come on, Fanny will help you."

As I tried to summon Jake's courage for him, Paddy knocked on the door. "You kids, open up now. Officer Kelly here wants to talk to you."

Jake took one look at me, swallowed hard, and jumped to the gable just as Fanny had. He stumbled a little and looked like he might fall off, but somehow he righted himself and ran to the shed roof.

My turn. I was quite a bit bigger than both Fanny and Jake. I had to squeeze to get through the small window, but somehow I did it. I jumped and ran without thinking, all the while hearing the innkeeper and Officer Kelly yelling for us to let them in.

We ran down side alleys and across neatly mowed yards. We didn't know where we were going, only that we needed to get out of sight of the inn. As tired as I was, the danger allowed me to find the juice in my legs to run like I'd never run before. We ran south and west for a long time. Before long we were on a small country two-lane road with nothing but fields of grass and sheep on either side.

I was too tired to keep count of time or distance. I knew only that we had to keep moving.

After what seemed like an eternity, we came to a thick woods just off the side of the road. It was looked primeval. It was dark and scary, but it was a place to get out of the open and hide.

We walked until we were far into the dense wood. Without saying a word to each other, we threw off our packs and fell down. I don't think we were awake for more than a minute. *Sleep while we can. This is only the beginning.*

22 ZOMBIE MAN WAKES

The day that his wife died, a large part of Liam Adams died too. Liam was like the stone foundation of a house, but Bridget was the fire that burned in the hearth. Without her passion for life fueling him, Liam reverted to the only other comfort he had ever known: Science.

Liam's only family was his sister Muriel, fifteen years his senior. He'd asked Muriel to stay with him for a while and help him to care for Emily. In the wake of his grief, caring for his child felt like a burden he was unable to carry.

Muriel didn't just stay a few weeks. She moved in permanently. And while Muriel chipped away at the beauty of both Liam's house and daughter, he threw himself into his work in theoretical physics at the University of Chicago. He became a zombie of a man.

But on that day that everything changed, Liam was jolted out of his zombie state. He came home from work and found his sister sitting in their parlor, an ice pack on her head. Her bags were packed and arranged neatly by the front door. Liam walked to the chair where she sat and stood in front of her. Muriel didn't look up at him as she handed him a note.

"I told you she's trouble," Muriel snarled. "Probably on drugs or something. You should have seen her when she attacked me. Her eyes were wild. She looked hyped up on something."

Liam said nothing and quickly scanned the note. He flopped his large frame into the worn chair across from Muriel and read it again. He searched each line for clues or hidden meaning.

"Was she with anyone?" he asked.

"Those two no-good friends of hers," Muriel replied.

Liam looked up from the note and looked at his sister. As soon as he looked at her, she screwed her face into a look of pain.

"Are you okay?" he asked.

"Okay? *Okay?* That brat attacked me! No, I'm not okay. You need to call the police, Liam. She needs to learn a lesson. If you don't nip this in the bud, she'll run wild all over you."

"Did she hit you?"

"Hit? Well no, not exactly hit."

"Then how did you get that knot on your head? Did she push you?"

"No, she didn't exactly push me."

"Dammit Muriel, what happened here?"

"I always knew she was strange. Just like her mother."

"Muriel, unless you want another lump on your head, you best leave off bad mouthing my wife and daughter."

Muriel's lips pursed tightly. Her 'baby' brother had never raised his voice at her or back talked her in any way.

"Just answer the question. Tell me how you got that lump," he said.

Muriel, still stunned, obeyed the request. "Well, you're not going to believe me. But she threw me."

"You mean to tell me that Emily picked you up and threw you?"

"Well no, not exactly. Maybe threw isn't the right word, but that's what she did but without touching me. She looked at me with a crazed look and I was thrown backward. Twice. The second time I fell against the wall. That blasted frame fell, hit my head and knocked me out."

It was Liam's turn to stare off to the horizon in a dazed silence. Any other father probably would think his older sister was cracked, the bonk on the head giving her brain damage. But Liam knew something that Muriel didn't know. Liam knew that his daughter had special talents.

Emily and Bridget thought that they had a secret from Liam. They had thought it was just between them. But Liam had known all along.

When Emily was not yet one, he came into her room in the morning to get her up and change her. As he walked in, Emily was sitting up in her crib and a small stuffed animal dog flew across the room to her. She didn't see her father there watching, but he could see her concentration on the dog. Before long it flew into her hands. She grabbed it, smiled big and played with the toy like it was the most normal thing in the world to make something come to you just by thinking about it.

Liam didn't say anything to his wife. He assumed it was a fluke, perhaps a trick of his own mind. After all, there had to be a reasonable explanation. Objects don't just fly around.

But as time went by, there were other flying objects. And Liam could swear that his wife and daughter communicated with each other without talking. He never said anything, and as time went on, Emily's abilities – and Bridget's too – became something that was 'between them'. Liam assumed that when Emily got older, she'd tell him about it if she wanted to. She never did. Liam had figured that maybe Emily had lost her strange abilities as she grew up.

When Liam heard Muriel's story about Emily 'throwing' her across the room just by thinking about it, it didn't surprise him in the least. In truth, Muriel's story made Liam smile inside. He supposed that Muriel deserved it. She had been nasty to Emily. *Perhaps she had it coming?*

Liam resumed his study of Emily's note. He read and reread.

"Dear Dad,

I'm leaving. Don't try to find me. I have important work to do. A mission. I can't tell you where I'm going. I can't tell you when I'll return.

I'm not running away – at least I don't think I am. I plan to come back. But you should know that I won't be putting up with Muriel anymore. I'm done with her pushing me around.

Don't worry dad. Love, E"

Not a lot of clues. Acting on an intuitive sense that Liam wasn't aware he had, he knew as he looked at the laconic note from his daughter that he didn't want to call the police. This was a family matter, and Liam needed to take care of his family and of the mess he'd created.

"We're not calling the police Muriel," he said calmly.

"What! You can't do this Liam. That girl needs to learn her lesson. You have to use tough love with dope heads," she said.

"She's not a dope head, Muriel. And no, she's had enough of your tough love. If I call the police, I should be calling on you for child abuse."

Muriel's face turned as white as stone. *That shut her up.*

"No, this is something that I need to take care of," he said.

No sooner had Liam finished his sentence and the phone rang. Fanny's mom, Esther, sobbed on the end of the phone line. She had received a similar note. Her husband was out of town on business and she didn't know where to turn.

"Come over, Esther, and bring the note from Fanny. We'll find them. But don't call the police. Not yet."

He hung up the phone and padded to the kitchen to put on a fresh pot of coffee. Liam was measuring the coffee into the filter when the phone rang again. Jake's mom cried on the other end. Liam invited her over as well.

Within a half hour, both mothers sat in Liam's parlor. Jake's mom, Carol, still in her nurse's uniform, bags under her red-rimmed eyes, sat on the couch with Jake's note held tightly in her hand. Esther quietly sobbed and grasped Fanny's note tightly in her hands. Muriel finished out the quartet. She seethed but kept her lips tightly shut.

"Ladies, I know this is a shock for all of us. But we have to keep our heads about us. I suggest we compare the notes and see if our kids left us any clues so we can find them and get them back where they belong."

"Liam, shouldn't we call the police?" Esther asked. "They need to find my Fan ... " She broke down sobbing again and Carol put her arm around Esther. Liam could see tears well again in Carol's eyes.

"I know it seems natural to call the police. But I'm asking you not to. The children weren't kidnapped. And it's clear from these notes that they intend to return. The police will classify them as runaways and these kids will be in all kinds of trouble when they get back. Carol, Jake needs scholarships for college, right?"

"Yes. Without scholarships, Jake will never be able to afford college."

"I don't want him to have a criminal record. Not if we can help it. And Fanny, her chances of sports scholarships will be jeopardized too," he said.

Esther couldn't speak but nodded her affirmation.

"And, well, I feel I need to take care of this. I'm not at all proud to say it – you may already know this – but I haven't been a very devoted father to Emily since Bridget died," Liam said. A tear came to his eye but he willed it not to fall. Both mothers reached and gently touched Liam's hand. It was the first time anyone had intentionally touched Liam in seven years.

"I understand," Carol said at last. "You need to find your little girl, Liam. And bring our Jake and Fanny back too." Again, Esther only nodded her agreement.

With that, they went to the dining room table to pour over the notes and try to find clues. Liam was worried, sad and mad. But he was also exhilarated. It was the first real emotion he'd had in years. It was the first time he'd truly cared about anything in years. Liam felt like he'd been in a foggy sleep but was waking. He was needed, and he was going to find his daughter and bring her home. He'd bring her home at long last.

23 LIAM SEARCHES FOR CLUES

Three notes. Three different handwriting styles. All pretty much saying the same thing. None said where the kids were going.

All three mentioned an urgent 'mission'. *What kind of mission could three fourteen-year-old kids from the Midwest be on?*

Liam thought that if any of them would leave a clue it would be Jake. Liam observed the neat handwriting of Jake's note.

'I'm sorry Mom. I know this puts you in a bind. But I've got to go help Emily with her mission. I'm sorry for the trouble this is going to cause you, but it's for the greater good. I know that when I return you'll understand.'

So it's Emily's mission. What mission could Emily have (besides running away from Muriel)?

Next Liam looked at Fanny's note. *Sloppy handwriting. Poor grammar and incomplete sentences. She better hope for a sports scholarship.*

'Don't worry mom and dad. Don't send my brothers after me. Not running away. Em needs me for urgent mission. She's my best friend. Know you'd do the same for a friend. Please forgive me and I know you're going to ground me for life when I get home.'

Again with the "urgent mission." And Emily needs her. It's Emily's deal, and they're just along for the ride. But what could Emily possibly have going on?

Liam read over Emily's note again. He hadn't turned it over before, but for some reason, he did then. In even sloppier writing, she wrote more on the back.

'Dad, I miss you so much.'

Miss me? She just left. As Liam thought about it more, he realized what she meant. *Oh, she means she had been missing me, even before she left.* Tears welled in Liam's eyes and he didn't will them not to fall.

'If I told you where I was going and why I was going, you wouldn't believe me. Something amazing has happened. I know you wouldn't understand. The ancient blood that runs in my veins is calling me home. Please don't come looking for me. I love you dad.'

Liam read the backside of the note over and over. There had to be a clue in there somewhere, but all he could see was a runaway note from his missing daughter. Guilt and shame threatened to blind him until he could see nothing else.

Liam dragged himself to the kitchen and rifled through the high cupboard above the refrigerator that only his 6'3" frame could reach. Liam hadn't had a drink in years, but it seemed to him the right time for a stiff one. He retrieved a bottle of scotch and poured himself a shot.

He swallowed the amber juice down in one gulp. The fire liquid set his innards ablaze but did nothing to clear his mind. He sat with his head in his hands, waiting for something to click. As he sat and contemplated how drinking shots of scotch wasn't going to help clear the thick fog in his brain, the words from the note suddenly shouted at him. 'The ancient blood that runs in my veins is calling me home.'

In a flash he was sober and alert like he hadn't been in years. There was a clue in that phrase. It was a big clue that Emily didn't know she had given. She didn't know she had left a clue because she didn't know what he knew.

Liam ran to the attic, taking the steps by two. In the far corner, covered in dust and cobwebs, was a special box. He had hidden it under clothes and other junk. He'd hidden it from Muriel and from Emily too.

It was the box of Bridget. His own box. He hadn't touched any of the things in over seven years. Liam's hands shook as he took the little box from under the pile of stuff and wiped off the years of dust. It was only a mundane shoebox. It didn't look like anything noteworthy would be inside, but the dusty, ratty box contained the contents of his heart.

When Emily spoke of her ancient blood, Liam knew that she was talking about Bridget's side of the family. It was a lineage filled with Irish blood. Bridget had once shown him a family history, actually drawn out by her like a tree. She'd kept it in the box that Liam held in his hands.

He gently took off the lid. On top were letters Liam had sent Bridget when they were in college at two different universities. He couldn't believe she had kept them all those years. She'd also kept pictures Emily had drawn for her while in preschool. There were crayon drawings of houses and flowers. The bright colors mimicked the paintings that Bridget had made. He sifted through concert ticket stubs and more letters and cards. It was strange to see someone's memories of their life, now over, laid in a box that way. Bridget's memories laid to rest in a shoebox coffin.

There were sketches she had done of orchids and other flowers. Finally Liam found what he'd been looking for. On the bottom was a small black notebook. He pulled the notebook out and laid the shoebox to the side. He opened the cover and only a few pages in he found the sketch of a family tree. Bridget's family tree. It was a complex and convoluted drawing with lines going here and there and everywhere and notes in the margins. She had spent hours tracing her family history. Bridget had her mother's side back to the 1500's. And then there it was. Ireland.

As soon as he saw the word, scribbled in large letters in black ink, he knew it was where Emily had gone. *Had she received contact from someone in Ireland and felt she had to go. But who?* Liam looked at the names of ancestors long dead. Unless a ghost had haunted her, he had no idea who could have contacted her. But he knew he had to get on a plane and go to Ireland.

He didn't know what he would do when he got there or where he would go. He knew only the single-minded thought to get on a plane and fly to Ireland. He knew only the need to search for his only daughter.

She's got Bridget's eyes.

Liam carefully put the cards, letters, ticket stubs and pictures back in the box and shoved it back under a pile of dusty clothes. He grabbed the little black notebook and as he stood up, a small sketch fell out of the notebook and landed on the floor. He picked it up and puzzled over it for a few minutes. It was an odd sketch of something that looked like a bracelet. Liam had never seen Bridget draw anything like it. She always drew and painted flowers and plants and trees. Her work was all about nature. *Why did she draw this odd bracelet, all twisted and?* Somehow it seemed to Liam that this drawing was related to Emily's 'mission', but he didn't know how or why he felt it.

As he looked at the sketch, fresh tears sprang to his eyes. It felt to Liam as though Bridget's energy zoomed from the strange drawing and straight into him. Salty drops dripped from his eyes. Until that day, he hadn't cried since the day she'd died.

"Bridget, I miss you so much. If only you were here, you'd know what to do. You'd know how to find our Emily. Let's face it, if you were here, she wouldn't have run away, would she?

"Bridget, I don't know if you can hear me. I don't even know if I believe that you still exist. You know I'm not a spiritual man. I don't know why I'm doing this." Liam buried his head in his hands and let the long quashed tears flow in rivers down his cheeks.

"Bridget, if you can hear me – if you're still there, somewhere, somehow – if you're there, Bridge, our little girl needs you too. If you're there, look over our Emily."

After a few minutes, Liam wiped his tears and nose. He folded the little sketch and tucked it back into the notebook. He'd have time on the plane to puzzle over the drawing and the notebook, the only clues he had to find his daughter amongst the entire population of Earth.

24 EMILY'S SEARCH FOR THE SACRED WELL

When I woke, it was the next morning. We had all slept through the afternoon and into the next day. We shook the sleep from our bodies and ate the day-old bagels we'd stashed in our packs. After our dry breakfast, Jake pulled out his maps and pages he'd printed off his laptop while Fanny cranked up the GPS app on her phone.

Jake had printed out pages that he'd found about different wells and sanctuaries dedicated to St. Bridget. It was a surprisingly long list. Over the years, the old goddess Brighid was turned into a Catholic saint, St. Bridget. The spelling was different, and she had become a saint instead of a Goddess. But St. Bridget was associated with wells, springs and healing waters just as the Goddess Brighid had been for thousands of years. There were wells and springs dedicated to her all over Ireland. When Jake plotted the wells and springs on his map, we could see a concentration of them in County Kildare.

"This is promising," Jake said. "There are at least two wells within walking distance of each other in Kildare town."

"Bingo," said Fanny. "Hey, do you think that town cop called in an APB on us and has the whole Irish police force out looking for us?" Fanny asked.

"I think we should be cautious. In a little town like that, digging up a grave at a religious site is probably a high crime," I said.

Fanny searched the web on her phone and found a bus schedule. We hiked to the next town and popped onto Bus Eireann. After two bus changes and six hours, we went about a hundred miles and got off in Kildare.

By the time we got there, it was about an hour before dark. But it was only about a mile from the bus stop to the first well on our list so we decided to press on.

Our most likely candidate for the Sacred Well was a small, somewhat touristy site that had a statue of St. Brigid and a walking path to a well. We walked down a newly paved road with a sidewalk and followed the signs to 'St. Brigid's Well'. Before long, a sign pointed down a long paved lane lined with towering old trees. When we got to the end of the lane, there were some cars parked there and about a half dozen people milling about the site.

We walked over a small wooden bridge onto a manicured lawn of intensely green grass. A statue of St. Brigid stood by a small stream, and there was a path with grey upright prayer stones leading to a small ring of stones.

There it was. A small hole in the ground surrounded by stones. It wasn't much to look at and didn't seem very sacred. And it wasn't a deep hole either. It looked to be only two feet deep. *I can't imagine this is a portal to another world.* Looking at the small ring of stones around a tiny spit of water, my doubt grew and I began to feel silly about the whole thing.

"Well, let's get this over with," I said. I reached into my bag for the box with the torc in it.

"Wait Em, you can't do that now," screeched Jake. "Not with these people around."

"Why not Jake? Nothing's going to happen anyway. These tourists will just think I'm a weird American kid."

"What do you mean nothing's going to happen? When you pull that thing out of its box, the portal will open up," said Fanny.

I laughed out loud at that. *They really believe this stuff.*

"Look at this," I said. I pointed to the small pool of water. "It's a pathetic hole in the ground. Admit it, this doesn't look like a portal to another dimension, does it?"

Fanny and Jake looked at the hole in the ground and at each other, then back to me. They couldn't say anything. They knew I was right.

"Maybe nothing will happen. But we stole that artifact, remember? I don't think it's a good idea to bring it out and wave it around in daylight with all these people around," Jake said.

Jake had a point.

"Okay, you're right. We'll wait 'til night when these people are gone," I relented.

"So what do we do now?" asked Fanny.

"Let's go back up to the town and have some supper. We'll come back at night."

We stopped at a small restaurant and had Guinness stew, brown bread and Coca Cola. All we'd had to eat that day were the dry bagels at breakfast. We ate like feral children. After the heavy dinner, I wanted to find an inn and crash instead of walking back to the well. But sleep would have to wait, at least until I satisfied Jake's curiosity. He wouldn't rest until I'd pulled the torc out and shown him that I couldn't open a portal. Then maybe he'd let me sleep.

We staggered back to the well and it was full dark when we got there. Instead of all the tourists leaving, an even larger crowd had gathered.

"What's up with this crowd?" I asked.

"I don't know. But look over there. It looks like they're going to light a huge bonfire in that field over there," said Fanny. She pointed to a pile of wood and kindling large enough to set a house on fire. There was a real festival atmosphere going on as more and more people gathered.

Jake walked up to a small round lady and asked, "What's going on here tonight?"

"Well, it's Samhein – All Hallow's Eve, don't you know? We're honoring the spirits of our ancestors. Join in the festivities, lad," she merrily answered.

"Oh, okay, thank you then," he replied. The lady shuffled off with her friends toward the bonfire.

Jake returned to where we were standing. "Doesn't look like a good night to open the portal, does it?"

"Ah, this bites," I said. "I'm so tired. I just want to get this over with."

"What do we do now?" Fanny asked.

We stood there in silence for a few minutes. We were all cold and tired beyond belief. As miserable as my home had been for me, at that moment I would have gladly taken another crack in the face from Muriel if it was followed by sleep in my own bed.

We stood there, half asleep standing up, when a large bird swooped down and almost took my head off.

"What the ... " was all I could get out before it came back and swooped down again, this time actually grabbing at my jacket with its beak.

"What kind of bird is that?" Fanny asked.

"Looks like a small hawk," Jake said.

"A hawk?"

All of us looked at each other jaws open, remembering what Hindergog had said. 'Follow the hawk.'

The bird came at me again, this time flying right at me. I wasn't sure the bird would pull up, but at the last minute, it did and flew across the grassy field just to the west of the well.

"Follow the hawk," said Fanny.

"Yeah, I know what Hindergog said," I replied.

"No, I mean do it. Follow the hawk."

All three of us ran and tried to catch up with the bird.

"Why are we following this bird exactly?" asked Jake.

"Because the little dude with the pointy ears told us to," said Fanny.

"Good point," Jake said.

The bird led us away from the crowds at the Well of St. Brigid and over small hills. After about a quarter of a mile, we were well away from the bonfires and revelry and came to a small clump of old trees by a small brook.

As we went down a little dip, we entered a thick grove of trees. My body went into overdrive. I felt chills up and down my spine. The hairs on the back of my neck and on my arms stood up. Even the hairs on my legs were on end. My heart pounded wildly in my chest. *What is this place?*

"Does anyone else feel that?" Fanny asked.

"What, you feel it too?" I asked.

"Yeah, all my hairs are standing up," said Jake.

And he was right. I looked over at him, and the hair on his head was standing straight up. Jake's head looked like someone had rubbed a balloon on it and made static electricity.

"Holy crap, look at Jake's hair!" said Fan. "Not a good look for you man"

We couldn't help but laugh at his ridiculous hair.

"Come on guys, this isn't time for jokes. There must be something near here causing this," Jake said.

We wandered around in the light of a full moon. The trees and vines were thick here, and it was a bit hard to pick our way through the wood. We couldn't see the hawk anymore and I wasn't sure we were going the right way. But we heard the hawk cry out and turned to go in the direction of its voice.

A few minutes later we came to a small clearing. And there, perched atop a rock, was the hawk. She was beautiful in the full moon, her brown feathers flecked with white and her chest nearly all white. Even though it was entirely dark, the full moon lit up her eyes. They shone like two rounds of onyx.

For some reason I can't explain, the urge to speak to the hawk overwhelmed me.

"Are you the hawk that Hindergog said to follow?" I asked it.

The bird didn't move but let out a short squawk.

"And is this the Sacred Well?"

Again, a short squawk.

"Amazing," said Jake. "Hey wait Emily, take out the torc."

I did as he asked and handed it to him.

"Look, the bird on the torc. It's the same kind of bird. It's a hawk."

Fanny took the torc and inspected the bird finial then looked at the hawk. She nodded, "Yep, it's a hawk alright."

Jake took out the flashlight and shone it around the ground. He shuffled his feet around the thick grass under our feet.

"There's a ring of stones here. This is it. This is the real well."

The hawk squawked again, only a bit louder. It was as if she was saying "That's what I said, stupid!"

The second well was smaller and less noticeable than the first. If I thought the first well was an unlikely candidate for a portal, the second was just plain pitiful. There wasn't even any water, just a small, broken ring of stones.

We stood in complete silence as we looked down at the pathetic, broken ring of rocks. But the chills going up and down my spine contradicted my conclusion that it was just a dip I the ground surrounded by ordinary rock.

All I could say is, "This is it." Fanny and Jake spoke not a word but nodded in agreement.

"Emily, put the torc on now," said Fanny.

"Yeah," chimed in Jake.

I knew they were right, that I should put the torc on. The racing heart and chills in my body showed me that we were in the right place. But I didn't want to put the hunk of metal on. At the well the hawk led us to, I began to feel as if the torc really would cause something to happen and I was scared. I didn't want to go into the little hole. *What if I can't breathe? What if I get ripped apart? What if I can't come back?*

"Come on Em," Fanny said. "What are you waiting for?"

"Well," I stammered, "what if someone sees?"

"There isn't anyone around here. They're all over at the bonfire. They can't see us," said Jake. Fanny nodded.

Fanny held the torc out to me. I reached for the arm bracelet, half expecting it to crawl itself up onto my arm or for the small hole in the ground to open up and swallow me whole.

But as I grabbed the torc, nothing happened. It didn't feel strange or magickal at all. It didn't vibrate in my hand or cause a static discharge. The well was still just a small hole in the ground surrounded by ordinary stones. The torc was still just an old arm bracelet made of twisted metal.

"What now?" I asked.

"I don't know," said Jake. "Hindergog said you'd know what to do."

"Yeah, well I don't! How am I supposed to know what to do with this thing?" I yelled. The hawk cried out.

"And I can't understand what the heck you're saying," I grumped.

We stood there and said nothing. None of us knew what to do next. After a long, awkward silence Jake said, "Look in the box Em. Maybe there are instructions in there or a spell or something."

Jake shone the flashlight while I searched the box. But I found nothing. There was no inscription or ancient writing. No pictures. Just an empty box.

Jake inspected the torc itself. He found nothing helpful there either. It was just a bunch of twisted coils of gold.

"Oh, this is useless," I said. "I don't know what to do."

Then Fanny chimed in, "Put it on."

"What?" I said.

"You know. Put it on. Around your arm like Hindergog said that Saorla wore it."

"Well I've been holding it and nothing happened. I don't see how putting it on is going to make a difference," I said.

"I don't know," Fanny replied. "But try it anyway. It can't hurt."

The hawk let out another excited squawk.

"Apparently she agrees with you Fanny," I said.

I took my jacket off. The torc was pretty large and it slid easily onto my upper arm. As I eased onto my upper right arm, something truly strange happened.

The torc tightened itself. On its own, the metal became slightly liquefied and molded itself to my arm until it fit me perfectly. Fanny and Jake stared in amazement, their eyes wide and their mouths open.

"Holy crap, did you see that?" Jake asked.

I couldn't answer because at that moment, my head began swirling. In a matter of seconds, I was no longer with Jake and Fanny. The ground around me moved and morphed. I stood in front of the same well, only I wore a long purple robe and white tunic instead of jeans and a sweatshirt. I didn't know if it was a vision or real, but I had become Saorla. I don't know how I knew I was Saorla, but I did know it. *I'm Saorla.*

My mouth opened and I heard myself speak. The voice sounded strange, as if it came from a far away place down on long tunnel. I spoke these words:

Ring of stones,
Circle of Moon.
Goddess of Fire,
And of the Light.
Lift the veil of illusion,
Open the door to truth,
For the good of all mankind.

As soon as the last word was spoken, the ground trembled beneath me. I didn't know if the ground trembled only in my vision or in the real world with Fanny and Jake. But as the earth shook, I heard thunder boom and the little indentation surrounded by stones grew. It widened and deepened until it was a proper hole, not just a depression in the ground. A strange silvery mist coming billowed out of growing hole. It was like fog only thicker. The silvery mist looked like a liquid blanket made of silver.

I heard Jake's voice. "You did it Em! That's the portal."

Jake's voice pulled me out of my vision. I blinked my eyes. I was back in our world. I saw Fanny and Jake, both looking at the wide hole in the ground with mist pouring out. *They see it too. I'm not just seeing things. It's really happening.*

"Are you going to go in?" Fanny whispered.

"I guess," I whispered back.

I took a few steps forward but stopped when Jake said, "Wait Em. Don't go yet."

"Why?"

"Well ... I don't know how long you'll be there," he said. "Or when you'll come back."

"Or if I'll come back." I felt tears come to my eyes. Jake looked like he might cry too.

"You'll come back, Em," Fanny said. "I know you will."

"I hope so. I'll miss you guys."

"We'll wait for you," said Jake. "As long as it takes, we'll wait for you."

"Look, it may be like I'm in and out in a second, or it may be years. Time may be weird there. Anyway, if I'm not back in a few hours, go to town and get a room. Take care of yourselves. Promise me that, okay. That you'll take care of yourselves."

"We promise," they both said.

"Okay, then wish me luck." We gave each other a group hug and said goodbye.

"Good luck, Em," they both said.

I began again to walk slowly to the large hole in the ground. I felt as if I was on a conveyor belt. Somehow I moved, but I don't remember telling my legs to go forward. I was drawn to the silvery mist billowing out of the small cave that the incantation had created. Step by step, I drew closer. I heard the hawk call out. Every hair on my body stood on end. My heart beat so fast, it felt like it would explode in my chest.

The breeze picked up and clouds swirled in the sky, blocking out the moon's light. The wind blew my hair about my head, and the chilly air increased the already copious goose bumps on my body.

As I crossed the threshold between our world and the new world, I heard the same low hum that I'd heard when Hindergog appeared to me. *Was that just three days ago?* It seemed like a million years since I'd first seen the little, furry guy.

The humming grew louder and sounded more like buzzing. *What is that sound?* It seemed familiar, but I couldn't quite place it. Then it came to me. It was the sound that I'd heard coming from power lines. *It's the sound of electricity. Am I going to be electrocuted?*

Though it felt as if I walked in slow motion, the entire journey from our world to an alien one took but less than a minute. As I contemplated the possibility that I'd be electrocuted by as I stepped across the threshold to another world, I began to have a thought.

What if I'm going to what people call the 'other side'? What if there really are spirits of the dead and I'm going to the place where they live? And if there is such a place, maybe my mom is there. And if she is there, maybe I'll be able to see her again!

Those thoughts displaced my fear about electrocution and what might come next. With thoughts of seeing my mother again whirling in my head, I picked up my feet and crossed the threshold between two worlds.

25 EMILY AND THE NETHERWORLD

As I entered the portal, I expected to be in a wormhole kind of thing like I'd seen in movies. I anticipated being sucked into a colorful vortex of swirling light. I imagined that I'd feel as if I was being pulled apart or maybe I'd disintegrate and then come back together (hopefully) when I got there.

But it wasn't like that at all. The truth is, I was disappointed in the journey. I simply walked from one world to another. I knew that I'd left our world only because I was surrounded by the same silvery mist and fog that we'd seen come out of the hole. The fog and mist was so thick, I couldn't see my hand in front of my face. I had walked into a dimension of fog.

I didn't know what to do so I walked. At least I think I walked. It's hard to describe, but when you can't see anything in any direction, when you're totally surrounded by mist and fog, you can't tell if you're moving or not. I moved my legs, but I can't say for sure that I went anywhere.

And there didn't appear to be any 'where' to go. It felt like hours that I walked through the endless fog and mist. I was on the verge of some serious tears. *What have I gotten myself into?* I was stuck in a place of nothing, and I had no idea how to get out.

Through my tears I cursed Hindergog, the only one I could think of to blame for my misery. "Darn you Hindergog, you evil troll!"

No sooner had a yelled those words into the mist, I saw a dark shape materialize in front of me. My heart began to pick up speed as the shape came closer and grew larger. But when the shape was a few feet from me, I relaxed as I recognized the familiar outline of pointy ears.

"I am no troll, my young mistress."

"Hindergog, oh thank God you're here," I said. I hugged him to me and found that he was as solid as any person in my world. "I've never been gladder to see anyone in my life."

Hindergog almost looked happy. He looked exactly the same in person as he did in the holographic projection. He had the same sad, droopy eyes. Same tweed vest and rolled up sleeves of his linen shirt. Same dog muzzle but with a pig snout on the end and same odd pig-like ears. I can't say that Hindergog was cute because he was a bit ugly. But just then, he was the best-looking thing I'd ever seen.

"Hindergog, you've come to rescue me from this place, haven't you?" I asked.

"Rescue you? From what?"

"This horrible nothing land that I'm stuck in. I was supposed to go to the Netherworld, but I don't know how to get there."

"You *are* in the Netherworld," Hindergog said. He began to walk.

I ran after him because I didn't want to lose him in the fog.

"This doesn't seem like a world at all. Where are these great teachers I'm supposed to 'train' with? I swear I've walked for hours and I haven't seen anyone or anything."

"This is a decidedly different kind of world than you are used to, young Emily. Your teachers are here, as are other entities, but not nearly so many beings as in your world. Here, you will not have the interference of the creations of so many others."

"Yeah, I don't think interference of others is anything I've got to worry about here."

"My young mistress, so human. You still see only with your eyes."

"Well, I am accustomed to seeing with my eyes, yes. What other organ should I use to see? My spleen?"

"I can see that you are getting frustrated ... "

"You think!"

"But please, dear mistress, try to calm yourself. There is more here than meets your human eye. We are on the way to meet your first teacher, but let's stop here for a moment. I don't think the elders will mind if I give you a short lesson myself."

I was happy to stop walking for a minute and to know that we were, in fact, headed somewhere. I was being a snotty brat but I wasn't in the mood to play nice. I felt like Hindergog had misled me into a strange and unpleasant place. It was as if I'd closed my eyes to sleep and woke up in a silvery cloud of fog. There was no color, no shapes. It wasn't light but it wasn't dark either. It was an insubstantial cloud of nothing.

"Mistress Emily, I ask that you close your eyes for a moment."

It seemed silly, but seeing as how I had nothing else to do, I did as he said and closed my eyes.

"Good. Now, imagine in your mind a path before you to walk on. Make it any kind of path that you would like. Make sure it is solid and smooth so that you will not trip. Think only of your ideal walking path. Have you imagined it?"

I nodded.

"Good, now open your eyes."

I did as Hindergog said and still found myself surrounded by fog. "Okay, that was fun. I'm still in a fog bank."

"Look down."

I looked down and there in front of me was a path - the path - that I'd imagined. Seeing the path that I'd imagined struck me so funny that I laughed out loud.

"What is so amusing to my mistress? Do tell me why you laugh so."

"Oh Hindergog, this is amazing. I didn't know what would happen, you know, so I imagined the first path that came to mind. It was a silly thought but I didn't really know what was going to happen, so when you said 'path' the first thing I thought of was something from an old movie." I could barely finish the sentence because I laughed so hard I had tears in my eyes.

Under my feet and ahead of me, as if I was on the set of the original movie, was the yellow brick road. I'd imagined Dorothy's yellow brick road and I stood on it.

After I finally quit laughing quite so hard, I pressed Hindergog on what had happened. "So, I imagined this path and it just appeared?"

"Yes."

"Just like that, I imagine it and it appears here?"

"Yes."

"Do you see it too?"

"No, I have my own path. They may look different, but at this moment, they are going to the same place."

"So right now, when you look around you, do you see the same foggy cloud everywhere that I see?"

"No, not at all."

"You don't? Teach me, Hindergog. Teach me how to replace this fog bank of nothing with something so I don't get bat crap crazy in this place."

"But I have taught you. Do you not see?"

"You mean I just imagine it?"

"Yes, Mistress Emily, you just imagine what you would like to see. But heed my words of caution. Be exceedingly careful of what you imagine here. In the Netherworld, there is no interference of ideas from others, no competition as it were for creation. And there is no buffer of time. Whatever you intend will manifest immediately. Beware of your fear. A fearful mind can create truly awful things."

I closed my eyes and imagined a sunny day, with just a few bright, white puffy clouds. I imagined green grass and rolling hills and flowers and trees.

I opened my eyes and found that all I'd imagined had come true around me. Instead of standing in a world of dove-grey fog, I stood on

Earth and it was a perfect day. Birds chirped and butterflies flitted amongst the flowers. I breathed a sigh of relief to be surrounded by familiar things.

But the brightly colored flowers reminded me of the reason I'd gotten my legs to walk me through the portal. The flowers were my mother's paintings come to life. As if he could read my mind (and I found out later he could), Hindergog coughed lightly. "Not all wishes can come true," he said. He continued walking. I didn't have time to ask him what he meant because I had to run after him so I wouldn't lose him.

I practically skipped down a yellow brick road behind a man that looked like a dog crossed with a pig. I half expected that Hindergog would take me to an Emerald City and that I'd be chased by a wicked witch. *No, don't imagine that! It may come true.*

Follow the yellow brick road.

26 AND LIAM MAKES THREE AGAIN

Liam was restless on his flight to Dublin. His mind raced with thoughts of where Emily could be and why she'd gone to Ireland in the first place.

He arrived exhausted, but there was no time to waste. He searched from youth hostel to hostel and hoped his guess about where the three had flopped was correct. Liam got lucky. On his fifth try, he found two familiar faces in the dark common room of an old hostel. Jake was busy at his laptop, and Fanny appeared to be asleep on a couch.

"Fanny, Jake – thank God I found you!"

Jake didn't stand but his mouth fell open almost to the floor. His eyes were red-rimmed and tired looking but he smiled brightly when he saw Liam. Jake kicked at Fanny's leg hanging over the end of the couch. "Wake up, Fan."

Fanny pushed herself up, rubbed her eyes and laid into Jake. "Leave off, nub. I'm trying to sleep." But then her eyes caught sight of Liam and she ended her grumpy tirade at Jake. She ran to Liam and hugged him.

"What? How did you find us?" Jake asked.

"It's a long story, but I got lucky I guess. Are you okay?"

"We're fine Mr. Adams, really okay," said Fanny.

Liam's eyes roamed the room hoping to see Emily. But she wasn't there. "Where's Emily? Still sleeping?"

Jake and Fanny exchanged guilty, worried looks. A wave of nausea overcame Liam.

"Emily's not here?"

"Nah, she's not," Jake said.

"Well, where is she?"

The two teens were again silent.

"Look you two, this isn't a game. All three of you are in serious trouble. Now tell me where she is!"

Jake and Fanny again exchanged silent glances, but then Fanny nodded to Jake.

"Mr. Adams, what we have to tell you ... well, it's going to sound impossible. You probably won't believe us," Jake said at last.

"In the last forty-eight hours my fourteen-year-old daughter assaulted my half-crazed sister and ran away to Ireland. I had to calm down two mothers who are, by the way, close to hysterical, flew from Chicago to Dublin, I haven't slept in over thirty-six hours and, oh yeah, I ran around Dublin looking for you guys. So try me."

"Okay, but we need to go somewhere private. What we have to tell you isn't for public consumption," said Fanny.

Jake and Fanny took Liam to their small room. Fanny plopped stomach down on a bunk while Jake told Liam an incredible story about a visit from an alien creature, a golden arm bracelet and a portal. Jake ended his story, "Then Emily walked into a hole in the ground and disappeared into another dimension."

Jake went quiet. He and Fanny stared at Liam with mute expectation. Liam did not speak, but his cheeks flushed red and a large vein in his neck began to bulge.

Fanny broke the silence. "Well, what do you think?"

"What do I think? What do I *think*? I think my daughter's missing, and you're telling me this crazy story to stall me instead of telling me the truth. That's what I think.

"Why are you two doing this? You think it's a funny game to play – mess with Liam? Look, I know I haven't been the father of the year, but this is a cruel joke to play on me. So what I think is that you two better cut out lying and tell me the truth or so help me, I'm turning you over to the police and let you deal with that!"

Fanny's eyes filled with tears. Jake too looked like he was on the verge of crying. With tears beginning to spill down her freckled cheeks, Fanny went to Liam, knelt down and took his hand in hers.

"Look, Mr. Adams, I'd like to tell you that Emily is in the bathroom hiding and that after you leave she'll come out. I'd like to tell you that we decided to help her run away from you and her aunt. I'd like to tell you just about anything other than what Jake said but the truth is, we don't have another story. Truth is, this is all we got."

Liam pulled his hands from Fanny's and slammed his fist on the table. "Well you better come up with something soon. I'm beyond losing patience!"

"What if we can show you proof of our story?" asked Jake.

"We've got proof?" queried Fanny.

"You have proof of a holographic alien and an alternate dimension?" Liam asked.

"Well I don't know if it's proof exactly, but we've got the box that the torc was buried in. It's still covered in grave soil."

Jake dug in his backpack and handed Liam a small metal box. It was caked in dirt, but the engraved tree on the top was visible.

Liam's hands shook as he took the box from Jake. He held it and stared at the engraved picture on the top. Tears came to his tired eyes.

"What's the matter, Mr. Adams?" asked Fanny.

"This box – where did you get it? Did you take this from my house?"

Jake and Fanny exchanged confused looks. Liam could tell from their reaction that they had no idea what he was talking about.

"I told you, Mr. Adams, the box is the one we found buried in the cemetery at Monasterboice. We can show you the grave too, and you can see that the ground was recently dug up," said Jake.

"Yeah, but I'd rather not go back there seein' as how we'll probably be arrested for grave robbing if we do," said Fanny.

"You're saying that you found this buried here, in Ireland, in an old grave?"

"Yeah, that's what we're saying," said Fanny. "Look, I know you're worried about Emily and wigging out with all this. We are too. But I'm not okay with you calling me a liar or threatening me so you either believe us or you don't."

"Fanny, cut it," said Jake.

"No, I won't cut it," she replied. "We've got serious business to get to and we don't have time to put up with this so you either believe us or you don't."

"Calm down, Fanny," Liam said. His voice had become soft and warm. "I'm sorry, to you both. But look at it from my side. I'm a physicist for Christ's sake. I deal in facts and logic, not magick. None of this makes any sense. You – this whole situation – is asking me to stop listening to reason. You're asking me to ... "

"Believe," said Jake.

"Yes, well that's not easy for me. Bridget was the believer."

"It's hard for us to believe too and we've been through it all. I still wonder if we actually saw Hindergog or maybe it was a dream that we all had or a hallucination. But then we came here and found things just like he said we would," said Jake.

"Yeah and then we saw Emily walk through that portal. We had our doubts that it would open, but she put that torc on and then we were all staticky, and our hair was on end – that was real. It really happened to us. And then we saw the ground open up and the silvery fog came out ... " said Fanny.

"What are you saying about static and silver fog?"

"We all knew we were onto something when we got to the well the hawk led us to because we felt our hairs stand on end, you know, like when you rub a balloon on the hairs on your arm? Only it was like that all over our bodies, and we all felt it, right Fan?"

"True chiz, we all felt it. And there was no storm or lightening or anything."

"And you saw a silver fog come out of the portal? What do you mean by silver?"

"You know, not grey or white – silver," Jake said. "I know it's kind of hard to picture, but imagine fog like flowing liquid silver."

"And this torc – the arm bracelet she put on. What was it made of?"

"I'm not sure. It looked gold, but it wasn't like we did an analysis on it or anything. Why?"

Liam sat quietly. To Fanny and Jake it almost looked as if he were in a trance. His synapses fired, his mind focused. There was something familiar in their description but Liam was just too tired to place it.

"I'm not sure yet, but the static and silver fog and the gold bracelet – I think they're connected and relevant, but I can't put my finger on it right now. But let me tell you why I got choked up when I saw this box."

Liam pulled Bridget's notebook out of his bag and showed Fanny and Jake the drawing of the tree and torc.

"This tree looks almost exactly like the one carved on the box," said Fanny.

"And that's the torc. Almost a perfect likeness of it. Where did you get these drawings?" asked Jake.

"They were Bridget's," Liam said. All three fell silent.

"So you see, there are just too many coincidences. My brain is in a tailspin guys. I'm not sure what to do with it all. My wife drew a picture of a tree before she died over seven years ago. Now you're showing me the same tree carved on a box buried over a thousand years ago in Ireland, a place she'd never been. And she drew a picture of an odd, twisted bracelet. Now you're telling me my daughter put a bracelet just like it on her arm right before she walked through a hole in the ground and into another dimension."

"Yep, some pretty heavy chiz," said Fanny.

"Yes, Fanny, heavy 'chiz,' whatever that is."

"I know it's a bit much to take in Mr. Adams, but here's the thing. We're up against the clock here. If Hindergog was right – and so far he has been right about all this crazy stuff – this Dughall guy is out there somewhere trying to find a way into the Netherworld too," said Jake.

"Yeah, and we don't know what he's up to once he gets there, but apparently it's something really bad 'cause that Hindergog dude came all the way from another dimension to send Emily on a journey to stop the guy," said Fanny.

"So we gotta help her," said Jake. "We gotta do what we can on this side to figure this out so we can stop this Dughall guy."

Liam's head spun with coincidences and information, clues and ideas. But he was too tired to piece any of it together into a coherent thought.

"Hey, you look whipped Mr. Adams. Why don't you get some rest for a few hours? Jake and I will keep working," said Fanny.

"You're right Fanny," said Liam. "Good kids. Both of you. I want to thank you both for taking care of my Emily for me."

"Ah, we didn't need to take care of her," said Jake.

"I don't mean just on this trip."

Fanny took Liam's hand again and he didn't withdraw it. Fanny nodded and Jake clapped him on the shoulder. It appeared that they wouldn't hold the zombie years against him. Liam had come when they needed him the most.

The newly formed trio shared a common goal: Find Emily. Their destination, as yet unknown.

27 EMILY'S FIRST MASTER

"Hindergog, where are we going?"

"To your first master, of course."

He gave answers as though they were perfectly obvious. But every answer he gave made me more lost than I was before.

"My master? Can't you tell me anything about him? Even a name?"

"Oh, I think you will recognize this teacher right away."

My heart picked up speed. *Someone I recognize. Can it be? Who else would I recognize here? It must be. My mother! My teacher will be my mother!*

"Miss Emily, your master is not human."

My heart sank. *He really can read my mind, can't he?*

It's hard to describe the way time worked in the Netherworld. It's like I'd walk for what seemed like a long time, but I didn't feel tired. And as soon as I'd think, 'I'm tired, I wish I was there,' I was there.

That's how it was at that moment. I thought, 'I'm ready. I want to meet this teacher, even if it's not my mom.'

I no sooner that it when out of the mist appeared a small building. As I got closer, I saw that it was made of wood and it was weathered grey. It had a roof thatched in straw blackened by time. The windows were covered in wood screens with old Chinese carvings, the lacquer aged to an almost blackish-red patina. A path of stone steps led to a carved redwood door. The little house looked like it had come out of the Chinese countryside.

As we approached the front door, Hindergog stopped. Panic seized me. *Is he going to leave me here alone without him?*

"Are you leaving me?" I asked.

"Yes, dear one, this you must do alone."

"But Hindergog, I don't know what to do. I'm scared and you're the closest thing to someone I know in this strange place. Please stay with me."

He shook his head and his dog lips curled into a small smile. "Dear Emily, you are in capable hands here. Your task is at hand. Learn well, young one."

With that, he vanished into the fog and mist.

Sweat pooled in my palms and I stood as still as a stone in front of the small, cottage door. I felt like an idiot standing there. A voice in my head said, 'Knock, moron'. I think that was Muriel's voice.

But I did as the voice said and I knocked. I rapped softly on the door, but I could barely hear it. The incessant grey fog seemed to suck up sound like a vacuum cleaner. I knocked again but harder.

No answer. I stood in the unearthly silence of the unearthly place and waited for something to happen.

Just when I thought that maybe I should leave, the door slowly opened. As the door swung open, I saw a small figure in the shadow of the doorway. A *very* small figure.

Although I'd never met her before, I recognized my teacher right away. She looked exactly as I'd pictured her when I listened to Hindergog tell his tale. My teacher was none other than Madame Wong.

I felt relief that the kindly, wise woman from Hindergog's story would be my first teacher. My relief was short lived.

28 MADAME WONG

"Are you going to stand there or come in?" she asked.

I told my feet to go in, but they didn't want to move. With great effort I got my lead feet to walk through yet another door to the unknown.

I ducked as I walked through her tiny door. The little house was dark inside but clean and sparse. There was a wooden table under one window, large enough for two. Two rickety-looking wood chairs flanked the table. There was a simple hearth with a kettle over the fire. In another corner rested a small bed made of knobby pine with modest, white covers over the mattress. Beside the bed was a diminutive table with a washbowl and pitcher.

It was like I had stepped back in time. No phones. No television. No electricity. No technology of any kind.

"Madame Wong? Are you really the Madame Wong that Hindergog told me about? The Madame Wong who taught the girls in the Sacred Grove?"

"I am."

"But how ... how can you be here? I thought the portal was closed."

"It was."

Apparently, not much of a talker.

"Then how can you be here if you were left behind when the portal closed?"

"Ah, Madame Wong starting from scratch here." She shook her head, went to the fire and poured hot water from the kettle into a small, porcelain teapot.

"Tea, Youngling?"

"Sure, I guess that would be okay."

"You guess, or you know? Tea or no tea. This is not a hard question," she barked at me.

"Okay then, tea, yes."

Another cup materialized on her table, seemingly plucked out of nowhere. I shouldn't have been surprised. I had, after all, walked into another dimension. But I had a hard time believing what I'd just seen.

"How did you do that?"

"What?"

"Make that cup appear out of nowhere."

"All of here is nowhere. Ask and it is given. So much to learn." She shook her head again as she poured tea into two, small cups.

"Sit," she commanded.

I did as she said and fast. After Hindergog's story, I knew that I didn't want to mess with Madame Wong.

We drank our tea in silence. Madame Wong watched me over her teacup with dark, brown eyes surrounded by copious wrinkles. She hadn't answered my question so I pressed her again.

"You never answered my question. How is it that you are here?"

Madame Wong put her cup down and squinted her dark eyes at me.

"You know nothing? Hindergog said that I had my work cut out for me." She wrapped her knobby fingers around her warm teacup and sipped again.

I knew she could pull and do me in before I could even scream. But I'd lost my patience. I couldn't get a straight answer about anything from anybody and I'd had enough.

"Look, I don't know anything. A few days ago I was worried about flunking math and dealing with the wrath of Muriel the Mean. Today I'm sitting in another dimension sipping tea with a woman that should have been dead over a thousand years ago. You're supposed to be the teacher, so teach me at least this one thing. How can you be here?"

Madame Wong gently put her teacup down on the table, but when she looked up at me, her eyes were ablaze. *Here it comes!* I knew I was going to feel the sting of a slap soon, just like when I mouthed off to Muriel.

"Because you are Youngling and know nothing, Madame Wong spare you insolence one time. But you not speak to me in that tone again. Madame Wong not Aunt Muriel. If you speak to Madame Wong like that again, Miss Emily will wish for her aunt."

I felt my cheeks flush scarlet. My mouth was full of cotton and I couldn't speak. She was small and had not raised her voice yet instinctively I knew that what she said was true. I nodded my head to show her I understood.

"Listen well as Madame Wong not explain again. This first lesson, youngling. Most humans see with eyes only. That is great failing of the species."

I nodded yes even though I wasn't sure I knew what she was talking about. I wasn't about to disagree with her.

Madame Wong swept her arms out wide. "This place, what humans call the Netherworld, is place of pure potential. If you allow it, Miss Emily learn things that have eluded most humans. Here you see with whole self, not just eyes."

I listened as best I could, by my mind was still back at the question of how Madame Wong was in the Netherworld when she should have been shut out when the portal closed. I wasn't following her, and it must have shown on my face.

"Oh, Madame Wong in for long life with this one." She shook her head and drank her tea.

"The Madame Wong from Hindergog's tale, her human body is of the earth now. The Madame Wong you see is a merged being."

"Merged being? I don't understand."

"Madame Wong, like many curious humans before her, stumbled into this world, like you did, many, many Earth rotations ago. Long before Saorla's time. Madame Wong met an entity who had left its body behind. They made agreement."

"An agreement? What kind of agreement?"

"Agreement to merge. To become one being. Part of their combined essence was projected into the body Madame Wong carried around with her in your world. Part stayed in this realm. Now, merged life essence all that remain. Body no longer."

"So, what you're saying is that you are not real? Am I imagining you?"

"Real? What is real?"

"Again with that question. I thought I knew what real was, but I'm starting to wonder what real is."

"Good!"

"It's good that I don't have a grip on reality?"

"Good that you begin to question what is real. Madame Wong more real than most of what you have known."

"But when you – I mean Madame Wong – when she had a body, how could she exist two places at one time?"

"Quite easy. Even smallest, simplest matter in your universe can do this. All things exist always in every possible time and place. It is choice. You choose where you want to be and be there now."

"Can you die?"

"Not sure if death come or not in this place of no time. Still here. That's all that matters. Madame Wong found a way to cheat death, no?" She chuckled softly. "Not all it's cracked up to be when all those you loved cease to be with you."

"I know what that's like."

"Yes, yes. You lost one most dear."

"She was dear, but I'm not so sure how I feel about her anymore."

"Yes you are."

"Am I?"

"There is no question here. If you did not love her, you would not have come. Miss Emily only come to Netherworld to see her mother again."

That was true. It's all I had thought about. I wanted to look on her face one more time.

"Hindergog, simple-minded creature. He lacks the courage to tell you himself."

"Tell me what?"

"Netherworld not the place of spirits, Youngling. You will not find Bridget Adams here."

I felt like I'd been shot. All hope drained from me. I realized then how much I'd been hanging on to that hope. Hope of seeing my mom again had kept my feet moving all over the hills of Ireland when I was so tired. Hope had made me walk through the portal in the first place. It was the only reason I'd come.

To be honest, at that moment I didn't give a rat's hind end about Dughall and trying to save the world. I just wanted to see my mom again. *Now, what's the point?*

"Selfish, isn't it?"

"What, to want to see your mom again? I was just a little girl. She was the only one who ever understood me. The only reason I came here was to see her. And now, you're telling me that she's not here," Hot tears welled in my eyes, broke free of my lashes and streamed down my face in torrents.

"You lie. Mother not only one to understand you. You lie to yourself much, Youngling. Bad human habit. Speak untruths, even inside their own heads."

"Okay then, you're the teacher. Tell me. Who else has understood me?"

Madame Wong did not immediately answer. She took another sip of tea, put her cup down, and said, "Look in your tea."

"What?"

"Look in your tea," she repeated.

I looked down into my teacup. The soggy black tea leaves at the bottom had arranged themselves into the shape of faces. Two faces stared back at me from the bottom of my teacup. Two very familiar faces.

Seeing Jake and Fanny in my tea made me feel like a turd for what I'd said. There I was, blubbering about my mom and thinking only of myself. But Jake and Fanny were out there somewhere, putting themselves in danger for my quest. And they understood me about as well as anyone could. At least as well as I'd allowed them to.

As I looked at the tealeaves in the shape of my two best friends, the leaves started to shift and change. The leaves again took the shape of a person. Zombie Man.

"Okay, Jake and Fan I believe. But Zombie Man? No, he doesn't get me. I can't agree with that."

"Tea does not lie." Madame Wong got up, walked to her washbasin, washed her cup and placed it on her small shelf. The small gesture of washing the cup and putting it away seemed odd in that place of dreams and fog.

"Why did you do that?"

"Do what, Youngling?"

"Wash the cup and put it away. You can conjure up a clean cup whenever you want to. Why clean that one?"

"There is joy in doing."

I'm not sure what was stranger. Meeting an entity in another dimension, or meeting one who washes teacups.

"You are tired. Long journey. Rest now, Youngling. When you wake, we begin your training. You sleep." Madame Wong gestured to the small bed.

The bed was a bit too short for my long frame and it wasn't very comfortable, but Madame Wong had been right. I was more tired than I'd ever been. I fell onto the bed and fell to sleep as soon as my head hit the pillow. I didn't dream about torcs or green hills or Madame

Wong. I didn't dream at all. Even in my sleep, I was in a place of fog and mist.

29 BREATHE

I woke to the crack of something hard against the bottom of my foot. *What the ...*

I opened my eyes, and in the blur of first waking, I made out the outline of a tiny woman. She rapped my feet with what looked like a bamboo cane.

"What the heck are you doing?"

"Time for Miss Emily wake up."

"Yeah, well you don't have to beat me to wake me up."

Have I slept for a few minutes or days? There was no time in the Netherworld. No sunrise or sunset. But I woke feeling refreshed so my sleep was long enough anyway.

I got up, stretched and ducked so I could get out of her small door without banging my head. There was less mist and fog than there had been before. Through the light haze I saw Madame Wong. She stood perfectly erect. It was as if there was an invisible string attached to her head imperceptibly lifting her body yet leaving her feet firmly planted on the ground. Her hands were at her chest, palms together in prayer position, her eyes closed. Her body, completely still, looked like a statue. I wasn't sure if I should interrupt her, so I just stood there like a mute for what seemed like an exceedingly long time, afraid to make a sound or speak for fear of startling her.

"You cannot startle me when I already know you are there."

Her ability to read my thoughts annoyed me.

"What will I do today?"

"Sit."

"Sit. That's it?"

"Sit. Breathe. No think. That is lesson."

I plopped myself down in front of her and sat cross-legged. During our brief conversation, Madame Wong hadn't moved anything except her mouth. She stood as still as a statue with her eyes closed.

"May want to make self more comfortable. Miss Emily sit long time."

I wasn't sure I could conjure things the way Madame Wong did, but I figured I'd give it a try. I thought of the most comfortable sitting I'd ever done. It was at Fanny's house. She had a cool chair in her room that was like beanbag chair, but it had a back to it. I could sit in that thing for hours. *That's what I'd like right now.* I felt the chair materialize beneath me.

I could get used to this having whatever I want thing.

The chair felt exactly the same as the one I'd sat in at Fanny's house. I wiggled and wedged my butt until I was comfortable. When I had settled in I asked, "Now what?"

"Sit."

"Just sit?"

"Sit. No think. No do. Just breathe."

"I just sit here doing nothing? This is way easier than I thought it'd be."

"Not doing harder than doing."

"Not for a teenager. This is the life." I kicked back and relaxed.

I'd say in regular human time, it took all of about five minutes for me to feel bored. Really bored. I was fidgety and anxious. I couldn't just sit there when my friends needed me. According to Hindergog, the entire free world was counting on me. *How can I just sit here when that dude Dughall is out there somewhere trying to start mayhem?*

"Look, Madame Wong, I don't have the time to just sit on my butt doing nothing. I gotta get the cliff notes version of your lessons and get back to stop Dughall."

"Miss Emily think she is ready to stop that dark one?"

"Well, no, I don't think I'm ready. So that's why I'm saying, you know, speed this up a bit. Give me the quick version so I can be on my way."

"No short cut to understand Akasha."

"Akasha? Who is she?"

"Akasha not a she. Or a he. Akasha is all that is. Miss Emily here to learn mysteries of Akasha. To learn of the great Web of All That Is. Now sit."

I groaned loudly at that. *How can sitting on my butt possibly help me learn about this Akasha or become a warrior or help my friends?*

But I did as she said and sat. After a few more minutes I could take it no more. "Look, I'm not a warrior. I just want to go home. I want to find Fanny and Jake and just go back home."

"Leave without training? Miss Emily not ready to defeat the dark one."

"I'm not the one, okay. Look, if you know so much, why don't you go defeat him? You, Brighid and little Hindergog. You shouldn't send a teenager to do this anyway."

"We exist in this realm, not in yours. A human must stop the dark one from his plan. Not our destiny. Destiny of one called Emily."

"Well then find someone else. There's got to be some other person that can do this job. I'm not hero material."

"You are what you believe yourself to be. Now sit. Breathe. Answers you seek will come to you. Lessons needed will be learned. Sit. Breathe."

I was so frustrated, I wanted to scream and throw things and kick Madame Wong out of her statue post. I'd envisioned learning how to use weapons and performing magick spells. Instead, I was told to sit and breathe, two things I was pretty sure I already knew how to do.

But seeing as how I didn't know the way out of the place, I flopped myself back down on my chair and pouted. *I may have to sit. I may even have to breathe. But I don't have to be happy about it.*

"Miss Emily stubborn one. Yes, very inflexible. Your resistance makes lesson more difficult."

I ignored her. I would sit and breathe. Best to do it quickly and get it over with so I could move on. The sooner I figured out what she wanted, the sooner I'd be able to get out of there.

I sat. And I breathed. My mind wandered freely. I thought about Fanny and Jake and wondered what they were doing. *I hope they're not still sitting by that well.* I thought about how I was ditching school and wondered if I'd missed much. But I decided a few weeks didn't much matter since I was close to flunking almost everything anyway.

Thinking of school and flunking made me think about Muriel and how steaming mad she'd be at me if I ever made it back. And my mind stayed on the subject of Muriel for a long time as I imagined how she might lock me in my room without food (one of her favorite punishments) or maybe she'd beat me with a cane like Madame Wong's.

I was startled out of my daydreaming by the sound of a shrill and familiar voice.

"Emily Marie Adams!"

I opened my eyes and about peed myself. Standing before me was none other than Muriel the Mean. She glared at me and she held a cane in her hand just like Madame Wong's.

"Get up off of your lazy butt this minute!"

I did as she said and as I stood, she rapped my legs with the cane.

"Go. Go to that table and study your math. You will study all night and all day and won't eat again until you have mastered the entire book."

I looked over and where there had previously been only mist stood a long, brown table. It looked a lot like the one in our dining room at home but it was longer, taller, darker and more menacing than the one in my house. I walked to the table much like the one I'd sat at doing homework and suffering raps across my knuckles and Muriel's icy stare. I was almost to the table but I stopped in my tracks.

"Wait. I don't have to do what you say. Not here. You're not real."

"What are you talking about, girl? Not real? Are you hyped up on drugs? Maybe a lash from this cane will show you how real I am." Muriel pulled the cane back, ready to wallop me with it.

As the cane swung forward, I grabbed it with my hand and wrung it from her. Muriel was stunned but only for a moment. Her icy glare gave way to outright fury.

"How dare you?" she said.

"How dare you treat me so badly?" I asked.

"You get what you deserve for your disobedience. You are a stubborn child, so unlike your father. If you were only more like him."

"If I were more like him instead of my mom, you'd stop beating me? Well, I'm not Liam. And I'm not Bridget either. I'm Emily. And I'm not going to let you beat me or starve me or mistreat me anymore. Now go away!"

In an instant, Muriel faded into the mist of the Netherworld as if she had never been there at all. I panted and my heart raced. *I thought I was supposed to be just sitting and breathing.*

"Madame Wong, what was that? Why did Muriel just pop in for a visit?"

Madame Wong still stood as still as she'd been before. Her eyes remained closed. She was nonplussed by what had just happened.

"I said sit. Breathe."

"Well I was sitting and breathing."

"No. Madame Wong also say 'No do. No think.' You thought."

"Well yeah, I was thinking. It's kinda' hard not to think if you have a brain. I don't exactly have a shut off switch for the thoughts."

"Oh, you do. Find it. Until you find switch, Miss Emily face whatever mind imagines."

"You're saying that if I think about something, it will appear? Good or bad, it's just going to show up?"

"That what Madame Wong say. Why Miss Emily need to repeat Madame Wong not know."

"But I can't control these thoughts. My mind wanders, and it often wanders to unpleasant things. Bad things that have happened or nightmares I've had."

"Then Miss Emily in for rough time. Sit. Breathe. No do. No think."

I whined at her. "But I can't help it that thoughts come to me. Other thoughts came. Like I was thinking about Fanny and Jake, but they pop in for a visit. Why only bad things appear?"

"No difference, good or bad. Thoughts like birds in mind. Some fly in. Some fly out. Some stay at water hole to drink. Beware of birds that linger."

I reflected on what Madame Wong had said and remembered that I had dwelled on Muriel for a while. My thoughts of her weren't fleeting.

"Now, sit. Breathe. No do. No think," commanded Madame Wong.

So I sat. Again. I breathed. Again. I tried not to dwell on any thought for very long. I let go. My mind wandered. I tried hard not to allow anything awful to come into my mind.

"If awful come, let it go." Madame Wong's voice sounded like it was coming to me from a far off place.

I got the rhythm of my breath. In. Out. I focused on my breath, repeating the words 'in' and 'out' in my mind in time with my breath.

The whoosh of my breath in and out, in and out reminded me of a sound from a memory. The whoosh, whoosh, whoosh got louder. It was no longer my own breath I heard but the sound that had haunted my dreams, both waking and sleeping, for seven long years.

Whoosh. Whoosh. That horrible sucking sound. Air being sucked in and pumped out.

I knew that sound. I didn't want to open my eyes. I knew what I'd see, and it was my worst nightmare.

How many times do I have to see my mother die?

30 RIDING THE WAVES

If I'd had any sense about me, I would have kept my eyes closed and thought of something – anything – else. But it was like driving by a car wreck and looking even though I knew I'd see something gruesome.

I opened my eyes and I was in my mom's hospital room. The last one. The one she died in.

My dad sat in a chair beside her bed. And on the other side of the bed was a little girl. Her long red hair looked unbrushed. Her eyes were wide open with fear and they sparkles with tears, but she looked completely focused on something. The room was silent except for that awful sound. *What's making that horrible sucking sound?*

The machine that looked like a bellows pumped up and down. It was the source of that awful sound. The contraption was hooked up to the little girl's mother by the tubes that ran into and out of the woman. The machine whooshed and pumped in a smooth rhythm. Below the bellows contraption was a clear plastic container that held a disgusting black, tarry substance. *What is that tarry stuff coming out of the woman? Or is it being put in?*

No kid should ever see her parent die. Yet there I was, reliving the nightmare again.

It was unbearable. The long seething wound deep within me was ripped open again. The horrid sight of the tar being sucked out of my mom. My dad, eyes red-rimmed, his face ashen gray. The little girl – my child self – focused on her mother's station, picking up her frequency for the last time. And present through it all, that incredibly irritating sucking sound.

I couldn't take it anymore. I rushed over to the machine and ripped at it like a mad person. "Stop sucking the life out of her!" I screamed at the machine as I knocked it over and pulled at the cords and wires.

"I won't see this again!" I swung madly at the air, trying to make the ghosts go away.

I fell to the floor, the plastic tubing still gripped in my hands. I sobbed great, heaving sobs. I cried so hard that I thought I might drown in a river of tears.

I'm no warrior priestess. I'll drown in my own tears before I have a chance to help anyone.

Warm arms wrapped around me. I was afraid to open my eyes for fear of what I'd see. The touch was small and soft yet unfamiliar.

I opened my eyes. Madame Wong's arms were around me and she cradled me in her warmth. She was the last person I'd expected to comfort me. She'd stood as still as a statue for so long, I'd begun to think maybe that's all she was. A statue. But her arms were substantial and warm around me.

I didn't speak and relaxed into her arms. My wailing gave way to soft sobs. As I relaxed into her, I almost heard her voice in my head. Pictures began to form in my mind's eye but they weren't pictures from my own life. Without speaking any words out loud, Madame Wong spoke to me of her life. Within a few seconds, I understood that Madame Wong knew more about my suffering than anyone I'd ever known. The human part of her knew.

In my mind, I saw a group of ancient Chinese houses. Rice paddies. Beautiful mountains in the distance. But the houses were on fire. I heard the sound of anguished cries.

There were other pictures flashing before my mind's eye. A baby that looked still as a stone. Another baby – no a child – being held by a gentle looking man. The child didn't move either.

I saw men and women dying by the hand of a sword and felt the anguish of a heart that had known considerable loss. And great anger. I saw an old woman finding her way through the mist of the portal and into the Netherworld. I saw her struggle with the lessons that I too struggled with. Of letting go of anger and of sadness. Of finding peace and happiness.

All this was a flash in my mind, like a movie being shown at super high speed. It was more like a knowing than a seeing.

Madame Wong. The tiny woman holding me had known enormous suffering in her human life. And she had come to the place of mist and fog and learned how to forget.

"No, Miss Emily. Not forget. You never forget. If you live to be as old as Madame Wong, you never forget."

"Then why did you choose to live so long – to allow yourself to go on – when you had such immense pain inside?"

"Ah, yes, choice. I chose to let ghosts stay in past. Past is history. Living is now. I sat. I breathed. I let past go. I let future go. I am. That is all."

"But didn't it take you many years to learn how to do that?"

"Have you not understood yet? Time here – it is slippery, no?"

"It seems not to exist at all, and still ... It's odd, in some ways, I feel like I've been here my whole life, but it also feels like I just got here."

"It is difficult for humans to stay in Netherworld because no watch, no rising sun, no setting moon. No markers for human mind to gauge its ever present need to know time."

"So if there is no time here ... "

"It is eternal."

"Then what is happening back in my own dimension? Has a great amount of time passed?"

"Miss Emily, you need only know that you need not worry about time. That is one you must let go like the ghosts of your past. Plenty of time to sit. To breathe."

Back to sitting and breathing.

I sat on my chair again and got comfortable, closed my eyes, and began again to breathe. I thought only of my breath. I opened my eyes briefly, and Madame Wong was back in exact same statue pose I'd seen her in before. It was like she had never moved. *Did I dream it? When she comforted me, was it a vision?*

But I let those thoughts go too and paid attention only to my breath like the waves of an ocean. Tide coming in. Tide going out. My breath was like the gentle roll of the waves, up and down my body.

I sat in meditation for a long, long time, reckoning as best I can about these things in a place with no time. I had more visions come to life, but they weren't as frightening or as momentous as Muriel or the hospital room.

Eventually I found that I was fully in control of my mind. Mostly I thought nothing at all, which I hadn't thought possible. For long stretches of time, known to me by the large amount of breaths I had followed like a wave through my body, I thought nothing at all. At other times, there were small thoughts that popped in, like the little birds Madame Wong had talked about. I told them to take flight and they did. It became easy to have a mind free of the distraction of a thousand thoughts and ideas crowding all at once like a busy market filled with people. My mind was instead like a vast, still meadow, waiting to see what would appear.

After immeasurable breaths into and out of my body, my long meditation was broken by the sound of Madame Wong's voice.

"You ready to become warrior priestess now," she said. "But first, Miss Emily sleep."

I opened my eyes and felt underneath me the rustic bed of Madame Wong's cottage. It took me no time at all to drift off to a dreamless sleep, my mind already so empty that it didn't have the material left to create dreams.

But just before waking I had one dream – or was it a vision? I couldn't be sure. In the dream I stood before a dark haired man with eyes like two lumps of coal in his skull. He was gaunt, his fingers bony, and his body was like a skeleton covered in thin skin. He looked smug and satisfied with himself.

The man's face was menacing and I knew instantly that he'd do me harm. I thought, "I should be scared." But I wasn't scared. Instead, I felt pity. *Why would I pity him?*

My eyes fluttered open and the dream faded. But I recalled the image of myself that I'd seen in the dream. At first I didn't think it was me. The girl seemed strong and powerful. She had a halo of buttery yellow light that glowed around her. Her face was determined with no hint of fear or smirk about it, just calm self-assurance. And in my dream the girl held a dagger in her hand. *Can this be me? But I don't own a dagger, and I never look that confident.*

I rose from the bed, ready for a new day with Madame Wong in the place of mist and fog, of dreams and shadows. I had a vision in my mind of a girl with a dagger that I wanted to meet.

31 WHY I HATE BAMBOO

I found Madame Wong in a perfect headstand in her spot under the large maple tree in the garden. I sat in patient mediation in front of her, waiting for her to start my lesson for the day. I listened to the burbling brook that tumbled past her small meadow, and I drifted off into a state of deep relaxation. It was a shock to the system when Madame Wong finally spoke, her high-pitched croak interrupting the perfect stillness I was becoming accustomed to.

"Miss Emily ready to become warrior priestess now?"

"I don't know if I'm ready for it, but I'll try."

"Only do or not do. Which is it?"

"Okay then, I choose do."

"Ah, good choice. Come." She gracefully exited her headstand and walked across the garden. I followed respectfully behind her a few paces as we walked through intense fog and mist to the babbling brook.

"Miss Emily has learned focus, yes?"

"Yes, I suppose so."

"NO, NO, NO! No suppose. Focus or no focus – which is it?"

"Okay, yes, for God's sake, I can focus! Jeez, no need to scream at me."

"Don't suppose. Don't guess. Know the answer and say it. A true warrior is sure of herself. Right or wrong does not matter."

"Well see that's the point now, isn't it? I'm not a 'true warrior'. And about the only thing I'm sure of is that I'm not sure of myself."

I looked down into her eyes. She stared up at me evenly. Stalemate.

"You know focus. Time to learn awareness."

I rolled my eyes, a knee-jerk reaction to the thought of spending more time sitting for days on end breathing. I was ready for action, not more doing nothing.

"Oh, you will have action, young one." Her lips curled into a sly smile.

"I'm afraid to learn the answer to this, but I'll ask it anyway. How do I learn 'awareness'?"

"By doing laundry," she said. Out of the nothingness appeared an enormous pile of clothes just like the ones Madame Wong wore. There were black linen pants with wide legs and a drawstring waist and long-sleeved dark blue linen shirts with cloth buttons up the front and a mandarin collar. There was also a large, metal washbasin, bar of soap and a washboard.

"I become a warrior by doing your laundry?"

"You become aware, alert and ready by doing laundry."

"So how long do I have to stand here scrubbing your clothes until you decide I'm sufficiently aware?"

"Until all clothes are washed and hung to dry." She pointed to a clothesline hung between two large oak trees.

"Then what?"

"Then cut the fire wood." She pointed to a pile of logs and a hatchet that I hadn't noticed before on the edge of the meadow. "Chop wood. Learn to be aware and alert." Madame Wong vanished into the misty air.

I wanted to rebel. I wanted to sit down on the ground and refuse to do anything. I wanted to be back at my house, even if Muriel was there.

But I caught myself and stopped thinking about Muriel before she reared her ugly head again. I picked up a shirt and began washing the old gnat's laundry.

I dipped a shirt into the stream, rubbed soap on it. Up and down until it was well lathered, then I swished it in the water and hung it to dry. Shirt after shirt, pant after pant, all the time trying to be 'aware', whatever that meant.

My mind was in a stupor then it wasn't. I was on my knees in pain, a burning sting surging from my calves and up the backs of my legs. There was a moment when I thought that the hatchet on the edge of the meadow had flown into the backs of my legs.

"What the ... " I turned and Madame Wong stood behind me with her cane, her face wearing a smirk.

"Did you just beat me with that cane?"

"Yes."

"Why?"

"Test. See if Miss Emily aware."

"Well? Am I?"

"Welts on the back of your legs. What you think?"

"That's not fair. I didn't know this was a game. You didn't tell me that you'd materialize and beat the crap out of me."

"If aware, you know it coming. If alert, you stop me."

"Well I'm alert now." I towered over her, challenging her with my look to try it again.

She stood stone still and eyed me just as I eyed her. We stood locked in a death stare for countless minutes. I felt focused and aware.

Suddenly, CRACK! That cane swung out of nowhere and bit into the flesh of my left thigh.

"Son-of-a-kraken. You did it again!"

"Miss Emily not aware." She disappeared again into the nothingness.

I flopped myself down and let flow the tears that had sprung up in the corners of my eyes. Caning is a barbaric punishment but it's still meted out in some countries. *I know why they still use it.* Only two swats with that little piece of bamboo had left me with the most painful welts and bruises I'd ever had. The pain, the fear, and the worry about my dad and Jack and Fan made me feel hopeless and beat down. I wanted to give up.

I heard a faint voice from somewhere beyond the mist say, "*No think. Do.*" The voice was right. If I dwelled on negative stuff, bad things would happen. I had to get up and do something – anything – to end my negative thinking.

"Your lessons suck, Madame Wong!" I yelled into the nothing. Screaming that out made me feel a little better.

More laundry. Wash, rinse, and repeat.

It seemed like I washed clothes for days. Every now and then, without any warning, the old bat would appear out of the fog and beat the crap out of me with that cane. I tried my best to focus on what I was doing as I finished the laundry then moved to the woodpile.

I can't tell you how many swats with that cane I got over the endless time that I did Madame Wong's chores. And I can't tell you how long it took me to figure this out, but eventually I realized that I could focus on what I was doing but at the same time be alert to my surroundings.

I chopped wood (not as easy as it looks), swinging the axe high then down into the center of a piece of wood. I split it clean in two. I felt a slight breeze to my left. I had my feet planted, but I swung my upper body to the left and held my axe in both hands, ready to deflect the coming blow of her cane.

But as I turned to my left she wasn't there. Just empty space. Then SMACK! The cane blow came across my legs to my right. I swung myself around and there she was, standing still and holding her cane like she hadn't just beat me with it.

"Aw crap! I heard you that time! You switched sides on me."

"Progress, yes. Alert. Aware. But too focused on what you *thought* was going to be. Don't think, just do."

"But if I hear something on my left, then I should think you're going to be on my left, right? I mean that's logical."

"Don't think! Logic not relevant. *Feeling* is way. Be in the flow of things, Miss Emily. Let go. Just be." She vanished again.

I'd come so far yet felt so frustrated.

But one good thing came out of all that wood chopping. I had long ago abandoned my long sleeved shirt and stripped down to my black tank top. I'd never been muscular. But I noticed that my shoulders were cut. I had deltoids and shoulder muscles. My arms were strong, not skinny and lacking any semblance of muscle tone like before.

I don't think that building muscles was part of the old woman's plan, but it made me feel good about myself. I was beginning to look like a girl that was strong enough to take care of herself. Maybe I could even stop that Dughall guy.

Back to chopping. Sweat poured down my back and my tank was soaked. The pile of wood grew. Focused but alert. "Into the flow Emily," I told myself. Swinging the axe.

I felt a ripple of air move. "Don't listen, be," I told myself. The air around me moved. The hairs on the back of my neck were on end. I swung my upper body to my left, holding my axe out and this time, it connected.

THWACK! I blocked her blow. My axe and her cane were locked together, each of us maintaining our stance and our stare.

"Miss Emily ready for combat," she said. Madame Wong backed away and bowed her head slightly.

32 SLICING AND DICING

When she said, "Miss Emily ready for combat," I almost wet my pants. It's one thing to fend off a blow from a cane, it's another to do battle. As always, Madame Wong kept me unsettled. Just when I thought I'd mastered something and felt balanced, she threw something else at me, and I felt like I'd topple.

"Come." She walked away from the stream and through the meadow to a path I'd never seen before. Before long a building appeared out of the fog. It was made entirely of wood and looked like it had been there for hundreds of years. Instead of a thatched roof like her cottage, it had a pitched roof covered in weathered tiles. I followed her as she walked up the steps to a wide wooden porch the length of the whole building, and then into a door opening (there was no actual door).

Inside was one large room, open to the rafters above. Windows from the second story rafters let a little light filter into the otherwise dark, cavernous room. To my right and to my left were walls filled with racks of weapons. There were broadswords, spears, daggers, lances and other sharp, pointy things that I had no idea what they were called. It looked like a weapon cache for a small army.

"What is this place?"

"My training room," she said quietly.

"But where did it come from? It wasn't here before."

"Building from my childhood." She walked to the right and inspected a row of swords. Madame Wong picked up one and swung it around gently a few times, then replaced it and chose another. She did this with several until she picked up a sword with a handle that looked like it was made of ivory and a thin blade that had lost its sheen, weathered like so many other things in Madame Wong's world.

"You trained to be a warrior as a child?"

"No, of course not. Girls not allowed. Madame Wong snuck in and watched her brothers train." She continued swinging her sword around in wide arcs and practiced thrusting her blade forward.

"Choose your blade," she said. She gestured to the wall opposite her, also filled with weapons of all kinds and shapes.

"Oh, I don't think so. Hindergog told us of your fighting skills. I'm not fighting you."

"How learn if not try? Come Miss Emily. I teach you ways of the true warrior." She had a mischievous glint in her eye. "Yes, long time since Madame Wong teach a warrior. This will be a good day."

She's excited to kick my butt!

I didn't know what kind of weapon I needed or how to choose. I inspected them all and finally settled on a broadsword. Its handle was wrapped in black leather and it had a curved, shiny steel blade with intricate carvings of a dragon etched into it.

I picked it up, and despite the fact that I'd built up quite a bit of upper body strength wielding an axe at the woodpile, it was so heavy that I almost dropped it. I teetered a little as I tried to hold it out in front of me, gripping the handle with both hands.

"That one too heavy for Miss Emily?"

"I'll be alright," I said. "Just need to get used to it."

"Best to be used to it now." She sprung into the air, did a somersault and landed in front of me, brandishing her ancient looking blade. I reacted as quickly as I could and tried to use my sword to deflect her, but her blade caught a bit of flesh at my ankle.

"You should block my attempt to cut you," she said.

"Really?" I gripped my ankle. My hand was covered in blood. "Son of ... You cut me!"

"Real warrior fights through pain," she said.

"Yeah? Well I'm not a real warrior now, am I? I've got to do something about this wound, or I'm going to bleed to death."

"No need worry about blood. Ready for battle." Madame Wong held her sword horizontally in front of her face, her legs planted and ready to go again.

"Look, I'm not like you, okay. I'm a real person – flesh and blood. So yeah, I've got to bandage this cut up so I don't bleed out."

"What cut? Miss Emily not bleeding."

"What ... " I looked down, and my ankle was fine, not a scratch on me. It wasn't even covered in dried blood. It was like Madame Wong's blade had never touched me.

"What the heck? You cut me. I know you did."

"Cut? Maybe. Wound no more."

"But how?"

"This is Netherworld. Now ready yourself." She backed up a few paces, planted right foot in front and left behind, then raised her sword in her right hand above her, her left hand out straight in front.

I moved out from the wall and toward the center, all the while keeping my eyes on wily Madame Wong. When we were about twenty feet apart from each other, I planted my feet like Madame Wong's and put my arms in the same position. The blade I had chosen was super heavy. My arm wobbled as I tried to hold it above me as Madame Wong was doing.

"Remember what you have learned, Miss Emily. Focus. Aware."

I tried to do as she said and focused on her sword, tuning everything else out.

"I don't know anything about this, you know. I never took fencing in school, and I wasn't exactly on the medieval knight team. What am I supposed to do?"

"Stay alive." No sooner had the words escaped her lips and she took to the air again. She did a somersault then kicked me in the chest hard. I flew backward about ten feet and landed flat on my back. Madame Wong landed gently on the ground at my feet.

"That's not fair. You can fly."

"Miss Emily can fly too."

"In case you didn't notice, I don't have wings."

"Madame Wong has no wings."

"Yeah but you're not human."

"Form of entity of no matter. Intention what matters. You want to fly you fly. Focus on what you want Miss Emily, not on what you do not want. Focus on doing, not failing. Ready?"

I got up and took the stance. It was like a showdown in the old west. Both of us stared at each other but neither made a move. The silence grew to the point that I heard my blood rushing through my veins.

If I had been watching with my eyes, I would have seen nothing. If I had been listening with my ears, I would not have heard a sound. But in the focused awareness that Madame Wong had taught me, I felt her coming.

I thought of flying away to the other side of the room, and I pushed off with the toes of my front foot. I sprang into the air effortlessly. I spun myself head over heels several times then gently landed facing her. I think I saw Madame Wong's lips curl into a small smile, a twinkle in her eye.

But there were no words of adulation or praise, only her little body coming at me, swinging her sword in tight figure eights as she gently glided forward across the grey tile floor. It was like watching a mini combine coming for me, the only sound was the swoosh of her sword like a wind turbine.

I took to the air once more, and as I turned mid-air to land facing her, I saw that she, too, had taken to the air and was right behind me. I reacted quickly enough to fend off a blow from her sword, and we were locked in battle, mid-air.

We came down with a thud as our weapons continued to clang against each other. I was working hard just to keep her from chopping my arm off. Madame Wong looked like she was hardly putting forth any effort at all. She stood entirely motionless except for her right arm, swinging the sword tightly as she thrust it toward me over and over again.

On the defensive, my arms quickly tired. I was so busy blocking her blows that I had no chance of mounting an attack. Then it happened.

Pain ripped through my arm as I felt the warmth of blood flowing in a torrent down my arm. My legs shook. I dropped my broad sword to the ground. It was like I was moving in slow motion as my head slowly turned to look at my left arm.

There was a gash so deep that I could see the bone peeking through. It was a wound so severe that it was a matter of seconds until I felt the lightheadedness that comes just before the world goes black.

As I slumped to the ground, my last thought was that I'd make a terrible warrior with only one arm.

33 SWORD OF THE ORDER

When I woke I was in Madame Wong's cottage, resting on the bed. My arm had been dressed in a white linen dressing, wound tightly. I saw no blood on the bandage so I decided to unwrap it even though I was scared of what I'd see.

I slowly unwrapped the cloth. As the linen slipped off my arm, I saw no blood, puss, or oozing sore. There was only the faintest of scars where a three-inch gash had been.

"Miss Emily come, take tea and stew," Madame Wong croaked.

I sat at her small table and drank the cup of warm tea in one swallow. I devoured the bowl of stew like I was starving. She said not a word as she refilled my tea and scooped more stew into my bowl.

"Madame Wong, I don't understand. How can I heal so quickly and completely here?"

"It is a world of no time and pure intention. We can have things exactly as we want them."

"Then why did you bandage me?"

"Because your mind expects a bandage. You feel you must *do* something to heal rather than *think* something to heal. I gave you what you expected."

I let her words sink in as I devoured the rest of my stew and tea. Every time she gave me an 'answer,' more questions rose from it.

"Look, I see how that may work here, in a place of no time."

"And a place of no place."

"Yeah, whatever. But when I go back to my world – the world where I have to defeat Dughall – well it most certainly is a place and has time. So none of what I'm learning here will apply there, will it?"

"If it didn't why would I teach it to you?"

"Well that's what I'm saying. It's like I'm wasting my time here."

"No time so no waste. Besides, all Madame Wong teaches works in human world."

"So I can defy gravity and fly through the air and have whatever I want? I don't believe that."

"Then you're not ready to return. Miss Emily, laws of universe same everywhere. Big or small. Here or there. No matter. Only thing that matters – your intention."

"Then why can't humans fly or just think of something they want and poof, it's there?"

"Because humans do not believe they can do those things. Because your world is a place of time. Because of time, your creations do not happen instantly. And that causes you not to believe, bringing you back always to the first thing."

"So when I go back there, I can do all the things you're teaching me here if ... "

"If you have belief and patience."

I wasn't there. I couldn't believe I could sail through the air just by thinking it. Not in my own world. I didn't believe I could conjure up a chair or any other object just because I wanted it. I wasn't sure that I would ever believe those things were possible in my world, even if I stayed with Madame Wong a thousand years.

"You not believe. You not ready to go. But you are ready to fight, no?"

I simply sighed and instantly we were back in Madame Wong's training room.

"Madame Wong teach about weapons. Miss Emily chose broadsword because it was shiny and pretty."

"That's not why."

"Yes it is, and Miss Emily knows it. Not good reason. Warrior must play to her strength. Broadsword is weapon for a brute man, not a medium-sized girl.

"You need a weapon for finesse, cunning. Come." She walked to the weapons rack. "Pick them up, swing them, listen to them. Choose the one that sings to you."

Singing swords? I glared at her hard but didn't argue as I picked up swords and lances and daggers and other objects of aggression. Most of them were too heavy for me or felt awkward to hold. Toward the end of the line, I saw a sword with a wood handle and a thin blade, much like Madame Wong's. The handle looked well worn, its wood polished to a sheen by the sweat of the hands that had held it before me. The blade was only about an inch wide and could be no more than an eighth of an inch thick. The handle was about a foot long, maybe eighteen inches and the blade about two feet. The blade was not corroded but not shiny either and covered in what looked like Celtic knots.

When I picked it up, I felt a tingly feeling run up my hand and into my arm. The hair on the back of my neck stood on end like it had when I entered the Sacred Grove. I swung the sword wide, and I swear I heard a single musical note hang in the air. The handle felt like it had always been in my hand. It felt effortless to swing it in a wide arc.

"That blade sing to you Miss Emily?"

"Yes," I answered in a whispered voice. "Madame Wong, this sword. Who owned it?"

"That sword have no owner but was used by last High Priestess of the Order of Brighid."

"Saorla."

"Yes, and many priestesses before her. Like the torc on your arm, it was crafted by the Fair Sidhe for the Order of Brighid."

I practiced swinging, thrusting and flying with the beautiful sword in my hand. It felt like an extension of my arm, like it was a part of me.

"Miss Emily ready for next combat lesson?"

"Yes." I continued to practice my moves.

"For a true warrior, life is sacred. A warrior with honor never kills unless she must. But when she must kill, a warrior is prepared to take the life of another – or to die – if honor requires it. Are you prepared to take the life of another? Could you kill Dughall if necessary?"

I hadn't thought of that. Up to that point my mission had been a bit abstract. *Kill someone?* The thought hadn't crossed my mind.

It's not like I'm against a person killing another to save their own life or the life of someone they love, but I never thought I'd be the one doing the killing. Doubt crept through my blood like a cold, dark shadow.

"I don't know Madame Wong. Honestly, I'm not sure I can kill someone, even someone as bad as Dughall."

"Even if it were necessary to save the ones you love?"

A scream pierced the air, breaking the icy silence that defined the Netherworld. A high-pitched scream that was familiar but also seemed like it was from a long-forgotten dream.

Fanny.

34 THE THREE LITTLE NINJAS

I ran from the training room and out into the mist and fog. Another scream and a shout.

"Help! Emily, we're here."

Jake. I ran toward the voices as fast as my legs would take me. I felt like I was in a dream, running and running but going nowhere. After a while it occurred to me to stop running and instead think about being where they were.

Out of the mist and fog another building came into view. It was a small cottage, much like Madame Wong's only slightly larger. I stormed through the door, the Sword of the Order still in my hand.

Inside it was dark like night, the only light coming from the grey haze of the Netherworld through the small window openings covered with carved wooden screens. In a corner of the large open room I had stepped into were Jake and Fanny, their hands bound behind them. They were lashed together with a thick rope, and their feet too were bound tightly.

"Emily, look out!" screamed Jake.

It was a good thing he warned me. I had been thrown off my guard, and was not focused and aware like Madame Wong had taught me. With Jake's warning, I sprung to the air and did a back flip so that I could see my attacker.

Correction. Attackers. There were three small men, dressed in black from head to toe, all brandishing large, curved broadswords like the ones Madame Wong had said were for brutes. The three little ninjas. They turned to face me as I gently landed on the wooden floor. I planted my feet, right foot in front, left behind. I held my sword horizontally in front of me, my left hand up and vertical in front of my face. *Focus. Breathe.*

They all lunged for me at once, charging like bulls, their swords swinging wildly as they screamed their warrior cries. I felt the blade coming before I could see or hear it, like the movement of the swinging disrupted the molecules in the air around me. I thought only of my blade connecting with theirs, and my arm swung powerfully in a large arc. There was the loud crash of steel as the Sword of the Order swung true and hit the first blade.

The man wielding it looked down in shock as he saw that my sword had cut clean through his thick broadsword. But he was a trained fighter, not a novice. It took him a matter of seconds to recover and grab another sword that he had strapped to his back.

In the meantime, my arm swung like it was a machine, connecting time after time with the blows coming from the three men. I lifted myself gracefully into the air and came down behind them. As one of the ninjas came at me, I thrust forward and dashed to the side so quickly that I cut his arm clean off. He screamed in agony but then vanished from the scene entirely. His cries of pain lingered even after his body was gone.

There was no time to think about it. The other two didn't miss a beat as they both came at me at once. I swung left and right, parried and turned. I took to the air, but they followed right behind, our blades connecting the whole time. Sparks flew, ignited by the steel grinding on steel.

As we touched the ground, one ninja to the left of me, the other on the right, I swung my arm in a tight figure eight like I'd seen Madame Wong do. I fended off the attempts of each of the ninjas to do me in. I sensed the one on my left was ready to thrust hard. I pitched myself straight up like I was shot from a cannon.

I looked down, and the one ninja's thrust landed straight in the heart of the other as the second ninja's sword, which has already been in the motion of a wide arc intended for me, swung clear through the torso of the first ninja. Both vanished even as the sound of their anguished cries lingered.

Then there was silence. My chest still heaved from the exhaustion of the battle with the three ninjas. But there was no time to waste. I had to get Jake and Fanny out of their bindings.

"That was amazing," Fanny said. I looked at Jake who said nothing, but his clear blue eyes showed their appreciation and awe.

"I didn't know you could fight like that," he finally said.

"I didn't know either." I cut the ropes around his wrists with my sword. When his hands were free, Jake caught my hand with his. He looked in my eyes with a look I'd never seen before. His hand was warm and as he held my hand in his I felt a slight tingle run up my spine. Time was frozen for a moment as I let Jake keep his hand there, the first true warmth I'd felt in so, so long.

But the moment was cut short by the sound of a large, low voice.

"You're not finished here, Youngling," he said. Instantly Jake's hands were once again bound together.

I turned and there before me was a large man, standing at least six feet three. His upper body was bare, his barrel chest smooth and rippled with muscle. His biceps were two of the most powerful guns I'd ever seen, his stomach a washboard. His dark hair was tied behind him in a smooth tail, his chin covered in a well-groomed goatee. His black eyes glared at me as he stood with his legs spread wide, his sword in his hand.

I hadn't finished getting Jake and Fanny out of their bindings, but that would have to wait. It occurred to me at that moment that I was going to have to keep fighting until I finished what I came here for.

I had to keep fighting until I killed.

35 THE KILLING TIME

The supersized ninja stood firmly, a devilish smirk smeared across his face.

"They'll be tied up here forever you know. If you want to save them, you've got to go through me. And from the looks of you, still a whelp sucking at your momma's breast, you'll give up. I'll take immense pleasure in killing them just because I can."

I didn't wait to take my stance or focus myself. His words had their desired effect. I was enraged and shot through the air straight at him.

"My ... mother ... is ... dead ... you tart monkey." I hurled the words at him as our swords clashed. My arms were already tired from fighting the three amigos, but I had to keep going. I wasn't sure if Jake and Fanny were real or an ephemeral figment of Madame Wong's imagination. But either way, I couldn't stand by and allow the guy murder them. Somehow I got my arm to swing the sword, more defensive than offensive. It was all I could do to keep supersize from cutting me in half. I was so unbalanced by his strength that I didn't have a chance to land any blows against him.

I took to the air and bounced from wall to wall, trying to give my arm a rest while I avoided his attack. Everywhere I landed, he was there. It was like he anticipated my every move.

Then I ran across the walls. I know it sounds impossible, but I was like an insect defying gravity using the walls of that cottage like a floor. I wondered to myself what would happen if I ran really fast and I thought only of making myself move so fast I was a blur to him. After a few seconds, I took a chance and looked at supersize. He had dropped to the center of the room, standing on the floor, looking at me. Or trying to look at me and find out where I was exactly. Somehow I was moving so fast I was a blur to him, winking in and out of the room altogether.

I didn't have a plan and wasn't sure why I felt the need to run. But I had unhinged him a bit so I guess that was as valid a reason as any.

"Get down here and fight like a man," he grumped at me.

"Ah, but I'm not a man. I want to fight like a woman." I swooped down from the wall and struck him with my sword across his back. I quickly flew back up to my wall and continued to run in circles around the room.

Supersize only grimaced and shrugged off the large gash across his back. Blood dripped from the slash across his naked back.

"If this is what you call fighting like a woman, then women are cowards." He ran up the wall and planted himself firmly like a fly on the wall, hoping I guess to stop me in my tracks. When I saw him there, I simply reversed direction so that I again came at him from the back. My second blow was a sword thrust to his back.

"Smart, not cowardly," I said.

I had hoped that my strategy would do him in for good. Problem with my plan was that the Sword of the Order got stuck in his large, thick torso. I tried to thrust and pull but as I pulled, the sword stayed. I fell backwards and dropped to the ground with a thud.

Supersize stood for a minute, his feet defying gravity, stuck to the wall like a fly on flypaper. Then he gently swooped down to the ground and faced me, his face taut with rage. He reached his left hand behind him and pulled the Sword of the Order out of his back. His face showed only the slightest twinge of pain as he pulled the sword out. Blood gushed from the deep puncture wound, but I noticed that the other wound I'd inflicted only minutes ago was almost healed. *I guess I'm not the only one for whom the Netherworld provides protection from injury.*

"Beautiful weapon," he said. He held the Sword of the Order in his left hand and inspected it while he held his own large broadsword in his right. "I will enjoy killing you with it." He swung both weapons in small arcs in front of him.

Supersize had two weapons. I had none. When I'd run the walls like a human fly, I had a surge of hope. But my hopes were dashed. *How can I kill a man if I have no weapon?* No time to think about it. Supersize was coming at me with both swords blazing. Time to make like a cricket and leap.

I sprung through the air in time to miss being chopped like tuna at a sushi bar but not before he landed a gash across my thigh. I felt the warmth of blood trickle down my leg. I knew it would stop soon, but it still hurt like blue blazes. I didn't know what to do with no weapon so I took to running again until I could figure something out.

Supersize wasn't going to let me just run in circles anymore. He took to the air and leapt from wall to wall, occasionally finding purchase, and I'd get a new gash here or a slice there. I knew there were phenomenal healing powers in the Netherworld, but I intuitively knew that if I got injured badly enough, my death would come before I had the chance to heal.

Then I heard a familiar voice come from what seemed like a long way away. Jake yelled out, "Emily! Over there." It seemed like it came from a dream. I turned my head to where Jake and Fanny were tied up, and I saw Jake point to the corner opposite from where they were bound.

There, by the fireplace, was a poker. It wasn't the Sword of the Order, but it was something. *No time to be choosy.*

I ran over and down the wall, picked up the poker, and went back to running like a mad thing around that room. We were both moved so fast that we blinked in and out. I'd see supersize in front of me. I'd approach and thrust but he was gone. Occasionally I'd get a slash in on him, or he'd get a gash in on me, but mostly we ran and flew around like idiots.

I was so tired I thought I'd drop. *This had to end.*

I glided down to the floor, beckoning him to join me. Sweat poured in rivulets down my back and between what little chest I had. My hair was soaked, and wisps of it clung to my face and neck.

When supersize landed I could see that our hours of fighting had slowed him too. His bare torso was completely slick, covered in sweat, his well-muscled chest heaving. If it weren't for the fact that he was trying to kill me, he would have looked hot. But it was no time for a crush. I had to kill this guy so I could free Fan and Jake.

As supersize caught his breathe, I planted my feet like I'd learned from Madame Wong. I held the poker firmly in both hands out in front of me, ready for his offense. I took a long, deep breath in, closed my eyes, and focused. *Aware. Alert.* I felt the molecules in the air shift, heard the sound of his blades swirling and opened my eyes. Acting on instinct alone, I let my arms do what they knew how to do. I trusted my body to protect itself and went with the flow, my arms moving independent of my conscious thought, fending off blow after blow.

Finally, the moment had come. I felt it before I saw it. His guard was down for the smallest fraction of a second, and I swung the poker in an upper cut that caught his chin, took him off balance and down he went. As his hulking frame fell backwards, the Sword of the Order flew out of his weaker left hand and slid across the floor.

I willed my body to do several front flips to where the sword had landed. I scooped it up before supersize could reach it. I leapt to the air and came down behind him, planted again and ready. With the Sword back in my hand, I felt a renewed energy course through my body. As I brought the sword out in front of me, clasped in both hands, I could hear it sing.

Supersize took to the air and so did I. No running away from him this time. I leapt for him before he could gain speed and blink out of sight. My sword caught his hand and his broadsword went flying. I didn't waste a single moment as I began hacking at him with my sword as he tried to run away. But I was on his tail and moving at the same rate that he was.

I did a flying somersault over him and landed in his path. Before he could even see me, I swung my sword low, taking his right leg off below the knee and sending him down to the floor, a river of blood flying in the air around him.

I knew that wouldn't do it. In this place of mystery and magickal healing, I knew that if I left him there, he'd just grow a new limb in a few minutes. Time to do what I'd been sent there to do.

I landed beside him and pulled my sword up high, ready to thrust it deep into his heart. His coal black eyes were not filled with hatred or sadness. They did not plead with me to spare him. He looked into my eyes with the eyes of a true warrior, knowing that he was bested and ready to accept his fate.

It was a small gift that I knew Dughall wouldn't give me if it were he that lay there on the floor. But I was glad of it as I thrust hard, swift and true. The Sword of the Order sang out as it struck Super-size in the heart. He didn't say a word or make a sound, but soon he began to vanish. His eyes held mine to the last second.

As he vanished, the Sword of the Order vanished too, swept right out of my hand and back to the aether from where it came. My body ached as it had never ached before. At that moment, I wanted nothing more than to be in my own bed in my own house and sleep the sleep of the dead. But a recess of my brain remembered that Jake and Fan were tied up, held against their will.

I turned and ran to them, surprised my trembling and wobbly legs could still move. Super-size had bound them even tighter, and I didn't have the Sword of the Order to rip through the ropes. I began trying to untie them with my hands, the rough rope giving me burns.

Jake caught my eye. "You were amazing," he said.

"Yeah, thanks Em," said Fanny as I worked on the knots. Once I had Jake's hands free, he worked on the knots at his ankles while I worked Fan's hands loose.

When they were finally free they stood and stretched, happy to be free of bindings that had held them for an unknown amount of time. I couldn't believe they were there. I didn't want them to leave. For a moment, I forgot about my T.V. receptor and how it came on when I touched people. I just wanted to hug them both to me and hold onto them so they'd stay.

With my arms stretched around them both the visions started at once. I saw a large explosion and Jake's lifeless eyes looking up at me, his head covered in blood. I turned and saw Fanny's leg sticking out of a pile of rubble.

I took my arms out of the embrace and backed away so the horrible scene would get out of my head. As I stepped back, the vision vanished. Then Fanny and Jake vanished too.

Tears instantly sprang to my eyes. Fanny. Jake. Gone.

The walls around me dematerialized as well, and I found myself once again in Madame Wong's meadow. The sound of the stream was so peaceful and comforting after what I'd just been through.

Madame Wong sat in silent meditation, her eyes closed. She looked dead.

Exhausted beyond reason, I flopped down hard and sat cross-legged, too tired to put my legs in a lotus position. I sat and breathed hard. It took several minutes before my breath became slow and smooth.

"Miss Emily succeeded?"

"You know I did. I wouldn't be here if I hadn't killed him," I said. She didn't open her eyes or say a word, but her mouth put on a small smile.

"Madame Wong, will it be time for me to leave soon – you know – to leave the Netherworld?"

"Your lessons with Madame Wong almost complete but not finished yet. When done here you must go to next Master."

"I'll have another teacher here? Who will it be?"

"Not Madame Wong's place to tell you that. You must find teacher on your own."

"But Madame Wong, that means that soon – soon I'll leave you?"

"Yes, Miss Emily."

The thought of leaving Madame Wong mixed with the emotion of seeing Jake and Fanny die in my vision then vanish before my eyes brought a flood of tears.

"There there Miss Emily," she said as she gently hugged me. "You crying to leave Madame Wong? You miss my lessons, yes?"

"I'll miss you," I said. "You have taught me so much ... "

"You taught yourself," she said.

"But Madame Wong, you don't keep the past. For you, memories are like ghosts. I'll be no more than another ghost that you lock away, won't I?"

"Memories not ghosts, Miss Emily. Just little birds. You will fly in from time to time. Madame Wong say hi then let you go. One of my little birds." She patted my hand and winked at me.

"Rest now, Miss Emily," she said. "After sleep, last lesson."

I bowed to my teacher and crept into her cottage for what would be the last time that I slept there.

36 THE DARKEST WOODS

I woke after sleeping the longest, soundest sleep I'd ever had. I went outside and found Madame Wong in the same place she'd been each day before, still as a statue in a perfect handstand. *How long can she hold that pose?*

I sat on the ground across from her as I had become accustomed to and waited for her to speak. I was just about asleep when I heard her ancient voice croak, "Relaxed, Miss Emily?"

"Well, yeah, I am actually."

"Good, good. For your lesson today, must be extremely relaxed."

"I'm ready for this lesson."

"Yes, Madame Wong agree. This lesson, hardest for some to learn. I ask you question today."

"Okay, I can answer a question."

"Who are you?"

"Who am I?"

"Is there echo in my mist? You have question, now answer."

"Who am I? Well, I am Emily, of course."

"No. That is a name. Does not answer question. Again, who are you?"

"Well, I'm a girl. And my name is Emily. I am a human ... "

"No, no, no. Names only. Does not answer. Who are you?"

"Well, I don't know then. I think I've answered your question."

"You think you ready, but you don't know who you are? Maybe Madame Wong put it to you another way. What are you?"

"Well isn't that different? Who I am. What I am. Two different things."

"No different. Same question. Answer now."

"Well I don't know. I'm molecules and cells. Water and carbon."

"You describe that thing you call body that you drag around with you. What are you?"

"I guess I don't what I am. If I'm not this body, then what am I?"

"Don't ask me! I thought you knew who and what you are."

"Come on, stop with the riddles. I don't know what you're asking me."

"Only you can answer who you are."

"Apparently I don't know who I am. How can I find out?"

"Ah, that is good question. That I have answer for. Come." She gracefully exited out of her handstand and began to walk.

I followed Madame Wong as she walked through her little yard and into a deep, dark wood. *I don't remember this being here before.* We walked silently for a long time, ever deeper into woods so thick you could barely see your way. We came to a small clearing, scarcely large enough for both Madame Wong and myself. There she stopped and gestured me to sit on the ground.

"Most important question, one you must find answer to, what you are. You will journey on your own now, to find answer. This wood will help you. Listen well to the trees. They will guide you. When you have answer to question, you will find me."

"But how do I find you? I'm lost here. I wasn't paying attention to how we got here, and I didn't mark my way."

Madame Wong rose from the ground and walked away. I was up in a flash.

"You can't just leave me here! I don't know what I'm doing. I could be here for days."

"Maybe months, even years," she added.

"What? This is going too far. Look, I've played along. But this isn't right. Jake and Fanny – even my dad – they need me. I don't have time to sit in the woods."

"Miss Emily. Such a Youngling. Your journey here will be long one I fear. You have seen you can create all that you need here yet you do not accept it. Yes, long journey."

"Well if I can create whatever I want, then I'll create a road out of this mess."

"Once you have answered the question, a path as clear as the morning sun will appear before you and lead you to next phase of your journey."

"I was afraid you were going to say that. Loophole."

"Madame Wong leave now, Miss Emily. Madame Wong return when Miss Emily have answer."

And with that, she was gone. No puffs of smoke or wave of a wand or anything. Just there one minute, the next vanished.

I stood alone in the darkest woods I could imagine. I didn't have any food or water, no flashlight or other provisions. Just me in the dark. With Madame Wong gone it seemed even colder and darker in the small clearing. All I could think about was getting out of there.

I wasn't interested in answering her question, but I figured by the time I found my way out of the woods, I'd have something worked out to say to her. Walking again, destination unknown.

37 AKASHA

I walked for what seemed like days. I never saw light shining from outside the thick wood. After a long while, I saw a clearing and I ran. I was so excited that I might finally be out of the woods.

When I got to the clearing I cried. I wasn't out of the woods after all. I was right back at the same clearing where Madame Wong had left me. I'd walked in circles.

I sat down with my head in my hands. "Get a grip Emily," I said to myself. I had to find a way out of that place.

I was determined not to go in circles. I got up and walked in a direction that was at a ninety-degree angle from the direction I had traveled last time. There was no way to end up back in the same place going in that direction. And as added insurance, I thought about a large bagful of peanuts in the shell. A bag materialized in my hand. *Something to eat and something to mark my way.*

Off I went again. I ate the peanuts and dropped the shells as I went. I walked like that for many hours. The supply of peanuts was endless. My stomach hurt from the pain of eating too much. *I have to be out of these woods soon.* I looked down and could not believe my eyes. I was walking on a path littered with peanut shells. And in just a few minutes I was back to that same clearing.

I had felt sad before, even depressed, but until then I'd never felt complete despair. I felt like I was at the end of my rope and it would never get any better. I was beyond tears. *What's the point of even crying?* I was in a living hell. I'd wandered in circles in a dark, cold wood, all alone. Utterly, completely, helplessly alone. And my friends were out there, somewhere, in our world wondering what had happened to me. *By now Dughall has probably succeeded in whatever evil plan he has.*

What can I do? What's the point of any of it? It was clear that I wasn't getting out of there by walking out. I'd just end up in circles again. I sat down on the ground and curled up in a ball and tried to sleep. I was lying there thinking about how pleasant it would be to at least have a comfy beanbag chair to lie on when one appeared. It was all fuzzy and so comfy.

Now that's more like it. Funny how a stupid beanbag chair could make life seem a little less hopeless. "How about a warm blanket," I said aloud. Bam, there it was. I'd conjured a fuzzy, peachy soft blanket. *Now for a nap.*

I lay there, curled up on the beanbag, snuggled in my blanket. I wanted so badly to sleep. But sleep didn't come. Instead, I just lie there fully awake.

"What am I supposed to do here?" I screamed into the woods.

No answer.

I'd rather spend my days facing Madame Wong's blade than sit alone in these dark woods by myself.

I was one hundred percent alone. No T.V. No cell phone. No computer. No people. Just completely, totally, utterly alone.

There were many times, living with Muriel the Mean and Zombie Man, that I thought it would be much better to live alone. But my experience of alone? Well, it's not what it's cracked up to be.

"Apparently I'm supposed to sit in this stupid clearing until I figure out – what was it that I was supposed to figure out? Oh yeah, who I am," I said aloud to no one but myself. *Talking to yourself – not a good sign.*

I sat on the beanbag chair, not quite asleep, but not quite awake either. I heard the sound of wind in the trees surrounding me. I thought I heard a voice. It sounded like it came from the trees. The breathy voice sounded like it was saying 'breathe'. "Listen to the trees," Madame Wong had said. So I closed my eyes and did what I thought I'd heard the trees say. I breathed. *Open the receiver.*

I concentrated on the rise and fall of air going in and out of my lungs. I found my mind got more and more quiet. If a thought came in, I just let it go like Madame Wong had taught me. *Little birds.* I concentrated instead on the steady flow of air going in and out, in and out, in and out ...

After immeasurable breaths, I felt weightless. No sound. The breathy whisper of the trees was gone. I didn't even hear the air going in and out of my nose. Complete emptiness. I knew instinctively that a part of me was no longer in the darkest wood.

Where am I? I knew that wasn't the right word. 'I' didn't seem to describe me anymore. *Am I floating?* Not so much floating as just being without any effects of gravity.

If I'd had eyes, I would have seen the most beautiful sight. It was like trillions and trillions of stars, tiny and large and miniscule and epic, all twinkling and pulsating and connected one to the other by what seemed like an almost invisible filament.

This cosmic string pulsated too. And it created a sound, like a low, melodic hum. As I tell this, I realize it's hard to explain in words what I felt. It wasn't just that each star was connected only to the next closest by this pulsating string. Instead, it was like all the lights were connected to each other all at once in every direction by this nearly invisible throbbing web.

I've seen graphics of the nerves in your brain and how there are those spiderlike dendrites that finger out to each other. It was like that, but all lit up and pulsating with life.

Do I still have a body? What am I?

I can say I looked, but it wasn't like I had eyes in that place. It was more of a knowing – a sight without eyes. As I 'looked' at myself, the being that I am, I saw that I too was one of those small, pulsating stars. And all around me, in every direction that I could fathom, was the fine mist of throbbing netting, touching me and surrounding me all at once.

If I'd had a mouth, it would have been beaming in the biggest smile it could make. If I'd had eyes, they would have cried from the rapture of unbridled joy. There is no feeling that I have felt in my human body that can compare to the pure bliss that I felt in that moment of being connected to all these twinkling stars by that lovely pulsating web.

I concentrated on the low, melodic hum. I found that I could pick out individual notes, like the strings of a cosmic instrument had been plucked. Here, one is lower. Over there, it is higher. Some were so clear and beautiful. There were a few though that sounded a little off key. But mainly it was the most beautiful music I'd ever heard.

And yet to call it music isn't quite right because in that place – if you can call it a place – I didn't have ears to hear with. I just knew that there were different notes all playing together.

What about my note? Can I tune into my own frequency?

I again put all of my concentration on these questions. Within seconds, I began to hear a separate distinct hum. It was stronger than the others to me. It was clear and not particularly high but not low either. It was my own vibrating string, unique and individual amongst all the others, yet resonating with them as well.

It was so beautiful. I didn't want to leave. In that place and time, I could see everything so clearly. I knew my own unique note. And I could see how I fit into it all.

In that instant, I knew. I knew who I am. I knew what I am. I am not a human. I am not a girl. I am not Emily or a daughter or a niece or a friend. In that instant of pure joy, I knew the true nature of myself.

"I know who I am," I said (or was it a thought, I can't be sure).

In an instant, there was a powerful whooshing feeling like I was being sucked up by a large cosmic vacuum and then spit out on that beanbag chair.

I felt like the wind had been knocked out of me and took a large gulp of air. I blinked open my eyes, and there I was, back in the clearing of the deep, dark wood. Only this time, there was a golden path. It was my yellow brick road. It lay before me, lit by bright sunlight.

Just a few minutes earlier – or was it days? – I'd wanted nothing more than to forever exit that gloomy forest. After being one with Akasha, I wanted nothing more than to go back to that place of pulsating webs and stars and beautiful, resonant humming. It was my true home and I wanted to return.

But I could see Madame Wong at the end of the path, her mere presence beckoning me. It all came flooding back, Fanny and Jake and Dughall and somewhere, my dad. All of them needed me. The pulsating web would have to wait.

I rose and walked calmly and serenely down the golden path to the waiting Madame Wong. *How did she know that I was ready to come out? How did she know that I realize the truth?*

"You ask that question? Why, when you already know answer. Annoying habit of yours asking questions to which you know the answer. Are you ready to answer your teacher's question now? Who are you?"

"Annoying habit of yours," I said, "asking questions to which you know the answer."

Madame Wong smiled a bemused smile, one of the few smiles I'd seen on her face. I knew though not to push it. It was important for me to answer this question aloud for my own ears to hear.

"I am Akasha," I said.

Madame Wong bowed her head gently. I followed her out of the darkest woods.

PART THREE

The Rise of Dughall

"The best way out is always through."

-Robert Frost

38 UMBRA NIHILI

"... To arise and live once more, flesh reunited with spirit, to walk again as a man, back from the *Umbra Nihili*, arise when all has been aligned to achieve your deepest desire."

These were the last words Dughall heard spoken before his thousand-year sleep. Cian uttered them as he completed his dark and forbidden magick at the end of Dughall's life.

Dughall and his army had wandered across Ireland and the whole of Europe searching for the chalice. Over time, the legend grew. Many came to believe that the chalice was the Holy Grail, the cup used by Christ at the last supper. But Dughall knew better. He knew the real power of the chalice. He didn't care if they had it wrong. The fools. All the better for him.

Little by little his army dwindled as his men tired of chasing a dream. They returned to their homes and families. Dughall had no family, only the quest.

For many years he wandered, searched and fought battles. Eventually he grew old and knew his time to part this earth was near. But such was his desire for power and to achieve his lifelong goal that he was not content to go quietly into history.

Dughall knew that Cian still had dark magick up his sleeve. As his last breaths drew near, he summoned the old wizard to his bedside to inquire of a particular ritual that he knew could help him achieve his deepest desire. Macha, ever faithful, brought Cian to his side.

"Cian, old friend," Dughall croaked. "I call upon you once again, as I did in the Grove those many years ago, to help me now with your dark arts."

Cian winced at the word friend. He couldn't explain why he had allowed himself to remain with Dughall all these years, but it surely wasn't friendship.

"I have no charms or elixirs that will prevent your death, Dughall. You are a mortal, like all of us, and it appears that you will soon draw your last breath."

The façade of charm was gone from Dughall's voice as he tried to raise himself up to confront Cian. "I know that, you old fool," he growled.

Macha flew to Dughall's side and urged him to lie himself down once again. "What Dughall means to say," interjected Macha, "is that he hopes that you have dark arts to help him direct his soul to that place that he longs to be."

"To Heaven?" Cian was incredulous. "Oh, malevolent one, there is no magick in this world or the next powerful enough to send your immortal soul to anyplace heavenly," laughed Cian.

"I'm not interested in Heaven or Hell," snarled Dughall. "Don't toy with me Cian. You know that I'm talking about the *Umbra Nihili*."

Cian grew quiet. The mere mention of the name brought chills to his spine.

"You do not want to go there," Cian replied.

"I do. I know that you know how to make it happen, Cian, so don't try to hold back on me. Your skill and knowledge of the dark arts is unmatched old wizard."

"Dughall, as much as I dislike you, and I truly do detest you to my core, I would not send my worst enemy to the *Umbra Nihili*. You do not fully understand what you ask."

"I understand that it is the only way," Dughall choked out. With desperation in his eyes and his voice, he pled with Cian.

"I am not done here," he said. "You know that I am not finished. It is all that I have dreamed of. All that I have hoped for. And I can feel that it is close. Closer now than ever before. I will achieve my dream, Cian, even if I have to sever my soul and wait a hundred years in the *Umbra Nihili*, it is a small price to pay."

Cian had never seen such desperation in Dughall's eyes. There was something more there, more than just a quest for power. The man was on a mission for something even deeper.

"You do not know what you ask," said Cian gently. "If you do this, you have no control you see. Your fate will be up to the gods, not your or I. And I do not know when, or even if, you will be able to come back. According to oral accounts, your soul will be reunited, and you will be thrust back into creation when all has been aligned for you to achieve your deepest desire. But that may never happen, you see. If you do this, you may have a fractured soul for all eternity, stuck in a place of nothing."

"I do not believe that will happen, Cian. I know that my quest will be achieved. I just know it. I need your help though, old man. You must perform the ritual so I can go to the *Umbra Nihili*."

Cian continued to plead with Dughall. "But you do not realize what you ask. It is not as if your soul will travel to heaven or even hell where you will be with other souls. You will be in the 'Shadow of Nothingness', in a place of no place. And you will be there entirely alone."

"That suits me well since I detest every living creature anyway," snorted Dughall.

"That may be true, but there is more that you need to know. You will not only be alone, but you will not have a body or ability to create. You will be a disembodied mind, alone with only your thoughts to torture you, perhaps, for an eternity."

"You may be tortured by your own thoughts, Cian, but I am not tortured by mine. My only agony is the endless prattling of others. My mind is set. I know what I am doing. Now will you help me willingly?

Or will I have to use my last breath to coax this favor from you?"
Dughall grabbed for the dagger he had stashed under his pillow.

"You are in no condition to test your strength against mine
anymore. Put that thing away before you hurt yourself. I will do this for
you, against my better judgment. It is probably what you deserve
anyway."

With that Cian turned to leave. "Where are you going?" Dughall
shouted out.

"To make preparations. You have used a fair bit of your remaining
strength to threaten me so I imagine your time draws near. Rest and I
will return to perform the ritual tonight."

Dughall flopped himself back down on his pallet to rest. His heart
beat rapidly with excitement. *Soon I will make the final journey to all that I
desire.*

39 MACHA'S PROMISE

Cian returned to Dughall's cottage that night with a basket full of linen strips, vials of potions, and herbs and other plants. It was just a few hours after dusk and Cian found Dughall sleeping fitfully. He was still alive, but his breath was shallow.

Macha was by Dughall's side. Her wings, always reflective of her mood, were a muted blue and grey. As Cian walked in Macha brightened a little.

"Do you have all that you need to do my master's bidding?" she asked.

"Yes, it's all here. Why you stand by his side all these years is beyond me," Cian replied.

"I would ask the same of you, antediluvian one," Macha retorted.

Cian ignored her taunt and moved quickly about his work. He took a stick of sage that had been wound tightly, lit it in the fire, and then walked slowly around the room in a sunwise direction three times. Cian swirled the smoke above his head as he walked and muttered incantations.

Once he had purified the air of the cottage, Cian pulled fine linen cloth out of his bag and dipped it into a bowl that had been filled with water that he had blessed and prepared with purifying herbs. He took the cloth and wiped Dughall's face and body with it, doing his best to purify Dughall's body before it drew its last breath.

He could see that Dughall undoubtedly was near his end, as he did not protest being touched and bathed by Cian. In his fragile state, Cian thought Dughall looked much like any other man about to die. There was no trace upon his face of the sadness and fear he had inflicted on others. There was no evidence of the battles he had waged and the lives he had taken. There was only an aged man, skin greying and sallow, overtaken by the illness that raged in his body.

Cian knew that he had to wake Dughall so that he could get him to drink the tonic he had prepared. He was hesitant to do so. *Perhaps I should just let him die.* It would be best for the fellow anyway – to pass to whatever realm best befit a man who had lived the life Dughall had chosen. *That fate would be better for him than the* Umbra Nihili, *would it not?*

But Macha was right. Cian had a strange allegiance to this wretched man lying before him. He did not know the reason a brilliant former Druid and dark wizard spent so many of his precious years in the company of Dughall and his deceitful, ever-present companion Macha. Perhaps the allegiance was forged out of a shared quest to achieve the domination and power each sought.

Cian had no time for philosophy. He had to make a choice, and he knew he would honor the request of his longtime companion.

"Macha," he said, "the time has come. Wake your master and have him drink this tonic. Make certain that he drinks it to the last drop."

Macha did as he requested and the small vial of bitter tonic seemed large in her small faerie hands. She woke Dughall and ordered him to drink the tonic. In his weakened state, he did not protest.

As soon as he had swallowed the last bit his head fell back against the pillow. "Trying to poison me again, hey Cian?" he asked.

"The tonic will prepare your body to more easily allow a portion of your soul to depart to the *Umbra Nihili*," replied Cian. "Rest now."

Dughall kept his eyes open. He was tired but felt warmth coursing through his veins. His body felt as though every fiber tingled. There was certain aliveness in him that he had not felt in years.

"Cian, this tonic is healing me. Now I am not ready to die, old man. Perhaps this ritual may wait another day." Dughall's voice carried with a strength it had not had for a long time.

"Yes, the tonic is working then. You feel alive and tingly now, but it is just the tonic preparing your body for its long rest. You are not healed."

Cian pulled another bundle of dried herbs from his pack and lit the bundle. As the smoke rose from the herbs, Cian walked in a widdershins circle and muttered another incantation. The herbs smelled bitter and made Macha wrinkle her nose in distaste.

"Must you fill the air with that foul stench?" asked Macha.

"The odor matches the work that I do," he said.

After Cian's bundle had burned to ashes, he worked quickly and mixed another potion for Dughall to drink before his last breath. "You will drink this right before you take your last breath." He handed the cup to Dughall. The liquid was thick and viscous. Dughall wrinkled up his nose as he smelled the vile concoction.

"Now this is most important," Cian instructed. "As you feel yourself fade, recite these words over and over again. As you drink that draught of potion, repeat these words in your head. Repeat them as you take your last breath. Repeat them with every fiber of your being. You must believe these words and repeat them as a part of you moves to the beyond."

"What are the words, Cian?" Dughall asked.

> "I sever my soul,
> I sever my self.
> Go to the *Umbra Nihili*,
> Oh part of me that is lost,
> So that I may gain
> All that the whole of me desires."

"That is it?" Dughall asked.

"Yes, that is it. But you must say it with conviction. And it helps if you picture in your mind your deepest desire. Picture in your mind that end that you seek as you say the words."

"Cian, what will happen to my body?"

"After you have stopped breathing, Macha and I will anoint your body, wrap it in medicated linens, and enshrine it in a stone box. We will travel north with your body, as far north as we can to the place where the gods cover the earth in white all of the year. There we will bury it deep in the earth."

"When all is prepared for me to achieve my deepest desire, how will I be able to come back to a long-dead body buried deep in the frozen ground?" asked Dughall.

"You will not be fully dead, you see, but frozen. Your body will be well preserved. In the moment that all conditions are met, the severed part of yourself will find its way back to its body and be reunited with the rest of you. You will be whole again and ready to wake."

"But how will he get out of the ground?" asked Macha.

"Yes, how will I escape my stony tomb?"

"Well, yes, that is a challenge, is it not," said Cian. "I will be long dead by then and unable to help you."

A silence surrounded them, broken by Macha's tinny pixie voice.

"I can help him."

"How? Even though faeries are nearly eternal beings, you will not be able to know when your master has arisen."

"I will if I am buried with him," she replied.

The thought was too gruesome even for Cian. Buried alive with Dughall's cold, lifeless body. He could think of nothing more horrible.

"You know how it is, Cian," Macha said. "In the cold, my body too will go to sleep. I can put a spell on myself to awake at the first stirrings of his body. I will be weak, but with my magick, I will be able to lift the stony lid and burrow us out."

"Macha, my dear little Macha," Dughall interrupted. "I knew that I could count on you. You will be rewarded well for your loyalty. When I achieve all that I desire, yes, you will be rewarded well." Dughall reached out his hand and lightly touched Macha's cheek. Her wings blushed pink and crimson at his touch.

"If you choose to spend an eternity frozen with this vile man, that is your choice," said Cian. "All is prepared."

They waited by Dughall's side for a few more hours. When the moon was high in the sky, Cian saw that Dughall's breaths grew shallow again. Cian lifted Dughall's wrist and could hardly feel a pulse.

"It is time," he said.

Dughall began repeating the incantation, murmuring it aloud over and over again. "I sever my soul. I sever my self. Go to the *Umbra Nihili*, oh part of me that is lost, so that I may gain all that the whole of me desires." He said it over and over again while picturing in his mind the vision of his deepest desire. He pictured himself entering the portal. He pictured himself victorious and powerful. He pictured himself with many subjects bowing before him.

"I sever my soul. I sever my self. Go to the *Umbra Nihili*, oh part of me that is lost, so that I may gain all that the whole of me desires." He knew it was time. He took a deep breath and swallowed the draught that Cian had made. As he felt the last of his breath go from his body, he repeated the incantation in his own mind. He pictured attaining all that he desired and fulfilling a promise made to himself, and to the dead body of his most beloved, all those years ago.

40 DUGHALL WAKES

Dughall awoke to an impenetrable darkness. He knew he was alive by the sound of his lungs coughing and wheezing as they sucked in the first air they had breathed in over a thousand years. As he lay in the dark rasping in breath, the reality of his new situation dawned on him.

It worked. He was in his own body, alive again after so many years. *But how to get out of this icy tomb?*

Dughall lay quietly for a few moments and tried to use as little air as possible. He heard a sound. It was muffled and sounded faint at first but grew louder. *Someone is pounding on my granite coffin.*

After several minutes, Dughall heard the lid of his stony coffin opening. Fresh, cold air wafted over him. As his eyes adjusted to his surroundings, he could make out the faint shadow of a tiny being. *Macha.*

Macha and Cian had built an underground tomb in the frozen wasteland. She had been true to her word and had put herself into a deep pixie sleep in the gruesome tomb. Besides the coffin, they buried items that Dughall would need when he arose. Warm furs to protect him when he exited the tomb; a torch and flint to light his way; cured meats and water sealed in airtight jars, and Macha herself whose magick was always of assistance to him.

"You are with the living once again," Macha croaked as Dughall stretched his arms. For her part, Macha looked exactly like she had a thousand years before except that her skin and hair were a dull, lifeless grey. Even her wings, once a beautiful iridescent rainbow of color, had become grey and without any hint of their former luster.

"Yes, Macha, I live," replied Dughall in a raspy voice.

"You will need to drink and eat to regain your strength. Your body is much withered from lack of sustenance."

Dughall looked down at his hands and arms and could see that Macha was right. He still had flesh, but it was wrinkled like a raisin and clung to his bones. His skin was brown and weathered like a mummy, yet he was not a mummy. He was very much alive. But he looked like no more than a skeleton with flesh covering it.

Fear gripped Dughall, a feeling that was most foreign to him. This was not what he had expected. He could not go out amongst the humans in that condition. He looked like a monster and would be tracked down and killed. How could he achieve his deepest desire looking like a mummy?

As if reading Dughall's mind, Macha said, "Do not worry. Your flesh will plump out again in time. With food and drink and the special cream that Cian left for you, you will look normal in a few weeks' time."

"A few weeks? We do not have that kind of time. I need to get out of here now!"

"You must stay in the chamber. You cannot complete your task in your present condition. Look at you," she said. In Dughall's mind he quietly conceded that irksome Macha was right. He could not even rise to leave his grisly stone casket.

"Eat the stored food and drink," Macha offered. "I will go in search of more food for you."

With that, she flew to the ceiling of their chamber and removed a large stone that had been left unsealed for their escape. Then Macha grabbed a small spade and dug furiously as she flapped and flapped her wings. It wasn't long until Macha had a small hole, large enough for her to squeeze through and poke out the top.

Macha flew down to Dughall and handed him a jar of cured meat and a sealed jar of water. "Eat this and stay here, Dughall," Macha said before she flew away.

Dughall had no intention of staying put, but he hadn't the strength to raise his body out of the coffin. *Cursed Cian.* The old wizard had completed the spell but had neglected to care properly for Dughall's body. Dughall had not bargained for being a cripple upon his return. He tried to scream out a curse in his rage, but it came out as a mere raspy strangled yell.

In utter frustration and with nothing else to do, Dughall opened the jar and grabbed a handful of salty cured ox. It tasted like leather that had been covered in salt. *Awful.* Dughall chewed and chewed, swallowing it down with the stale water from the other jar.

When Dughall's jaw tired from chewing on the leathery meat, he lay back and envisioned his next steps. While in the *Umbra Nihili*, Dughall was still connected to the aether and the web of all existence. Even though he could interact with it in no way, he was able to know all that took place in all of creation.

Dughall knew well why his soul chose to come back together at this time and place. Modern humans were building a most magnificent machine. "They think they are so clever," thought Dughall. "They haven't even dreamed of what that machine of theirs can do. So lacking in imagination, these modern humans."

Dughall lay in his cold, hard home of the past thousand years, smiling a gruesome smile to himself. *Soon, all that I have worked for will be mine. Soon, my most beloved, we will be reunited.*

41 THE FACE IN THE BUCKET

It was a whole night and day before Macha returned. In that time, Dughall had forced himself to eat all of the briny meat and putrid water. Macha had been correct. His skin was plumping up. He looked slightly less gruesome than he did but still not acceptable to walk among humans again.

"Macha, my favorite gnat. What have you brought me to feast on?"

Macha flew down through the small opening to Dughall, all the while levitating several dead rabbits tied together by their legs. Dughall thought he saw one of them still twitching.

"The Devil take you pixie woman, I am not eating half-dead hare."

"Raw meat has more energy in it," Macha replied. "It will help you regain your strength faster. Blood is good for one like you."

"I have already tested my ancient gut as much as I care to by swallowing that retched ox. You will cook those for me."

"If you wish, but it will prolong your stay in this crypt, my intolerant one," Macha quipped.

With that, she began her work. She used her small but extremely sharp knife to skin the hares and gut them, removing the entrails. With the wave of her hand, she produced a large copper pot and set it over a fire that she conjured with the clap of her hands. She made a horrific stew of the rabbits in the pot with melted snow from outside. The stewing rabbits produced an odor most foul. Dughall was certain that his ancient intestines would surely seize up and cause his demise in one bite of Macha's putrid stew.

Macha practically forced the fetid stew down Dughall's throat. For two more days, Dughall endured her force-feeding him the blood, guts and meat from the poor hapless hares that happened to have been in Macha's path.

Dughall also endured Macha rubbing the rank cream that Cian had created for him all over his body. Her small hands were more like cold claws than human hands. It felt like nails scratching him all over on his delicate mummy skin.

But for all the torture that Dughall endured, the results were nothing short of miraculous. His hands looked more and more normal. The skin, less yellow and more white and luminous. He no longer looked like a skeleton but instead like an extremely thin older man. Dughall was finally ready to see what his face looked like.

"Macha, fetch me a bucket of water so that I may look upon myself."

As Macha placed the bucket in front of him, Dughall braced himself for what he might see. He sucked in his breath and looked down into the smooth water of the bucket.

The man he saw staring back shared little resemblance with the face of the man that he once knew himself to be. The man in the bucket had long, shaggy hair, not well-groomed short hair in the Norman style. The reflection had sallow cheeks and all the bones in the skull were clearly visible under the thin, papery skin. It was not the firm but fleshy masculine face that he once knew. To Dughall, he looked like the lowliest old beggar.

But at least he looked human. He would need to set aside his vanity. *Bide your time, Dughall,* he thought to himself.

"I am ready." He said it to himself as much as to Macha.

With that, he put on the fresh linen clothing and furs that had been put in his icy tomb so many years before. Covered from head to toe in fur, he looked the part of an old nomad from the north.

Macha levitated Dughall out through the opening in the ceiling and into the wide-open snow covered north. Dughall squinted and covered his eyes. *So much light.* Slowly his eyes adjusted to the light of life again.

Dughall wasted not a minute more. He knew he must make his way south. He trudged, Macha flittering beside him, for many days as he made his way to the ancient continent of his ancestors and of his former self. On to his destiny.

42 THE MACHINE

As Dughall made his way back to human civilization, he was amazed at how little the humans around him saw. Macha was with him for the entire journey. Color had returned to her skin and wings, though less vibrant than it had been before their long sleep. But the humans did not gasp in awe or hazard a second look their way. Not one human that Dughall encountered inquired about his pixie companion. *How is it that they cannot see this diminutive yet strong presence beside me at all times?*

The more time Dughall spent among modern humans, the more he knew the answer to this perplexing observation. The humans were so busy with those things they called 'cell phones', with the tiny pads of letters, and looking at their small glass windows with moving pictures and words printed on them, that they did not notice much of the world around them. The modern humans constantly moved and talked. Dughall noticed that they seemed to live in a world built upon rationality and thus dismissed evidence of the magickal and mystical events and things around them at all times. Dughall doubted they would notice a fire-breathing dragon scorching their arse until it was too late.

All the better for him. *A distracted mind is a mind easily fooled.* He only hoped the humans at CERN were as distracted and easily befuddled as the humans he had encountered along his journey south.

Within a few weeks, Dughall hoodwinked, swindled and downright stole food, clothing, money and all that he required not only to survive, but also to fund his way to the French/Swiss border. Dughall had a sharp mind wizened by the extraordinary amount of time he had been alive. He also lacked the conscience to deflect his attention with considerations of right versus wrong. Dughall easily worked his will on anyone he encountered.

It wasn't long until he found himself in Merino, Switzerland, site of CERN and the Large Hadron Supercollider, the LHC for short. *All is working according to plan.*

Between his own formidable powers of persuasion and the help of Macha's pixie magick, Dughall easily usurped the persona and credentials of the lead scientist on one of the collider experiments. Dughall was in charge of the most powerful machine humans had ever built.

Even Dughall had to admit that the humans had achieved something quite remarkable in the creation of the LHC. The sheer size alone was commendable. There was no hint above the ground of what was happening below.

Dughall delighted in the idea of the deceptive nature of the machine. Above, farmland and rolling hills. A mile below, a machine so powerful that it would force beams of particles to travel to within a fraction of the speed of light and smash into each other in violent collisions.

The human scientists said that they wanted to look into the 'face of God' to see the beginning of the universe. Billions upon billions of their dollars spent to build a twenty-seven kilometer tube of superconducting magnets, some five stories tall, all for a hope to see back in time.

Dughall laughed within himself at the thought. *Humans, always so preoccupied with their past and their own existence.* 'Who are we?' *What a stupid question to ask,* Dughall thought.

As Dughall's eyes swept over the computer screen in front of him full of numbers and formulas, he couldn't help but have a smirk come over him. *They are so focused on questions of their past and their existential nature, they miss out on the opportunity that lay right under their noses. If only they knew what will soon happen,* he thought. *So wrapped up in their computers, charts, formulas and self-importance. They may not even believe it when they see it.*

As Dughall waited for the computer to catch up its calculations to where he wanted it to be, his mind wandered. Wandered as it had done so often in the thousand-plus years he spent in the *Umbra Nihili*. Plenty of time then, and now, to remember his own history and the reason he risked his very soul to go to the *Umbra Nihili*. Time to contemplate his soul's most fervent desire.

It won't be long now, my dearest one. Dughall recalled in an instant the suffering he had endured that brought him to that place of the deepest of human longing, a longing large enough to cause a person to commit the most despicable acts in the name of love.

43 DUGHALL'S STORY

Dughall remembered his childhood as though he had lived it just yesterday. He could close his eyes and inhabit the body of his youth as easily as if he had slipped on a pair of slippers. It was a trip he had taken many times during his long stay in the *Umbra Nihili*. While there were many much more pleasant memories he could have dwelled on, Dughall chose to focus his attention on the day that everything changed for him. It was the day that the true Dughall was born.

He peered at the world out of deep brown eyes and watched as his mother gathered water from the town's well. To say that he was close to her would be an understatement. He felt he was a part of her, and she a part of him. The slave's life of abject misery can do that to two people who find themselves suffering through it together.

Dughall was born into nobility in a small town in the beautiful Mediterranean countryside. His people grew grapes and olives and made wine known to all as a most excellent elixir. He was born into what could have become a relatively blissful existence, but such was not his destiny.

One fateful day, a marauding band of soldiers came to his village, intent on taking what did not belong to them. Dughall's father died protecting his family, cut down by a blade to his unarmored chest. Dughall's mother wielded a small dagger and hid her boy behind her as two marauders approached her. Dughall never knew that his life was spared only because no soldier could bring himself to end the life of such a beautiful creature, Dughall's own mother.

A quick death may have been preferable to the life that followed. Dughall and his mother were sold to a middling merchant and into a life of slavery. In those days, slavery was rampant. It was not confined to a particular color, creed or town. There were only the conquerors and the conquered. If you were not the conqueror, you were as likely to be sold into slavery as to be killed.

Many slaves toiled in fields or worked in a wealthy merchant's home doing domestic chores. Still others endured a life far worse than any field hand or household slave. Such was the life of Dughall's mother whose beauty was sold for the pleasure and use of the highest bidder.

There were many nights that Dughall's mother lay there, enduring the basest form of indignity and defilement, wishing for death to come rescue her from her horrid existence. The only thing that prevented her from taking the dagger of her nightly 'companion' and doing herself in was the knowledge that her son – her only ray of light – laid in the next room.

Her son. He needed her, and that alone kept her alive from day to day.

For Dughall's part, his heart slowly hardened, day after day, week after week, seeing the suffering endured by his beloved mother at the hands of her master and those he so callously sold her to. She tried to stifle her own tears around Dughall, but he knew that her heart was dying inside her.

The only pleasure of their day was in the quiet moments when no one else was around. Alone in their small quarters, she taught him. They both knew that it was strictly forbidden for her to teach her slave son how to read or write or to provide him any education. But Dughall's mother used her waning energy to impart to Dughall all that she knew. She would not let her son, born of noble and educated parents, go through life an ignorant.

She also taught Dughall about survival and patience. Even though he had learned to speak in the way of nobles and kings – and surely knew as much about writing and mathematics and astrology as any of them – he spoke to his master and to all others save his mother in the guttural language of peasants and slaves. He followed orders and endured the lash, given frequently not because he disobeyed but merely because it pleased his master to know that he could.

"Bide your time, my dear son. You will rise above this place. I know that you will. You will grab upon the opportunity when the time is right," his mother said one day.

"How do you know, dear mother?" asked Dughall. "How do you know I will ever be anything but a slave?"

She took Dughall's hands in hers and looked deeply into the dark brown eyes of the only one she loved. "When I look in your eyes my son, I do not see the soul of a slave. I see in you a fearsome fire, not one easily extinguished by the lash of a slave master."

It made Dughall's heart soar to hear such powerful and hopeful words from his dearest one. He believed in his mother with all his being and so when she stated with such conviction that she believed in him, he instantly believed in himself too.

From that day forward, his spirits were lifted a little higher for he believed wholeheartedly in his mother's prophetic words. "Bide your time, Dughall," he would say to himself when times got tough.

But as the years passed, it became more and more difficult to endure what was surely his largest torture. Each night he lay on his small cot beside the hearth while in the next room, he heard brutes use and abuse his mother. The anger welled and his heart blackened. He swore to himself vengeance most cruel on his master who he held responsible for his mother's daily suffering. And as he grew closer to manhood, he felt the time was coming when he would have his vengeance and he and his mother would escape their brutal bonds.

"Bide your time, Dughall," he said to himself in the dark. "Bide your time."

44 A PROMISE

It was a day like most of the others that lay behind him. As usual he went to his master's main grounds and cared for the livestock and repaired the buildings. It could be worse, he well knew. Mainly he was left alone to do his work in outside areas, away from others. Left on his own to ponder and think all day and plan his escape.

He had decided that day was *the* day. He quickly finished his assigned tasks in record time. He could go home early. He planned to find his mother in their small quarters, through with her morning chores of gathering water and food and readying their evening meal. She did all this before she went to her own 'work'.

When he had left that morning at the first light of dawn, his mother's 'work' was still with her, loudly snoring in the small room his mother slept in. This happened occasionally. *The lousy oaf was too lazy to get up and out when he was supposed to.*

That day, as he approached the door to their small apartment, he felt coldness come over him. His belly tightened and seized up. With a huge feeling of foreboding, he ran to his home.

The door to their dwelling was wide open. He stopped in the small doorway and instinctively listened. He dared not call out to his mother. He was small and quiet on his feet. If an attacker were still there, he would have the element of surprise.

The abode was so small that it took but three steps to move from the entryway to the doorway of his mother's room. As his eyes adjusted to the dark, he peered inside. He quickly surveyed the situation and found no one in the room. He was about to turn around and leave to look for his mother when he heard a small whimper.

He spun back around and quietly walked the two steps that it took to go to the other side of the small bed in the room. For all the years since that day – and there have been many – Dughall wished that he could excise from his brain the memory of what he saw.

There, a mass of human flesh. Its face so black, blue and swollen it was barely recognizable as human. One arm dangled, lifeless, from the body. The other was bent at an odd angle, surely broken in two. And on the floor, a pool of blood that oozed from the pile of flesh.

A part of him wanted to back away and to run. He wanted to run as fast as he could from the horrible sight. Run until he was sure that it was a nightmare and he'd come back to find his dear mother cooking their evening meal as always.

But then he again heard a whimper and he knew it was real. The pile of broken and oozing flesh was his own mother, his only love, the flesh of his flesh. His reason to live. She was beaten and tortured beyond the capacity to rise again.

Then a tiny voice, rasping and choking and trying to speak. He bent down nearer what used to be his mother's face, nearer to hear what may be her final words.

The power of his touch on her arm as he bent in close seemed to give her the strength to speak. "My dearest son," she choked out. "Remember all I taught you." She coughed and stopped. Dughall thought she had stopped breathing.

But then she started again. "Your time is now my son. You will walk a path of greatness, my love." Her breathing labored, gasping for air.

"You must do something for me now, my son. Honor your mother," she rasped.

"Of course my most beloved," he said. His tears choked his words and blinded him. "Anything you ask my mother."

"Take your small knife, my son, the one you use to cut rope. Use it now, my love, and plunge it deep into your mother's heart. Use it, dear son, to end my pain."

Dughall felt he could do anything for her. He could kill their master with his bare hands. He'd smash the skulls of the slave owners in the whole province. He could do anything but the task she had asked of him. *How can I silence the beating of the one heart that ever loved me?*

"Please," she croaked. "Please ... "

As he looked at the rasping heap of flesh that was once his mother, he knew that he had to release the one he loved from her broken shell. Dughall grabbed the small, dull knife from the pack around his waist. His master didn't allow him to own a dagger, sword or weapon of any kind. The small knife was so dull it would barely cut bread. But it was all he had. He knew that it would be the power of the force of the thrust not the sharpness of the blade that would complete his task.

With that thought, he summoned all the strength and love that he had. With a powerful thrust, he slammed that small knife into the still beating heart of his only mother. From the sound of her shallow breaths he knew that his knife had swung true. Within seconds, she drew her last breath then laid still, her glassy eyes still open.

Dughall's hand was still clenched around the knife handle while, with his other hand, he closed the lids of his mother's eyes, never again to look upon her loving countenance. In that moment, his hand still on the hilt of the weapon that had taken the life force from his mother's body, any love or compassion that Dughall may have had within him died. In that moment, the Dughall that would fight his way to the top ranks of the Norman army was born. The Dughall that would lay waste to entire villages on his quest for power was born. The Dughall that would one day risk his soul to bide his time in the *Umbra Nihili* was born. On that day, the Dughall that sits at the control panel of the most powerful machine humans have ever built was born.

And on that day, in that moment, kneeling beside the dead body of his only love, Dughall made a pledge. Perhaps never before or since has one made such a fervent promise, a promise that would ring through the ages. A promise that would bind a person to risk their immortal soul. A promise that had the power to resurrect one long ago dead. A promise so strong, the desire to fulfill it blinds its maker to the risk of death to those around him, even to the whole of the planet, perhaps to the whole of the solar system in which the beautiful blue planet swirls.

"Hear me now, any gods there be. Hear me now as I pledge this solemn oath, with all my heart and soul. From the depths of my being, hear my promise. I will find you, my beloved, and we will be together again. I will find a way to bring you back to my side and together, my mother, my queen, we will rule over all those who have had a hand in our suffering, and over their kin for all generations to come. This I promise to you, my love."

Having made his oath, Dughall rose and swiftly left the small dwelling where he had lived since he was an infant. He considered himself free and would no longer live the life of a slave.

It was payback time.

45 DUGHALL'S REVENGE

As he sat at the LHC control center, Dughall's musing became enjoyable to him. He brightened as he remembered going to his master's home, intent on revenge. He had the element of surprise as he had always been a dutiful slave, not one to backtalk or show any signs of rebellion. His mother prepared him well for just such a moment.

"Why are you barging in here boy," the master bellowed as Dughall kicked through the door. "You belong out with the hogs and filth, not in your master's home."

"Maybe this will be my home now," he impertinently responded.

"What?" his Master yelled. His eyes raged at Dughall. "You will leave my sight at once and go back to that hole with your whore mother before I beat you to within an inch of your life."

"You will take back what you said about my mother just now, you swine of a man, or so help me," Dughall responded with fire in his eyes.

"You have gone too far slave. You have lost sight of your place in life." The master reached for his sword lying on the table beside him.

But the old, fat merchant was slow, his reflexes dulled by hours of drinking wine. Dughall knew it was his moment. He leapt for the sword with impressive speed and agility. Before the merchant had risen fully from his chair, Dughall had the sword in his hand.

"Look here boy, you can barely hold that blade, let alone wield it," the merchant sneered at Dughall. "Lay the weapon down and I may choose to spare your sorry life," the merchant pled.

Dughall had to admit that it was, in fact, difficult for him to hold the sword. It must have weighed more than twenty pounds. He was strong for his age but being only fourteen, it took all the strength of both his arms to hold up the sword. But Dughall's desire welled up from his core, a will forged by years of suffering and abuse.

There are some who live such a life and in their suffering, they grow immense compassion and peacefulness with all of existence. In others, the years of torment and observation of ill will among their captors breeds a hatred and anger that is unmatched.

From that place of ultimate despair and sadness over the loss of his only love, from that place of deepest desire to have her revenge, from that place of wholly unchecked anger and hatred, Dughall summoned a strength of body and will that surprised even him. Dughall lunged at the rotund merchant and plunged the man's sword deep into his belly. The merchant's dull eyes were filled with surprise as the warm blood that had pumped through his portly body spilled out, great torrents of crimson.

Dughall stepped back a few paces as he watched the merchant fall to the floor. Dughall stood by and watched with a rising feeling of glee as the life force once powerful in the large man spilled across the floor.

The merchant sputtered as he said, "Help me. Help me, boy."

Dughall laughed heartily at the merchant's words. "Help you? Help you?" he said incredulously. "Old man, I'm the one who put the blade in you. Why should I bother to take it out until I am assured that the last breath has passed from your rancid lips?"

"But what of your immortal soul, boy? If you kill me, what will come to your immortal soul?"

Dughall bent down so he could look the dying merchant in the eye. He smirked the smirk that would become one of his defining features, born in that moment.

"Well, old man, I suppose your soul, if you have one, awaits the same fate as mine then."

"But I haven't killed anyone," the merchant choked out.

"Ah, but you have. You killed my mother."

"No, I didn't," the merchant pleaded with Dughall. "Please, you have to believe me. I didn't get anywhere near her. I didn't kill her. It was someone else then."

"You may not have been the one who beat her and bloodied her and left her in a heap for me to find, barely recognizable as my own beloved. But you are the one who sent her each night to her real death, the death of her soul. And you are the one who sold her life for a price to the one who did her in. How much did you get for it, huh? How much you filthy rotten pig?" Dughall took the hilt of the sword and twisted it.

The merchant choked out muffled screams of agony as Dughall inflicted pain to his once master. "Please," the old man pled. "I am sorry," he whimpered. "Please ... "

"Too late you fetid scum. You shall die here, alone and broken and suffering, just as she did. And if you do have a soul, it surely will rot in a hell worse than any you can imagine for the horrible crimes you have committed in your life. And while it is indeed a pleasure to watch you die in agony, I must be off."

With that statement, Dughall gave the sword one last painful twist and turn before he drew it out of the near dead body of the merchant. He took the merchant's napkin and wiped the blade clean of its owner's blood.

"A fine sword," he said aloud. "It shall come in handy on my quest."

With those words, he turned his back on the merchant and left him to die. Dughall had taken the first steps on his path to becoming a bloodthirsty conqueror. He found killing far too easy and in a way pleasurable. In the years to come, he would find that with each new death, it became easier and easier to end the life of another like one would swat a gnat or a fly. Anyone who stood in the way of all that he desired was to him like a mere insect, of no consequence. In time, he stopped counting the number of human lives he took along his path to conquest.

Sitting at the control panel of the LHC, it was no different. All the humans around him, the team of thousands, they were of no consequence to him. Even those in the nearby towns and villages above, what should he care if they too perished when he implemented his plan?

There was a slight gnawing feeling in the pit of his stomach, a feeling foreign to him for so many years. *What is this?* He could not place it, but it seemed a bit familiar. *Why do I feel this edge in my gut?* Perhaps it was something he ate or a human virus trying to bring him down with an illness.

Just then Macha appeared by his side with news. It was upon casting his eyes on her face that he realized what that horrible feeling was in his stomach.

Dughall felt a pang of guilt. He was slightly amused with himself. He didn't realize he could still feel that. Apparently he had a pang of guilt over the probable loss of Macha.

To be expected, after all, he reassured himself. *She entombed herself for over a thousand years just so she could help me to resurrect when the time was right,* he thought. *She has been a faithful servant.*

Of course, if she hadn't entombed herself and put herself into the deepest pixie sleep, she probably wouldn't be alive today, he rationalized. *Yes, that's true. She would have gone the way of all the other pixies and faerie folk. Vanished with the rest. Vanquished by humans and stamped once and for all out of existence.*

The faerie people were so blind to the nature of their own condition. As times changed and humans left their ways of nature worship and chose the one God, the faeries retreated away from humans to survive, never fully realizing that they needed the interaction with humans to exist.

Macha may, in fact, be the last of her kind, thought Dughall. But his mind could go no further down the road of guilt or sympathy. For Dughall, that road was short indeed and a dead end.

The sacrifice of one pixie, it is no matter if I can achieve my most fervent desire, he thought. *In fact, Macha is probably prepared to sacrifice herself for me.* With that thought, the pinching feeling in his belly ceased. He sat upright and with a clear purpose.

Nothing would get in his way, not even the death of the world's last pixie.

46 PIECING IT TOGETHER IN DUBLIN

As Liam drifted to sleep on the small bed, he hoped that he'd wake from his nap to find myself back in the States, the whole thing just a crazy nightmare. Instead, he woke to find Fanny flopped on her stomach on the other bed, maps spread out in front of her. It looked to Liam like she was trying to look busy rather than actually doing anything.

On the other hand, Jake was the picture of concentration, intently reading a webpage on his laptop. His hair was more tousled than usual, his eyes rimmed in red and bloodshot from hours of looking at a computer screen.

Liam stretched his arms above his head and breathed deeply. He wasn't in a dream after all. His daughter's life depended on his belief in their outrageous story.

"Jake, you found anything interesting?" he asked.

It took Jake a minute to register a voice from the outside world. He slowly turned and ran his hands through his shock of now jet-black hair, pausing as if to collect himself.

"Well, I don't know if I'm getting anywhere with this, but I have an idea. It's a bit off the wall."

"Off the wall? More off the wall than our best friend disappearing into another dimension?" asked Fanny.

"Okay, well maybe not *that* off the wall. Okay, check it. Dughall's supposed to want to get to the Netherworld, right?"

"Yeah, that's what Hindergog said."

"Sure but what's he after? I mean, why does he want to go there?"

"That's the mystery, isn't it nub?"

"Don't be short with him Fanny."

"Yeah, work with me on this. What I'm saying is we have to know what this guy is after. What does he think he can find in the Netherworld?"

"I don't know. Hindergog didn't say anything about what the psychopath wanted."

"But the story he told had clues."

"What kind of clues? What do you think he's after, Jake?" Liam asked.

"Well he was power hungry, that much we know. And he clearly didn't care who got hurt in his quest for power, so we know he's dangerous."

"Yeah, but Jake, we don't know what's in the Netherworld really. We may have to wait for Emily to come back to answer that," Fanny said.

"That's what I was thinking too, but then I started to think about what Dughall might think he'll find there. You know it doesn't matter what he'll actually find there, only what he *thinks* he'll find."

"Okay, that's riveting, but we don't know that either."

"I think we do have some clues about that. Dughall heard the story of the well from that guy that he killed – what was his name?"

"Cormac," offered Fanny.

"Yeah, Cormac. Anyway, according to Hindergog, Cormac told Dughall all about the Sacred Well and the portal and the torc. And then there was the pixie ... "

"Macha?"

"Yeah, Macha. Sounds like she knew a lot. She probably told him things too. He probably knew a lot about the Netherworld, or at least what people thought was on the other side of that Well."

"That's some good deduction, but I'm not following what you think that tells us about why Dughall wants to enter the portal," Liam said.

"Yeah, or how you think he's going to do it. He doesn't have the torc you know. Hey, you know, come to think of it, if he doesn't have the torc, he can't get through the portal, so what are we worrying about?"

"Ah, you see, that's just the question I had. We know he wants to go to the Netherworld and badly. And if Hindergog and those in his world are so worried, they must know something we don't and that must mean there's another way in."

"Right, some other portal," said Fanny.

"Or, a way to create a portal," Liam said.

"Exactly Mr. Adams! That's what I'm thinking. And here's the biggest clue that Hindergog gave us. He mentioned a large machine being built by humans."

"We build a lot of big machines," said Fanny.

"Yeah, but not many of them have any capability of opening a portal to another dimension. There may, in fact, be only one ... "

"The super collider!" Liam shouted.

"That's right. The Large Hadron Collider at CERN."

Jake and Liam locked eyes for a moment while the truth of what they'd said passed between them. The butterflies in Liam's stomach and the chills up his spine told him that they were onto something.

"Okay, would one of you like to let me know what we're talking about?" screeched Fanny.

"Mr. Adams, you do the honors?"

"Sure, Jake. Well Fanny you may have heard of atom smashers before."

"Nope. Doesn't ring a bell."

"Oh, okay. How to explain this? Well scientists – physicists mainly – build these giant machines called colliders or atom smashers so that they can do experiments on the nature and structure of matter."

"Still not following."

"They smash atoms together Fanny to see what happens," said Jake.

"All right, you don't have to get all testy with me."

"You should pay more attention in science class."

"You should stop being such a nerd."

"Okay, stop fighting you two. Fanny, atoms are extremely tiny, but they contain a lot of potential energy. Our understanding of atoms is what enabled us to build atomic bombs."

"Oh, those kind of atoms."

"Well, everything is made of atoms and atoms are made of smaller bits of stuff. Particles. And when you collide these particles you get massive amounts of energy and observe what comes out of the collision. That's what scientists are doing at the LHC. They want to see what is produced by the collision of particles at near the speed of light."

"But if they do that, won't it make an explosion like a bomb?"

"No, they aren't colliding whole atoms, only subatomic particles. There won't be bomb-size explosions, but when they smash the particles the mini explosions produce even smaller bits of matter. And that's what they're studying, those mini bit particles."

"I sorta get what this collider thing is doing, but what does this have to do with Dughall?"

"Well, if Jake's theory is right, and I'm betting it is, Dughall may be trying to use the LHC to create his own portal."

"Not following," said Fanny. "I thought this thing was smashing particles. They plan to open up a doorway to another dimension with this machine?"

"Well no, that's not in the plan. I don't think anyone is even theorizing about that," Liam said.

"It's a long shot, but it's all we've got. Fanny, remember the static electricity we felt at the portal?"

"Yeah. It was like we'd been rubbed with a giant balloon."

"And remember the silvery mist we saw?"

"Jake, I'm not a science geek like you. Just spill it already."

"Okay, here's what I'm thinking. The static electricity and the silver mist are both related to mega amounts of electromagnetism."

"Yes," Liam said. "That's right. And where is there more concentrated electromagnetism than anywhere else in the world?"

"The LHC," offered Jake.

"What do magnets have to do with the colliding thingy?"

"It's complicated Fanny, but essentially the collider uses immense magnets, five stories high, to accelerate the particles through a massive circular tube twenty-seven kilometers around. The magnets both accelerate and bend the particles around the huge circle to get them to great speeds before they collide."

"Yeah, so the most powerful superconducting magnets ever built are at the LHC."

"And so you think Dughall will use these magnets ... "

"To open a portal," said Jake.

"But how?" asked Fanny.

"That I don't know. Do you have any ideas, Mr. Adams?"

"Well, first of all, I don't see how he'd get anywhere near the LHC. I mean this is a huge compound with hundreds, if not thousands, of people around all the time. And the collider itself is a mile underground. And it's not like you just flip a switch and turn the magnets on or off."

"Yeah, I was reading about it," said Jake. "It takes weeks to cool it down enough to operate at full power."

"Exactly. It has to be super cooled to -271° Celsius to be operational. And there's a whole command center with many people and oversight. I just don't see the possibility of Dughall being able to use the LHC in any way."

"We may not see how he'd do it, but we can bet he'll try to find a way," said Fanny. "Mr. Adams, you weren't there to hear Hindergog, but from his story, one thing's for sure. This Dughall guy is pure evil and he's smart. If there's a way, he'll find it."

"I agree with Fanny," said Jake. "We have to assume he'll find a way."

"So we don't actually need to know how he's going to do it. All we need to do is make sure he doesn't get anywhere near the LHC," said Fanny.

"You're right Fanny. You know what that means?" Liam asked.

"Road trip," said Jake.

"Exactly. You guys up for another road trip?"

"As long as we're not walking," said Fanny.

Jake was already packing his laptop.

Liam knew they had to go to CERN, but it meant leaving Emily — or at least the place where she was last seen. He felt doubt about whether he was doing the right thing, but he knew he had to do something. Sitting around a small hotel room with Fanny and Jake wouldn't bring Emily back.

By late afternoon, they were on a plane to France where they would get a train to the small town on the Swiss/French border that was the headquarters of CERN.

47 A PRESENT FOR MISS EMILY

"Miss Emily, are you ready to go now to your next Master?"

It was Hindergog. Even with my eyes closed in silent meditation, I knew his voice.

"Ready? I don't know if I'm ready exactly. But you're here, so I guess it must be time to move on."

"Lies again Youngling. I thought we were through with lies," croaked Madame Wong from her resting spot under the large maple tree. "You know you are ready."

"Yeah, okay. She's still busting my chops though," I said as I smiled at Hindergog.

"Come, Miss Emily. I will take you."

"Okay little guy but just give me a minute to say goodbye to Madame Wong."

She rose from her lotus position but still came only to my chin. I had to bend down to embrace her.

"Thank you." Tears came to my eyes. "I'll never forget you, Madame Wong."

"Madame Wong will be ghost that haunts your memory," she cackled.

"Yes," I laughed. "You will haunt me for sure."

"You will be my special little bird, Miss Emily," Madame Wong said then disappeared. Not only did Madame Wong disappear, but her little cottage, the giant maple tree, even the well, meadow and stream were gone, swallowed by the insubstantial mist and fog of the Netherworld. It was like it had never been there at all.

"Hindergog, where did she go?"

"Hard to say."

"But she was here, right? I'm not going *loco* am I? There was a little Chinese woman here, and a small house and a tree?"

"Yes, those things were here."

Hindergog walked away from me into the silvery mist that engulfed us again.

"Hindergog, where are we going?"

"I must deliver you to your next Master."

"Yes, but who is it? Who am I going to see? What will my next master be like?"

"You will see," he said as he scurried along in front of me.

After a while, Hindergog stopped. He turned to me with a most serious look on his face.

"What is it Hindergog? Do you have something to tell me?"

"Something to give you," he said. He pulled a small item out of a pocket hidden on the inside of his tweed vest. The parcel was wrapped in beautiful purple cloth.

"What's this?" I asked as he handed it to me.

"This ... this is something that will help you. Something I made many, many Earth rotations ago. Something I made for my first mistress."

I gently opened the cloth and couldn't believe my eyes. Inside was the most elegant dagger. It had a smooth, sharp silver blade, but the hilt was gold and encrusted with precious gems, some of a type that I had never seen before. The gem at the top was perfectly round and set in gold. At first it was milky white like an opal, but as I studied the jewel it began to change and flicker. The gem became perfectly clear and seemed lighted from within. Then I began to see pictures in my mind like a movie in my mind's eye. Fanny and Jake were on a train. Fanny was leaning on a man that looked familiar. *Who is that?*

Dad! It was my dad, and he didn't look like a zombie anymore. It was my own dad, back from the undead. And he was on a train with Fanny and Jake. *But going where?*

The jewel then clouded over again and became milky white. "Hindergog, I just had a vision. Did the jewel at the top here – did it make my vision happen?"

"The Sight Stone. It's exceptionally rare indeed. Probably the last one of its kind in all the universe. Yes, it enhances the sight."

"But these visions I have, are they telling the future or showing the past?"

"Sometimes the sight shows us things as they are. The truth of a situation. Sometimes the possible future, sometimes past."

"But how do I know? I mean how am I to know which is which? How can I be certain of what I'm seeing?"

"Ah, that is the trick now, isn't it? With experience, Miss Emily, you will know what you see. What did you see?"

"I saw Fanny and Jake on a train and the weird part was, they were with my dad."

"Why strange for your friends to be with your father?"

"Well, because my dad has been sort of lost since my mom died."

"Lost? I thought he lived with my young mistress."

"Yes, well he lives with me but you know, it's like he's not quite there. He walks around and goes through the motions, but he's not present. Do you understand?" I could see that his brow was furrowed.

"I think I understand your meaning. You did not expect to see your father in the crystal. What do you think they were doing?"

"I'm not sure. That's why I'm asking you for help. They were on a train. But is that something they're doing right now? Or something they already did? Or something they're going to do?"

"The one who has the vision is in best place to answer that question. I did not see your vision. I do not know the meaning of it.

Reach out with your feelings about it. What did you feel when you saw the vision?"

"Hope. Yes, I felt a surge of hope."

"What think you then of the vision? Past, present or future?"

"I think it's present. I think I was seeing what they're doing now in our world."

"Probably right then."

"But it still doesn't answer the question. Why would my dad be on a train with Jake and Fanny?"

"Only time will answer that riddle," said Hindergog.

We walked along in silence for a while. But then I had to ask a question that had been burning in my mind.

"Hindergog, was this Saorla's dagger?"

"Yes."

"The one she took her own life with?" I asked as I held it gingerly.

"Yes."

"But Hindergog, how did you get this? You were here and Saorla in my world."

"It does not matter how it came to me, but it did. It found its way back to Hindergog," he said as his eyes misted up.

"But Hindergog, I can't take this. You loved Saorla very much, and this is the only thing of hers that you have. You keep it, little guy. I can't take it."

"You must have it Miss Emily. It belonged to Saorla, but it was forged by my hand for my first mistress and was held by every High Priestess since. You must have it now," he said.

"This is an honor, Hindergog, truly. But I'm not a High Priestess yet. I don't feel ready for such a valuable thing."

"Miss Emily, you are next High Priestess. You must have the dagger. It will help you. Like the torc about your arm, the dagger has much magickal energy. You need it more than old Hindergog."

"What magick does it have Hindergog?"

"You have experienced the Sight Stone. It is a sacred stone from my own world, the only one that still exists. It will help you with the sight, not that most of the High Priestesses of the Order of Brighid needed much help with that."

"Well I do. Do I have to do anything special to use it?"

"Just by holding it, you will receive a boost to your own sight and inner guidance. But there is more. It is more than just a dagger. That object you hold can become any object that you need it to be."

"What? It will change into whatever I want? Oh, is that just here in the Netherworld?"

"No, mistress, even in your world its alchemic powers are the same. It will become whatever is needed by the person who holds it."

"That's amazing," I said as I looked at it closely.

"But know this Youngling. If the holder of the dagger ever seeks to use it for their own selfish ends instead of for the highest good of all, then it will cease to have any magickal powers at all. It will become a useless hunk of metal."

"So basically use it for good, not evil. Got it."

"It's more than use it for good, Miss Emily. Do not use if for your own selfish purpose. That is the key."

"Don't be selfish. Okay, I can do that. Thank you, Hindergog. This truly is a wonderful surprise." I bent down to hug the little guy.

Hindergog seemed a bit flustered and like he didn't know what to do. Finally, he lightly patted my back with his furry hands.

I let him go and he smoothed his vest and walked again.

"Miss Emily is ready now to meet her master." It was more of a statement than a question.

"Yes, I'm ready," I agreed.

For what I wasn't sure.

48 EMILY'S SECOND MASTER

"Miss Emily, I must leave you."

"You can't leave me," I whined. "I'm stuck in this blasted mist again. I need you to help me find my way."

"You must find your final master on your own," he replied.

"But how, Hindergog? You gotta' give me some kind of clue."

"From your desire to learn all that you need to learn to fulfill your destiny. When you have that in your heart, your master will appear to you."

"I should know by now that nothing here is easy."

"'Tis quite easy if you concentrate. Just focus, Miss Emily. I am away." He began to dematerialize.

"Hindergog, wait! Will I see you again?"

"You will see me again if the fates allow." He disappeared into the fog.

What now? I stood there for a few minutes, not sure what to do next. I decided to focus on my task and began to walk again.

I soon found myself rambling along rolling hills and green meadows, with stands of large oak and ash. There were little medieval cottages with straw-thatched roofs, and I walked on a path made of stones. It was a majestic place.

As I walked I pondered my destiny. I had learned so much, but I still didn't feel ready to face Dughall. I wasn't sure what I needed to learn, but my time with Madame Wong had taught me that there was so much that I didn't know and even more that I didn't understand.

As I pondered those things, my surroundings began to change. My stone path changed to a modern sidewalk. The small, medieval cottages replaced with midwestern homes made of brick or clad in white siding.

My pace quickened along with the beating of my heart. This sidewalk was all too familiar. *Could it be?*

Up ahead a house. A house well known to me.

I began to run and before long found myself at the front of my own house. But it wasn't the house I'd left. No, the house before me had beautiful red petunias and sweet William growing in the flowerbeds. And there was a smell wafting from the house. I sniffed the air and smelled chocolate chip pancakes and coffee and bacon.

I practically leaped to the red door. Red, just as my mother had made it. My heart felt like a train rolling down a track in my chest. My throat was dry. I don't think I could have spit if my life depended on it. My hand reached out to the doorknob. I hesitated a minute then slowly turned the knob and opened the door.

I stepped inside and my feelings were confirmed. Muriel wasn't there. Wherever I was – whenever I was – it was a place and time before Muriel entered the scene. The house was filled with the golden walls and the vibrant hues of my mom's Technicolor paintings.

I somehow found the voice to yell out, "Mom?" There was no answer.

I walked from the front hallway to my left into the formal living room. It was exactly as I remembered it from when my mom was alive. Nothing changed. But it was empty.

Back out to the hallway and straight across from the formal living room into the dining room. It too was exactly the same – frozen in a time past. The large, round antique oak dining table and worn Oriental rug over the wood floor juxtaposed with my mom's large, brightly covered canvases. But that room was empty too. There wasn't a sound in the place.

She has to be here. She just has to be. I followed the scent of the pancakes to the kitchen.

I didn't slow my pace, but my feet felt like they were walking in quicksand. As I walked through the kitchen door, I saw her. Her back was to me, but I'd recognize that hair anywhere.

"Mom!" I ran across the room to hug her.

She turned to me. My heart nearly stopped. The woman looking at me was my mother. Same golden red mane of wavy hair cascading down her shoulders. Same emerald green eyes. She smiled the same warm, embracing smile I remembered from my childhood.

She wrapped her arms around me, and it should have been one of the most incredible moments ever, but –

"Wait, this isn't right," I said. "You have the face of my mother, but you are not my mother, are you?"

"What do you think?" she asked.

"I think you're like a shadow of her, but you're not real."

"You have been told that this is not the world of spirits."

"I know, I know. It's just that, I want so badly to see her again. Why do you appear to me with her face? Why torture me with the sight of her?" I was at the point of tears.

"I torture you not, dear child. You see the face that you want to see. If it is torture, then it is you that torture yourself."

"Who are you then?"

"I am the one your ancestors called Brighid."

"You are the goddess?" I asked incredulously.

"I am a goddess to some," she replied. Her voice was soft and melodic yet strong. It was strange. Even though her lips moved, the voice seemed to come from someplace other than the body in front of me.

"I don't think I've ever really believed in God," I said.

"You are experiencing me here, now, with your senses. What do you believe now?"

"My world has been turned so upside down ever since I first saw Hindergog. I don't know what to believe anymore."

"That's a fine answer Emily. Yes, keep your mind open. Observe. Consider. Answers will come to you in time."

"Goddess, I would like to see your true face. Can you show me who you truly are?"

Her whole body and demeanor changed. She seemed to grow larger and yet at the same time less substantial. She became a shimmery vision. Instead of the common clothes of a human in my time, she wore a long gown that seemed to skim her body yet be a part of it as well.

But it was her face that caught my attention the most. Her face was my mother's face, but then it was Saorla. As swiftly as it became Saorla, it changed yet again to another woman with auburn hair. Her face would stay one person for maybe a few minutes, no more, then swiftly morph to another woman's face. There were women who looked much like Saorla and my mother, but there were others with dark hair and eyes. Some had dark skin, others had fair skin. At one point I even recognized the face of Madame Wong. I was glad to see the familiar visage that I had come so accustomed to. But as soon as I got excited, the face morphed yet again into another unknown woman. Each time this bizarre metamorphosis happened, the head of this being glowed a different color.

"Who are all these women? I wanted to see your true face."

"This is the true face of the goddess. Each woman from your world who has visited me here has envisioned me as she would. The goddess is created in the likeness of humans."

"Wild. I always thought we were created in the likeness of God. But Goddess, I want to see your true form. Please show me your natural state."

"My natural state is one that cannot be readily accepted by your human senses," she softly replied.

I was totally mesmerized by Brighid. At first her gown seemed like a silky material gently blown about her in a breeze that didn't exist. But the material — and that isn't quite the right word for it — was like nothing in our world. It was as if someone had spun pure silver into a fabric then woven throughout it an iridescent material in shades of blue and turquoise and purple, then set the whole thing into motion. It was like she wore a shimmering, iridescent liquid.

Being in her presence I felt content and at peace. I wanted to stay there, with the Goddess, forever. I was with a presence of pure love. I could create anything I needed or desired. *Why ever leave?*

"Emily, you will leave when the time is right. You cannot stay forever in the Netherworld."

"But why do I have to leave? Here I am in your presence and I feel a happiness and contentedness I've never felt before."

Her entire being became even brighter. She smiled and said, "Oh yes, and I enjoy your company too. I have always relished my time with your ancestors and the other humans who have found their way here. Such fascinating creatures, humans. Few of your kind realize the wondrous miracle of being human. To exist in your glorious bodies. Within those shells of water that house your Anam, you can create. That is a rare gift."

"But here in the Netherworld I've created anything that I want."

"While it is true that while here you can think and therefore conjure those things that you would like to have. But surely you must have noticed by now that your creations here are but a pale comparison to that which you create in your own space and time."

I hadn't thought about it before, but it was true. I created chocolate chip pancakes in the Netherworld, but they lacked something. It wasn't quite right.

"I shall enjoy our time together, dear Emily, as I hope that you do as well. But your corporeal world needs you."

I had learned and done so much in the Netherworld that at times it was easy to forget why I was there and what I'd left behind. The faces of Fanny and Jake and even my dad flooded my mind. Thinking of my friends and my dad brought a wave of sadness over me. Madame

Wong had kept me so busy, I didn't have much time to stop and think about home.

"I do miss my friends. I think I may even miss my dad."

"We shall begin your training then, dear one, so you may return to your world and those that you love."

"I have been here so long, at times it feels like I've always been in the Netherworld. But in all this time, I honestly don't understand exactly where I am. Am I in a dream?"

"No, not a dream. You create dreams in your own mind and are not shared with others. This we are experiencing together."

"It feels so dreamlike."

"The Netherworld is what your scientists might call a parallel world. If you think of space, your Earth and the Netherworld exist in the same space."

"What a mind trip. I'm not sure I understand it. Are there other worlds like this one?"

"Oh there are many other realms though no two are exactly alike. Your world is a fairly rare occurrence in the great scheme of the web of all that is."

"Can people from Earth go to these other worlds, like I've come here?"

"Yes."

"But that's another question. How exactly did I get here? What happened?"

"Yes, these things seem difficult to humans. You were there, in your world, standing on what felt like solid ground. The next minute, you were here in an ephemeral world of mist and fog. You have these magnificent bodies with your ability to create and then fully encounter through your senses the delights of your creations – or the horrors of your creations as the case may be. Your bodies and minds are incredible, but they also limit you as well.

"Humans say 'I have to see it to believe it'. Instead, you must believe it before you can see it."

"Are you saying that I needed to believe in the Netherworld in order to come here?"

"That is helpful, yes, to believe. If all humans believed, all could go anywhere they wanted. In order to come here, you had some help though.

"The Sacred Well of your ancestors was sacred because it was known to be a place where what your ancestors called the 'veil' between our two worlds is thin. Your scientists may find that there is a higher level than usual of electromagnetic energy at the Sacred Well."

"I don't think my ancestors knew anything about electromagnetic energy."

"Oh, they did not have those words for it, but they were more in touch with the unseen than modern humans. They could feel the same things you felt. The hair rising on their bodies, the tingling sensation. They knew there was a strange and magickal energy in that place. And the ancient torc that you wear on your arm helped you to come here as well."

"The torc is magick?"

"Magick is your human word for it. It is no mistake that the torc is made of twisted, coiled gold. Gold is an excellent conductor of energy."

"I never thought of it before, but it looks kind of like a bundle of wires."

"There is a reason the transport objects for electricity in your world are made of coiled wire."

"So the torc is like a conductor?"

"It helps the wearer to achieve the resonant frequency required to come to this realm."

"Goddess, you have revealed so many faces. Have you been visited by many humans?"

"Yes, I enjoyed my interaction with humans for millennia."

"What happened?"

"Humans changed."

"How so?"

"They stopped believing. They stopped having faith. They want 'proof'. Everything they must see with their eyes. All experiences come through their body now. They have lost touch with Akasha."

"Yes, I see what you mean. I didn't know that before I came here. But now, seeing what I've seen, knowing what I know ... "

"That is it. Now you know, not just see."

"Yes."

"As humans lost faith, their need for gods and goddesses faded."

"But on Earth now, there are religions with billions of followers who believe in God."

"There may be a few that truly believe with their Anam that there is a life after they leave their body and many more hope that there will be such an existence, but even fewer still know that they are infinite beings, part of the web of all things. You do not have to believe in a god. You are god."

"I wish everyone could have the experience that I did in the dark wood."

"All can have that experience and know what you now know, if only they open their heart."

I had wanted so badly to have these questions answered, and I was so riveted by our conversation, that for a while, I forgot why I was there. But then the vision of Jake and Fanny with my dad on a train came back to me.

"I'm so glad that you have answered my questions. These are things that I've wondered about since I came here but I was afraid to ask Madame Wong. She probably would have hit me with that darned cane of hers."

The Goddess softly chuckled. Her laugh filled me on the inside and brought a smile to my lips. "Yes, Madame Wong lacks the patience for questions."

"But I'm not here with you just to have my questions answered, am I?"

"You tell me, young one. Are you ready to fulfill your destiny?"

"I don't feel ready."

"If you do not feel ready then you are not ready."

"What now?"

"Now you delve deeper into the mysteries of Akasha."

49 THE DUGHALL ENIGMA

"We must talk young Emily about our friend Dughall."

"From what Hindergog told me, Dughall is no friend of mine."

"A wise human once said, 'If you know neither yourself nor your enemy, you will always endanger yourself'. You have learned much about yourself here in this land of mist and fog, have you not?"

"Yes, Goddess, I have."

"Then it is time for you to learn about your enemy. What do you think he is after?"

"I thought you knew! You must know."

"It is a simple thing to know the hearts of humans, but not so simple to know the plans of one who is no longer quite human. Dughall spent many years in the *Umbra Nihili*, perfecting his ability to hide his thoughts and plans from all, including me. I have ideas about this dark one. But you Emily, must understand him if you are to stop him."

"I don't think I want to know anything too deep about him."

"If he is successful with his quest, it will surely lead to the destruction of your world and perhaps even this one. If you are to end his quest, you will need to know something of the man that you are destined to meet."

Brighid told me Dughall's story. I learned about his enslavement as a child, the horrible life of his mother, his escape and the *Umbra Nihili*. It was hard to listen to it. At time, I found myself feeling sorry for him. But as the story went on, my anger rose.

I lost my mom too. Okay, she wasn't a slave and wasn't killed at the hands of another. But I watched her be tortured by the alien tar being. My dearest one got snatched from me too. I didn't go on a murderous rampage.

"It is one of the mysteries of humans. Infinitely fascinating creatures."

"What mystery?"

"That two different individuals, in similar circumstances, can choose such divergent paths. You walk the path of yellow bricks. Dughall walks a path paved with the broken and scoured bones of his enemies.

"Now you know his story. What do you think he is after?"

I reflected on the story. It was clear to me that Dughall wanted power and revenge. But there was more to it too. After a while it dawned on me. Maybe he was more like me than I cared to think. And maybe like me, he wanted to be reunited with one he lost. As soon as I thought it Brighid's robes shimmered ever brighter.

"He wants to find his mother," I said.

"Yes, smart girl."

"But why does he want to come here? I have learned that this is not the place of human spirits."

"No, it is not."

"Maybe he is mistaken. Maybe he thinks it is and boy will he be disappointed when he gets here. He'll find nothing but mist and fog."

"Ah, that would be the fates playing a cruel joke on one who deserves such a joke."

"Do you think that is what will happen then, if he makes it here?"

"The portends of the future speak of another possibility."

"Then what is it? What could he hope to find here?"

"Ah, that is one of the mysteries for which we will need to go deeper."

"Mysteries? You mean there is more to this place than I've seen?"

"Much more to the mysteries, my Youngling. Much more."

"You will teach me then, won't you? If I'm to defeat Dughall, I have to know all there is to know about this place."

"You will learn the mysteries that you need to complete your task. Perhaps someday you will return to learn more mysteries. Now, it is time."

"Time for what?"

"Time to learn about the mystery of time."

"Time is a mystery?"

"Time, space. Here, there. Yesterday, today, tomorrow. All just different names for one. If you learn this lesson, you will have a most powerful weapon. One that will help you defeat Dughall."

As always in the Netherworld each question was answered with a riddle wrapped inside an enigma.

"More riddles Goddess."

"What is life without riddles young one?"

I thought that I'd seen every strange thing there was to see in that place. I was wrong.

50 PUT YOUR BOAT IN

"Your scientists say that nothing can travel faster than the speed of light," said Brighid.

"Yeah, I think it was Einstein that came up with that."

"Very limiting, isn't it?"

"Well it's a limit set by Mother Nature."

"Nature set no such boundary. The true boundary is the one created by the human mind. Einstein was a bright man. Very smart, but very wrong."

"Wrong? You're saying Einstein was wrong? So we can travel faster than the speed of light?"

"You can be anywhere that you want in an instant."

"But how is that possible? We haven't even made it to Mars."

"Emily, you have seen the truth of my statement, yet still you allow what you have been told to limit you. Did you not experience the web of all things?"

"Well, yes."

"You knew what it was and could sense it with all your being even though you had left your human body behind. That is because you are the web and it is you."

"Yes, I knew that. I could feel it."

"Why then child do you question your ability to be anyplace within the web whenever you want?"

"You mean right now, if I want to, I could be on Mars in an instant?"

"Yes. But you may want to leave your human body behind for that journey. Mars is not particularly hospitable for humans."

"But how?"

"It is a choice. Your Anam is not limited by space or by time."

"Wait a minute. Time? Are you saying we can also travel through time?"

"Time is a fiction created by the human mind. You have also seen that for yourself. You have been living in a world without time."

"I'm not sure I understand what time is. It seems impossible to go back in time because the past is over. And it seems equally impossible to travel forward to something that doesn't exist yet. And Madame Wong's always croaking about being in the 'now.'"

"Madame Wong's advice is accurate as always. It is best to stay in your present moment and let the stream take you. But time is much like a stream."

A stream appeared before me. It babbled over rocks and meandered through a meadow and disappeared into a thick wood.

"I have created a stream so very much like one you may find on your planet. Do you see how the water flows?"

"Yes, but it flows in only one direction."

"'Tis true young one, 'tis true. But what you see around you when you are in the stream, do you agree that what you observe of your surroundings depends much on where you put your boat in?"

I had to think on that one a minute.

"So if the stream is like time, then if I put my boat in – back there, by the big willow ... "

"Then that is what you observe."

"And that's like the past."

"Yes."

"But if I put the boat in way up there, by that big oak ... "

"Then you are with the oak at that moment."

"And that is like the future?"

"Precisely."

"I can put my boat in the stream wherever I want to. So are you saying that the same is true of time? I can go to any time that I want simply by choosing it?"

"Your Anam is eternal. You already exist in all places that ever existed and all time that ever was or will be. Once you fully incorporate this into the core of your being, your Anam will then be able to travel to any place that it wants to because, you see, you are already there."

"Akasha."

"Yes."

I felt like I had to sit down. A sturdy chair appeared behind me. I fell into it and sat in a brain fog stupor.

"Your bodies and all your creations seem so solid, permanent and real to you. So hard for you to accept that you can cast it aside whenever you like and be wherever and whenever you want solely by your desire to do so. And even harder to comprehend that, with practice, you can even take that body with you. This lesson has been the hardest for the humans I have met."

I was barely listening to the Goddess at that point. My mind raced. If I could be anywhere or anytime that I wanted I knew exactly where I wanted to be. Home. And not the one that included Muriel the Mean and Zombie Man. No, I wanted to go to the home with a mother singing and painting vibrantly colored flowers and making Sunday breakfast.

"Yes, you can go there. But the past is a tricky business for the soul traveler."

Her voice brought me out of my reverie. *What is she saying about tricky business?*

"What do you mean 'tricky business'? I though you said I can go wherever and whenever I wanted to?"

"Oh you can but that does not necessarily mean that you should."

"But I was happy then. I want to feel that way again, if only for a minute or two. To see her smiling face. To hear her laughter, like a million bells ringing. To feel her hug ... "

Tears sprang from my eyes. My longing to see my mother again was so great that I don't think Brighid herself could stop me even if she wanted to.

"Perhaps the best way for you to learn the tricky business of which I speak is to experience it for yourself. Yes, humans do seem to learn best by doing, even if it is painful."

"So I can go there now?" I could barely contain my excitement.

"You are already there."

"But how do I go?"

"The same way you let yourself be one with the web of all that is. You simply let go of your conscious mind. Be one with all that is and choose your time and place. You will be there instantly."

I still sat in the chair that I conjured. I sat back and relaxed my whole body. I followed my breath as Madame Wong had taught me. I focused on the in and out, in and out. My breath like a gentle wave. Once I was in a deeply relaxed meditation, I imagined a stream and I pictured myself in a rowboat. I paddled my rowboat slowly. The water lapped at my boat and the paddles made little ripples in the water. I traveled down the stream. I imagined that the stream was a path to the house of my childhood. As I relaxed and focused on my breath and the stream, I felt the chair beneath me disappear, but I didn't fall to the ground. *Focus Emily.* I knew that if I lost focus, I was likely to fall on my keister.

The boat followed the current down the placid stream. Soon I was enveloped by a thick fog and couldn't see more than two feet ahead of me. It seemed like an eternity that I drifted slowly in that fog, all the while I concentrated as hard as I could on the house filled with my mother's laughter.

The mists cleared and the fog lifted. I was no longer in a boat floating down a gentle stream. I was walking up a very familiar sidewalk toward a very familiar house.

It was like déjà vu all over again. *Will I finally have what I've hoped for?*

51 THE SLIPPERY SLOPES OF TIME

As I walked up the wooden steps and onto the creaky porch, it felt different than when I'd first met the Goddess. The house was no longer shrouded in mist. This was utterly familiar. Same red door. Same snapdragons and sweet William in the front flowerbed.

My face lit up in a huge smile. I was home.

I opened the door and the smell of chocolate chip pancakes filled my nostrils. Coffee, bacon. Sunday morning breakfast at my house.

I practically ran to the back of the house and to the sunny kitchen. I couldn't wait to hug my mom once more. I wanted to wrap my arms around her and bury my face in her hair, all earth and spice. And I wanted to hear her laugh.

But as I neared the kitchen, I stopped and listened to their voices. I heard my mom laugh as if at the funniest joke ever. My dad chuckled and flipped the page of his newspaper. *My dad chuckling?* I couldn't remember the last time I'd heard my dad laugh.

And another familiar voice. I knew the voice as if it was my own. *It is my own.*

I crept down the hall and peered around the corner to get a view of the kitchen scene. My mom stood with her back to me and flipped a pancake on the griddle. My dad was hidden behind his paper with a cup of steaming coffee in front of him. He wasn't a zombie back then, but he did bury himself in his paper every Sunday morning.

And sitting at the breakfast bar counter was another familiar face. It was a seven year old me. I was holding court, trying my best to make her laugh. I loved to see her smile. And from the looks of it, I was doing a good job of it. I had my cheeks stuffed full of pancake and was acting like a monkey while eating. *I loved making her laugh.*

A dilemma occurred to me. If I barged into the kitchen, they were going to wonder who I was. They may not believe me. And if they did believe me, I couldn't very well pick up my life where I left it off. *I'm fourteen now, not seven.* The past already had a me in it.

What do they always say in science fiction movies? If you go back in time, you can screw up the whole time line and change the future. What if my little seven-year-old self saw me and that screwed up her head to know her future?

My heart thumped loudly in my chest. I wanted to run into my mom's arms. She was so close. And it was really her, not a goddess or ghost of her. Her arms would be warm and soft and real, just like I remembered. I wanted just one more hug. One more look into her eyes. One more smile on her face just for me.

Maybe there is a way.

I crept back down the hall and outside. I took a deep breath and rang the doorbell. I knew my dad wouldn't take his nose out of his paper to get the door. And my mom didn't let me answer the door when I was little. *She has to come. She just has to.*

I closed my eyes and waited. I tried to remember to breathe so I didn't pass out.

I heard the door open. I opened my eyes. There she was.

"Hello. Can I help you?"

"I hope so." My voice cracked.

"Do I know you? You look familiar."

"You know me very well, Mom."

She lost her easy smile and all the color drained from her face. She didn't exactly look frightened, but she took on a serious tone.

"Emily?"

"Yes. It's me. Seven years from now."

She yelled back into the house, "I'll be back in a minute. Liam, can you take your pancakes off the griddle?" She shut the door behind her and stepped out onto the porch.

"I'm not even going to ask how, but I do want to know why. Why have you come here?"

What to tell her? If I told her the truth, she'd know she was going to die. That seemed a heavy thing to lay on someone. And then there was the rest. If I told her the truth, she'd know her daughter would be in such grave danger.

"I had to see you again." Tears began to roll down my cheeks.

Then it came. It was the thing I'd missed most about her and the thing I'd most longed for. She enveloped me in her arms and wrapped me in her warmth and her scent. I had grown a lot since I was seven and was almost as tall as her. My head came to her shoulder and I rested it there. I breathed in the warmth of her body and the earthy spiciness of her. She held me for a good long time and I let her. I let her hold me and stroke my hair as I cried and cried and cried.

I didn't want to learn more about streams of time and Dughall and the Netherworld. I didn't want to save the world or be a warrior or a priestess. I wanted to stay there, in that place, with my mother.

I wanted to find a way to stay. *I could be a long lost cousin. That's it! A cousin that they took in.*

"Emily, tell me the truth. No lies between us, ever. Right?"

"No lies."

"Okay then. Why are you here?"

I couldn't get the words out.

"Does something happen to me in the future?"

I nodded yes.

"I see. And you came back here to see me again because you miss me?"

Again, I nodded my agreement with her words.

"But there's more, isn't there? You're involved in something. It must be something big. How else could you do this – I mean be here?"

Again I nodded.

"Are you in trouble?"

"Not exactly trouble. Danger maybe, but I'm not the one causing trouble."

"Good. I mean that you're not in trouble. But danger, I don't like the sound of that."

"I don't want to be in danger anymore. I don't want to go back and save the world. I want to stay here with you."

"Oh Emily, I know you do. I know you do sweetheart." She lightly stroked my cheek. "But you can't stay here. This isn't your time any longer."

"I know, but I can be a cousin or something. We can make up a story, no one will know any better."

"But if you have a mission in your own time and you don't go back, who will complete that task in your place? And what if the task isn't completed at all?"

I didn't have answers for those questions. Okay, I had answers, but I didn't like them. The truth was, there wasn't anyone to take my place. *I can see it now. I'm the only one in my own time and space with the knowledge to take Dughall down.*

"But ... I miss you so much," I sputtered out through huge tears.

My mom's eyes misted too. This was pretty heavy stuff for her to take in. But she handled it with grace as always.

"Emily, listen to me." She put her hands on my shoulders. "You are my daughter, and no matter what time or place we're in, we are always with each other. Don't you know that by now? Don't you know that I'm always here?" She put her hand on my heart.

"I know, I know." Tears spilled down my face. "But it isn't the same. No amount of enlightenment is going to take away the fact that sometimes I just want a hug from my mom."

She hugged me tightly to her again. "I know, dear Em, I know. It must be so hard for you. We're so close."

"You don't know the half of it." I remembered in a flash my years of torture at the hands of Muriel.

"Muriel? Oh no. Well, please try to remember that you are stronger than her Emily."

"I don't know about that. She packs a pretty mean back hand."

"I don't mean just physically. I mean your spirit. It's strong. Inside, Muriel is quite weak."

"I don't think I have to worry about her anymore. Before I left, I think I taught her to back off from me."

"So you're going back?"

"I'm going to have to do the right thing here, aren't I?"

She simply nodded and her eyes filled with tears.

"Don't cry. Oh please, I don't want to see you cry."

"These are just a mother's tears of joy and pride. Look at you! What a beautiful and radiant girl you're growing up to be."

"I don't feel beautiful. Mostly I feel awkward and out of place."

"Oh, that will pass. You're almost through that, I promise. Stand tall and remember who you are – the real you – in here." She again pressed her hand gently to my chest. "And remember Emily, I'm always with you."

"I know. I know that now."

"Good. Now, I have to go back inside and tend to a precocious young girl and what is probably a pan full of burnt pancakes."

"Yeah, he didn't take those off, did he?" I said with a chuckle.

"Emily, take care of yourself. You're stronger than you think."

"Yeah, probably."

We hugged for a long while and finally our tears subsided. She stepped away, turned her back and walked into the house. As she closed the door, I saw her smiling face one last time.

I stood there for what seemed like an eternity. I wasn't sure it was physically possible for me to move my feet, but eventually I got them to walk down the sidewalk.

As I walked, I thought about my mom and how happy it made me to see her again. But soon my thoughts wandered to the Goddess and to Dughall and then to Fanny and Jake and Zombie Man. They truly needed me. They were counting on me, and I couldn't let them down.

As I was thinking that, I realized that I was back in the mist and fog. I looked up and there was Brighid, her shimmering face changing and morphing.

"You found your way back."

"You sound a bit surprised."

"Perhaps. You long so much to be in the presence of the corporeal form of your mother. I admit that I doubted whether your devotion to your friends and father was enough to draw you back."

"I'm not sure what drew me back, but I'm here anyway."

"Yes, and I am glad that you chose to come back. Did you enjoy visiting your past?"

"Well yes, in a way. But I see what you meant. It is tricky business. There was no place for me there. So I'm guessing if I go to my future it will be the same. I'll already be there?"

"Yes."

"I'm afraid I gave my mom too much information. She knows that she's going to die. Will that affect the timeline? Will it change things?"

"It unfolds how it unfolds."

"I'm not sure I'm ready, Goddess, to take on Dughall. I don't know what to do yet. I feel lost."

"You will know when it is time."

"But that's just it, we don't have time. I need to act now. I've already been here so long."

"Emily, you know and yet you do not allow yourself to see. Did you not just experience with your own senses your ability to slip into any time that you want?"

"Yes, but if I'm already there – well, I hardly see the sense of it."

"Ah, but for many months of your Earth time, you have been here, not there. Here in a place of no time."

The realization of what she was saying took root in my brain. She just said many earth months.

But then that second part. If I had been in the Netherworld, then I wasn't really in the human world. *Will the mind trip of this place never end?*

"So you're saying that I can just slip into whatever time I want since I left and voila! Problem solved?"

"Yes. You know this to be true."

It was like a large weight lifted off my shoulders. I didn't have to hurry. I could take my time. There was no time in the Netherworld. All the time and yet no time.

"Okay, so now what? What else must I know before I can take care of our Dughall problem?"

"Now fair Emily, you must rest. It has been a long time since you allowed your body to sleep. Rest and when you wake, we will complete the training you need for your task."

The Goddess pointed to a door that appeared out of the mist. I opened it and went inside to a cozy room with a large bed covered in pillows and a plush duvet cover. I crawled in, covered up and drifted off instantly to a deep sleep.

I needed that rest. It was the last time I slept for a very long time.

52 DUGHALL AT THE LHC

"Sir, I think there's a bit of any error in your instructions for the experiment."

"There are no errors," Dughall coolly replied.

"But Sir, if we enter the codes you wrote, it will pulse the particle streams at a very high frequency."

"Yes."

"But Sir, we don't know what will happen to the machinery at such a high frequency pulse."

"I do."

The young man stood with his mouth hanging slightly open. Was his boss a mad man? Or was he as in command as he seemed?

"Are you going to input the program or shall I find someone more capable?" Dughall asked.

"I ... I can do it. I will do it. It's just ... well I have to tell you my concern here. No one has tested this. We don't know what will happen down there."

"Mr. ... what's your name?"

"Schaeffer, Sir. Ted Schaeffer."

"Mr. Ted Schaeffer, I am well aware of the capabilities of this machine. I would not order this program if I was not sure of the outcome. Now, you have exactly one minute to get to your station and click at the keys or I will find someone to replace Mr. Ted Schaeffer."

Ted Schaeffer practically ran from the room. He was uneasy going about the day's work, but he was even more uneasy staying in the room with his project supervisor. He knew it was crazy, but he had a strange feeling that his boss wouldn't just fire him from the project, but meant to harm him if he didn't comply.

Once Ted Schaeffer had left the room, Macha said, "Dughall, you're enjoying every minute of this, aren't you?"

"Why, whatever do you mean dear little Macha?" Dughall batted his eyes coyly at her.

"You know what I mean. Toying with the humans."

"Toying with Mr. Ted Schaeffer? Why ever would you say that?" Dughall had a hint of a smirky smile on his face. When Dughall smiled he looked like a cross between a snake and hyena.

"You enjoy sitting back, like the cat with a mouse, stringing them along, luring them step by step to your trap."

"Ah, I am not setting a trap for them, Macha. They are of no consequence to me one way or the other. But if they get caught in a trap, well so be it."

Dughall sat back and monitored the progress of Mr. Ted Schaeffer. He had never seen a human move his fingers so fast on the keys of a computer machine. The man typed as if his life depended on it. Dughall smiled to himself at this thought because, of course, Mr. Ted Schaeffer's life did depend on it.

53 HOSPITALITY, CERN STYLE

Liam, Fanny and Jake arrived at CERN but made it no farther than the first security gate.

Fanny had suggested that they arrange for a tour to get inside. But Jake said that plan was too 'Scooby Doo' and Liam had agreed with him.

Instead, they went with Liam's straightforward plan. Since Liam was a theoretical physicist, he suggested that he ask to speak to someone inside. He had thought that they would listen to him.

But Liam was wrong. Apparently CERN thinks anyone who shows up at their gate claiming there's a terrorist inside their compound is either a loon or a terrorist themselves.

Why the guard gate went for option #2 when approached by a middle-aged guy and two teenagers from Chicago, one can never know. They weren't sent away, but they weren't allowed in either. Instead, they were escorted to a separate building by military-type security guards.

Liam felt like he was being hauled to Guantanamo Bay. Branded a potential terrorist meant CERN could throw them in a room without windows, no one phone call, and pretty much hold them there was long as they pleased.

"This is crazy!" Fanny yelled when they were finally alone in their 'hospitality suite'.

"Shh! You want them to hear?" Jake scolded.

"I don't care if they hear. They've got their heads up their butts so far they're probably hearing bowel sounds. Oh, sorry Mr. Adams."

"It's okay Fanny. I have to say I agree with you."

"I don't care where their heads are, we gotta' get out of here," Jake whispered.

"Captain Obvious, as usual," Fanny replied. "And why are you whispering?"

"'Cause, Einstein, this place is probably bugged like crazy."

The three looked at each other silently.

"Jake's probably right," Liam whispered. "If you think you have terrorists in your custody, you'd want to spy on them while you're giving them your 'hospitality.'"

That's what the guards called it. They said, "Please enjoy our hospitality while we check out your credentials," then they locked the door of the small tin can of a building. It had only one room filled with four bunk beds and a small bathroom.

The situation seemed so improbable to Liam. *What kind of credentials are two fourteen-year-old kids supposed to have anyway?* Their reality hit Liam like a ton of bricks. He was harboring two runaways, one of who faked a passport (federal felony) and both of who recently robbed an ancient grave of a protected antiquity (an international crime).

"What was I thinking, bringing you two here with me? I was trying to keep you kids out of trouble. I may have just gotten you into even bigger trouble," he said.

"It's not your fault, Mr. Adams," Jake offered.

"Yeah, we came 'cause we wanted to," said Fanny. "We'd have followed you here even if you said we couldn't come."

"But this isn't your fight. It's mine now."

"Wrong. It's our fight. We promised Em. We're not going to abandon her now," said Jake.

"Yeah, we've come too far to be dealt out," said Fanny.

"Well, now I don't think you could be 'dealt out' even if you wanted to be."

"If only they believed us," Jake said.

"Yeah, 'cause if they don't, then they're going to get an unwelcome surprise." Fanny made a slashing motion across her throat.

"Gee, Fan, no wonder we were thrown into this tin can. You're going around making threatening statements and talking smack."

"I'm not threatening. I'm just saying we told them the truth. If they'd bother to remove their head from the dark place it's in, they might investigate and find out there's a guy in their facility that wasn't there a few weeks ago. And if they'd only check they'd see he doesn't quite add up." Fanny raised her voice to make sure any listening ears would be sure to hear her.

"You're probably right Fanny," Liam said.

"But what's he going to do here, Mr. Adams? And if he's here, how'd he get in. As we've seen, security is high."

"My guess is he faked credentials to get inside."

"Prolly killed someone," Fanny offered.

"Now why would you say that? You're so melodramatic."

"You heard Hindergog's story. This guy's like evil incarnate. He killed plenty of people back then, in Saorla's time. You think he wouldn't kill some wimpy scientists dude and steal his cred to get in here?"

"You've got a point," Jake conceded. "Okay, so maybe he could find a way in. But then what? I mean, how could he open a portal? For Em to cross over she needed to be at the portal at the Sacred Grove and she had to have the torc *and* say a magick spell."

Liam had pondered Jake's question nonstop since they'd left Dublin. He felt close to an answer, but it was still hovered just outside his reach.

The three sat in the bunkhouse for several hours before Liam gave in to exhaustion and stretched out on one of the bunks and dozed off.

Liam slept fitfully on the hard cot and dreamed. He was jolted wide-awake by the words 'pulsed resonant frequencies' repeating in his mind. It was as if someone had shouted the words into his ear and woke him up.

Fanny and Jake were asleep. Liam bolted up and shook them both awake.

"I've got it. I know how he's going to do it," he nearly shouted.

"What? How?" Jake asked sleepily as he yawned.

"By pulsing resonant frequencies," he stated matter-of-factly.

Fanny and Jake looked at Liam as if he had suddenly sprouted a second head.

"Huh?" asked Fanny.

"The giant magnets of the LHC. That's why he's here. If he pulses the frequencies of the magnets at an extremely high rate of speed ... It might just work."

"I don't get it," said Jake. "What would that do?"

"Well, it has been largely theoretical you see. The Philadelphia experiment and other more fringe stuff is based on this principle. It's theorized by some that if you rapidly pulse and focus really large electromagnetic frequencies, you could transport an object to other places instantaneously."

"Or people?"

"Yes, or people. At least that's what some have theorized. But it has been fringe science, not something that anyone with credentials has worked on."

"Okay, you lost me at the word pulse," said Fanny sleepily.

"Shut up Fan, this is serious."

"Don't get your tiny pants in a twist Jake. I don't follow all you're saying Mr. Adams, but if you think you've got it, I believe you."

"Thanks Fanny. But I don't know what good any of it does us when we're stuck in the hospitality suite."

54 DUGHALL AT CERN

As Liam, Fanny and Jake tried to find a way out of their situation, in a room littered with dirty coffee cups and half-empty Coke cans, a bored young security officer listened to the idle chatter of his American 'guests'. He spoke very little English so he didn't see the point in him being the one assigned to this task. *These people must not be much of a threat or else they would have assigned someone else.* He was low man on the totem pole so he always got stuck with the cession de merde.

Little did the three American 'guests' know that they needn't hush their voices or whisper to keep secrets. They also didn't know that loudly emphasizing a point wouldn't help either. For all intents and purposes, their communication was completely unmonitored, a fact which proved to be a helpful turn of events for Dughall.

Mr. Ted Schaeffer's hands worked feverishly as he typed the coded instructions to make the machine a mile underground perform as commanded. The instructions were highly unusual and Ted Schaeffer knew it.

Most of the experiments at CERN were straightforward enough. Power it up, cool it way down, and when everything was a go, accelerate particles, collect the bits of stuff created by the collisions, then send all the data to a huge conglomeration of computers around the world to crunch numbers.

An immense and complex machine but a relatively straightforward idea. Spin, collide and collect.

But the experiment that his strange new supervisor handed him was unlike anything else. He would have gone over Mr. Dughall's head too if it weren't for the nagging feeling that his life depended on his fingers quickly and accurately entering the codes commanded by his new boss.

Ted Schaeffer wasn't a physicist so it wasn't his job to know all the intricacies of the reason for an experiment. But he was an engineer, and he knew the machine. And because he knew the machine, he knew that oscillating the frequencies of the magnetic energy created underground in the collider as rapidly as requested by Mr. Dughall could have disastrous effects.

But the guy seemed like he knew what he was doing. He was so sure of himself. *Maybe I'm wrong.* Ted Schaeffer cast his doubt aside and typed like a madman.

Even at the feverish pace that Mr. Ted Schaeffer typed, it took days for him to enter the complex instructions required to order the machine to perform as Dughall required. Dughall's impatience almost got the better of him. It took extraordinary self-control, not to mention a swift kick from Macha, to keep Dughall from strangling Ted Schaeffer a few times.

"Remember your prize," Macha said. Her tiny body delivered an amazingly strong kick to Dughall's behind just in time to stop him from putting his hands around Ted Schaeffer's neck and squeezing the life from him.

It took weeks of work at CERN, not to mention over a millennium in the *Umbra Nihili*, but finally the day was at hand. All was aligned. Finally, Dughall would triumph.

"Macha, repeat to me the instructions one more time so that I am sure that your tiny faerie brain gets it right," hissed Dughall.

"After more than a thousand years of putting up with you, I still do not know why I do, you awful piece of rotted human flesh," Macha retorted. "I will repeat your instructions though even a faerie with half its wits would find it no harder than beating their wings."

"Just tell me woman. We have only one shot."

"All right, all right. It is simple. In one hour, you will make your way down to the accelerator and drink the potion I brewed for you. Remember, the protective effect will last only five minutes at most, so you must be right on the mark. If you are there any longer, you will freeze instantly."

"I know that Macha. You are telling me my part. What I am concerned about, my little gnat, is that you remember your part."

"At exactly the appointed time, I will press that green button and put in the code you have typed for me. I will hit the enter button then sit back and watch all hell break loose."

"If all goes right, yes, you will have quite a show. Hundreds of crazed humans will go insane with fear at the same time. I am only sorry that I will miss out on the fun."

"If all goes as planned, you will be through the portal and on your way. But Dughall, if this works ... "

"What do you mean if? My calculations are exact. It will work."

"Yes, well when it works, what will happen here? The portal you create will be tremendously unstable. It could rip the fabric of space time."

"That is the idea my dear Macha."

"But what will happen to it? Will it grow? Or collapse on itself?"

Dughall had expected her question and was surprised that it had taken Macha so long to ask it. She was an annoying flea of a faerie at times, but she was exceedingly bright for her kind. The tiny remnant of humanity still hidden somewhere inside Dughall had some unpleasant feelings about what may happen to Macha when he created the anomaly.

The truth was that there would be a mighty explosion that would destroy the machine the humans had spent so much money and time to create. But since it would occur a mile underground, it likely would have no effect on the humans up top.

But that wouldn't be the end of the story. And he couldn't bring himself to tell Macha the truth. If creating the portal took the life of Macha as well as all the others at CERN that was of no matter to Dughall. It was a sacrifice that he was willing for them to make.

55 STUCK INSIDE A TIN CAN

"We can't stay in this tin can forever," whined Fanny. "We have to do something."

"How long do you think they can legally hold us here?" asked Jake.

"I don't think they're concerned with the legality of holding us," said Liam.

"These idiots aren't going to stop Dughall. We've got to do it," said Fan.

"Do you have any ideas? Because the last idea I had got us into indefinite detention," Liam said.

"First we gotta' escape this place."

"Good luck with that," said Jake.

Fanny ignored Jake's remark. "I've been laying here looking up at that vent and thinkin' I can fit into that. It's got to go somewhere."

"And what about the cameras up there watching us?" Jake pointed to the security cameras mounted from the ceiling.

Fanny thumbed her nose directly at the nearest ceiling mounted camera.

"Nice, real nice. We're in serious trouble and you're being a wise ass. Are you trying to get us sent to prison?"

"Okay, genius, since you're so smart, why don't you come up with a way to divert their attention while I shimmy my butt through that vent so I can try to find a way to get us out of here."

Jake and Fanny's bickering became like a background buzz to Liam as he concentrated on the potential of Fanny's plan.

"Hey, you two stop arguing for a minute. The cameras don't move"

"Yeah, so?" asked Jake.

"So, that means that we can move them. Then, when none of them are focused on the vent, Fanny can get into it without being seen."

"Brilliant Mr. A," said Fanny.

"I don't know about brilliant, but it's worth a shot."

Liam boosted Jake up so that he could adjust all the cameras, taking care not to be seen while doing it. It wasn't easy, but within a half an hour, they cameras were repositioned so that none of them looked directly on the vent Fanny planned to climb into.

"Ready, Fan?" Liam asked.

"As ready as I'll ever be. What should I look for?"

"A room without anyone in it would be nice," Jake said.

"I know that nub. I mean, any particular kind of room you can think of?"

"If you can find a supply room or equipment room, that might be a safe bet," Liam offered.

"Okay, the man with the plan, that's what I'm talking about. Well, here goes."

Jake and Liam boosted Fanny up to the vent. She easily opened the vent screen and hoisted herself into the airshaft.

"Yuck! This place is disgusting."

"Oh please, it can't be any worse than your room," said Jake.

"Shut it nerd."

That was the last thing they heard Fanny say. Jake and Liam sat quietly and listened to Fanny's body banging the metal airshaft as she shimmied along. After about five minutes, it was once again silent as

Fanny disappeared into the bowels of CERN. All they could do was sit and wait for Fanny to return with a key so they could escape their tin can prison.

56 DUGHALL'S PLAN IN ACTION

With the help of Macha's enchantments, Dughall was able to slip past any watching eyes and into the elevator shaft. He rode the elevator for many minutes as it made its way a mile underground to the belly of the giant collider. Dughall had synchronized his watch to the collider's clock many times. He'd waited over a thousand years to achieve his goal. He wasn't about to let a stupid mistake stand between him and the portal.

Patience was not Dughall's forte, but the task required precision. He could wait a few minutes.

As he stared at his watch, it seemed as though time moved backwards. He waited by the door to the collider corridor for the right moment to down the draught Macha had brewed for him. He stared so intently at his watch that it almost hypnotized him. Dughall nearly missed the exact moment to drink the potion.

It is time. Dughall chugged the vile and viscous liquid down in one big gulp. *Macha made this taste foul just to spite me.*

As planned, Dughall waited exactly one minute then detonated the explosive he had planted at the door hinges. The small explosion was enough to blast open the time locked steel door. It was time to test whether Macha's potion worked or not. At -271°, if it didn't work, he wouldn't have time to think about it.

Dughall pushed the door off of its blasted hinges. He knew as soon as he did that Macha's potion had worked. If it hadn't, the deep chill of the collider would have frozen him nearly instantly. Instead, it was as if there was an insulating bubble around his body that protected him from the deep freeze. But Dughall had not a second to spare. He raced down the interior corridor of the circular collider as fast as his legs could carry him. He knew that it was about a quarter mile to the five-story high mega magnet that he was looking for. He had timed himself and knew that if he ran as fast as he could, he could make it there in about two minutes.

Dughall didn't need to search for the magnet. Dughall knew as soon as he saw it that his plan had worked. He had reached his destination. He could see the portal and there was no one to stop him.

Though he had only about one, maybe two minutes to spare, Dughall couldn't help but stare at the tremendous sight. The giant superconducting magnet was itself enough to inspire awe. Though built by human hands, it was a masterpiece of technology and had a beauty of its own. Miles of wires, circuits and electronics bound together in a colorful symmetry.

But topping it by far was the extraordinary beauty of the portal that lay before him. In the center of the giant magnet was a small hole, no larger than a small child, dwarfed by the size of the magnet itself. A silvery mist poured from the hole. It was both ethereal and majestic. Dughall also heard a faint hissing sound, like electricity flowing through power lines built by humans to conduct electricity from one place to another.

In the few seconds that he had stared at the portal it grew twice its size. He knew that he had less than a minute before it became unstable and was gone forever. *I must act now or lose the opportunity I have waited so long for.*

If anyone else had been in the corridor with Dughall at that moment, they would have seen something truly rare and a bit disturbing. Dughall smiled.

57 ESCAPE FROM A TIN CAN

Fanny had been gone only about half an hour when Jake and Liam heard what sounded like a large clap of thunder.

"What was that?" asked Jake.

Liam quickly walked the five steps required to reach the tiny barred window and looked outside. *Not a cloud in the sky.*

"There's no weather out there. It must have been an explosion," he said.

They looked at each other in silence for a moment. Both knew that what they had heard was an explosion and they knew who had caused it.

"Are you thinking what I'm thinking?" asked Jake.

"If you're thinking that that clump nugget is trying his best to blow this place to smithereens, yes, that's what I'm thinking."

"And are you also thinking that we can't sit here one more minute?"

"Yep, I'm right with you. We may have a chance now. With the explosion, they're probably distracted. Old Dughall might have given us the diversion we've been waiting for."

"Right. But we're locked in here."

"The only way out is the way Fanny left and there's no way I'll be able to fit through there," said Liam.

A few minutes later, they heard a scratching and thumping noise from overhead.

"You're not locked in anymore," said Fanny. She jumped down from the air vent.

"Fan, it's good to see you and all, but you were supposed to unlock us from the outside."

"Don't get your shorts in a knot, Jakester. I've got the keys." Fanny jingled the keys at Jake. "We can unlock it from the inside. I didn't want to be seen coming in that way."

All three ran to the door. Fanny's fingers shook as she tried to work the keys to find the right one to unlock the door.

"Hurry, Fan," said Jake.

"I'm going as fast as I can man. There's like 20 keys on this thing. Hey, did you guys hear that explosion?"

"Yes," answered Liam.

"You guessing it's that butthead Dughall?" Fanny asked.

"That's our guess."

"Yeah, so hurry. We gotta' get to the control room of this thing and make sure they're shutting down everything before the whole place blows," Jake implored.

Fanny found the right key and the door swung open into a deserted hallway. They ran down the corridor and found the door to the outside. They had been holed up in that tiny room plus a bath for days. All three took a moment to breathe in the fresh air and feel the warm sun on their skin as they stepped into the outdoors. But they knew time was not a luxury for them at that moment.

"This way," said Fanny. "When I was taking my little trip through the air shaft I think I found out where to go."

They ran as fast as they could, following Fanny closely. They weren't the only ones running. People were coming out of every building at the facility running to exactly the spot Fanny led them.

"By the looks of it, we're heading in the right direction," Liam said.

They followed the crowds and, like salmon swimming upstream together, soon found themselves in the thick of command central. It would seem that after an explosion in their facility that CERN would go to high alert for terrorists. Instead, the explosion and ensuing alarms and shut down protocols made such a huge distraction, the trio was able to breeze into the main operations room without anyone trying to stop them.

In the middle of it all was one poor young guy getting his rear chewed out by a whole gang of scientists. Security guards surrounded his chair as gray-hairs fired question after question at him. He looked like he was about to vomit on their shoes.

The three fought their way through the crowd to get a closer look.

"You entered these codes, even though you knew that they were likely to cause a problem?"

"Yes, Sir ... I mean Mr. Dughall ... well, he ordered it, Sir. And I figured he knew what he was doing as he's the physicist here, not me."

"You figured? Well you figured wrong, young man. Now we have a class A mess down there. The whole of magnet number two is blown to bits and who knows what else is destroyed."

"Yeah, it will take weeks for it to warm up enough for anyone to go down and have a look," offered another scientist.

"What do you want us to do with this fella?'" asked one of the security guards.

"Probably ought to take him to a holding room until the police can question him thoroughly about this," said the man who appeared to be the head of the operation.

"Wait," Liam shouted.

All at once, the grey-hairs turned to see who was interceding in their business.

"Wait," he said again as he approached the small crowd around the poor chap in the chair. "We have to stop him," Liam said.

"Stop who? And who is this guy? Hey, you don't have credentials to be here," said the head scientist.

"Look, we came here to warn you about Dughall, but your security guards there wouldn't listen to us. We've been here … how long have we been here?"

Jake looked at his watch. "Two days."

"Yeah, like he said, we came here two days ago to warn you about this guy and your fellas there locked us up in one of your 'hospitality suites.'"

The head guy swiftly turned his eyes on the security guards and glared even harder at them than he had glared at the poor man in the chair.

"You knew of a possible breach in our security two days ago, and you did nothing!" he shouted.

"Well their story Sir, if you heard it, well we thought they were either kooks or terrorists themselves trying to make a diversion."

The head guy turned to me. "Who are you?"

"My name is Liam Adams. I'm a theoretical physicist from the University of Chicago. It's a long story how I got this information about Mr. Dughall, but you have to believe me, that small explosion was just the start. We have to get down there to stop him, now."

"Mr. Adams, I don't know how you know something that our so-called intelligence here didn't pick up on, but if you're a physicist, then you must know that we can't just pop down there. The temperature will kill anyone who tries to enter the corridor. If your Mr. Dughall tried to go down there, he'd die instantly. So I don't think we have to worry about him any longer."

"Well, on that you'd be wrong," chimed in Fanny.

"Who is this girl and why is she here?" asked the scientist.

"She's with me. Look, I know this is hard to believe. I didn't believe any of this at first either. But this guy Dughall, he's not exactly … human."

There was a silence in the room so thick you could cut it. Then the small group started with furtive looks at one another. The security guards said, 'See, we told you he's a kook', with just their eyes.

"He was human, like a thousand years ago, but now ... well he's been brought back from the near dead so I guess you'd call him a mummy." said Jake.

"Or a zombie," offered Fanny.

"Okay, I've had enough of this. I don't need any more distractions. Security, take Mr. Schaeffer here and these American guests back to holding for questioning by the police."

Just as they were about to be hauled off again for another stint of detention, there came a loud shout above the noise of the crowd.

"Sir, Sir. You gotta' see this. You're not going to believe it," said one of the security guards at a monitor on the other side of the room. The whole crowd shifted to the other side of the room where the guard was watching a security tape.

"What have you got?" asked the lead scientist.

"Here is the tape from the camera focused on magnet housing number two, the one that exploded. Look here at two minutes, ten seconds before the explosion."

All eyes stared at the screen as it clearly showed a tall, dark haired man walking toward the magnet. The camera was trained on the magnet housing so it showed the man only from behind. But clearly there was a man walking toward it.

Within seconds, a more extraordinary thing showed on the screen. There, in the magnet itself, a small hole was forming. It wasn't a hole from an explosion, but was instead like a window opening that appeared to look into another world entirely. As each second passed, the opening grew larger and larger as what appeared to be fog billowed out.

And then, clear as day, Dughall ran into the center of that opening and disappeared. He was there one instant, gone the next.

Within seconds of Dughall's disappearing act, the portal that he had created exploded. The camera picked up the fire and shrapnel coming toward it, then nothing. The explosion knocked out the camera too.

For a second time in less than ten minutes, you could hear a pin drop in a crowd of no less than twenty-five people. And then all eyes turned to Liam, Fanny and Jake. There was an awkward, stunned silence until the lead scientist spoke in a hushed voice.

"I don't know how you knew these things, Mr. Adams, but all that you stated appears to be true. I've seen the evidence for it, but I still can't believe it. But somehow this man ... or thing ... was able to breach our security, obtain a willing partner to enter his malicious code, and enter a facility cooled to minus 271° without freezing to death.

"And to top it off, he created an anomaly that somehow created what appears to be a wormhole or transportation device of some kind. The perpetrator of this horrendous crime has fled from justice."

"Sir, I don't mean to stop you, but the other truth is that what he created down there is extremely unstable. I've done some calculations while in your holding tank and we need to act fast to get this thing under control. We're wasting precious time here."

"You've already started calculations?" he asked.

"Yes, well, as I said, I had a pretty fair idea what he was up to. I started working out calculations for what would likely happen if he succeeded and, well, it's not a pretty sight."

"Mr. Adams, I sincerely apologize for all that you and your kids have been through. I need to impose on you again though and ask if you can please work with my team here. Share with them all that you know. Bring them up to speed so that we can nip this thing in the bud before it causes more damage."

It was the invitation Liam had waited for. Liam was in his element when working on a problem or solving equations. He had felt so helpless and incompetent at helping Emily. *Now I can be of use to her and hopefully bring her back safely.*

"I'm happy to help however I can."

"Okay then, let's get going," said the lead scientist. He immediately created teams and divvied up work.

Liam dove in and got to work with his team. But after a few minutes, he remembered Fanny and Jake. Liam went over to the corner of the room where Jake and Fanny stood, their eyes tired and their faces pale with lack of sleep.

"You guys are dead on your feet. Why don't I see if there's an expendable intern or someone here to take you to town, get a hotel room with a comfy bed and some warm food?"

"I'm not going anywhere," said Jake firmly.

"But Jake, there's no reason for you kids to stay here. You've done everything you can. Besides, it's safer back in town."

"I'm not leaving," said Jake.

"Yeah, we've come this far. We want to be here if Emily comes," said Fanny.

"She'll be here, Fanny," Jake said testily.

"Okay, okay Jake. Don't knot up your panties again. I'm just sayin', I thought she'd make it here in time to stop him. I'm worried about her."

"I know you want to do everything you can to help Emily. We all do. But right now, there's nothing you can do here. This is work for an old fart scientist like me," Liam said with a wink. "The best thing for you to do right now is to get some well deserved rest and food."

"Mr. Adams, don't you get it? I'm not leaving without Emily," Jake said.

Liam knew he'd lost the battle. "Okay, okay. You can stay. But just hang out back here, out of the way. And promise me if there are more explosions that you'll run, okay? Run as fast as you can out of here and don't wait for me or for Emily. Do you promise?"

Both Fanny and Jake nodded.

Liam wasn't sure it was the right thing to do to let them stay. *Maybe I should have fought harder to get them to safety.* Not only did he feel responsible for them, but after all they'd been through together, he had begun to think of Jake and Fanny as part of his own family. He just wanted them to be safe. But if he didn't get back to work and find out how to stop the anomaly, they wouldn't be safe even at a hotel in town. No one would be safe.

58 DUGHALL AND THE PORTAL

Dughall expected pain or at least some discomfort from passing through the portal like he had felt going to the *Umbra Nihili*. Instead, it was painless. It was like walking through a door. One moment he was running through the collider corridor toward the large magnet. The next he was running in a land made entirely of silvery mist and fog.

The entities of the Netherworld, thinking they can send a mere child to stop me. What fools they are. And where is she? The whelp did not even make it to the collider.

Dughall briefly considered that he should look for her, but he quickly dismissed it. He didn't need to worry about her or anyone. No one knew where he was going. All that was left to do was to still his mind and focus on the time and place he longed to be. He knew he would end up there instantly so long as he could focus his mind. He had no worry that he would not be able to accomplish the proper concentration. He'd had over a thousand years in the *Umbra Nihili* to practice focusing his mind.

Dughall remembered the time and place he wanted to be. He had obsessed about it for so many years that it was easy to put himself there in his mind. All he had to do was close his eyes and picture the scene.

It was a bright, sunny day in a small village in the south of Italy. He was a fourteen-year-old boy walking home from his morning duties for his master, ready to enjoy his midday meal with his beloved mother. He smelled the scent of the cedar trees mixed with the smell of olives and honeysuckle climbing the walls of the cottages he passed. He was jubilant because it was the day he planned to take his mother and escape their slavery.

Dughall knew exactly where to jump into the stream of time. He had dreamt of it for years. Dughall longed to see the eyes of his mother's attacker and take the man's life. Dughall looked forward to boundless joy when he finally did what he'd wanted to do for countless years. He would plunge a knife deep into the man's chest and twist it. He looked forward to watching the man suffer as the man had Dughall's mother to suffer.

Dughall took a deep breath and opened his eyes. Before him was the familiar room of the confinement of his youth. There was a small hearth but there was no midday meal cooking. He did not waste a second lingering in the small outer room. He knew the action was in the next room.

Just as he had done so many years before, Dughall walked as quietly as a leopard, taking care not to show himself. But he heard no whimper from his broken mother. *Excellent. I am here in time.*

His knife was at the ready. Dughall could have brought with him a very sharp, excellent hunting knife from the future time. He chose, instead, to use the same type of dull work knife of his youth. Anything too sharp and precise would hasten the jackal's death.

He turned the corner knife in hand, ready to take the man by surprise. But as he entered the room, he did not see the man who he intended to kill. What he saw instead was a surprise to him, and a most unfortunate complication.

59 HIS DEEPEST DESIRE

I don't think Dughall could have looked more surprised. His dark hair and heavy eyebrows rested over a gaunt face that looked like it had been chiseled out of stone. His eyes landed first on me. His look of surprise quickly gave way to a look of pure rage. I think he would have leapt upon me and killed me on the spot if his mother hadn't spoken.

"Is this my son?" she asked incredulously.

Dughall's eyes immediately shifted to the woman standing across from me. At over six feet tall, his frame towered over her mere five-foot body. Her jet-black hair was matted to her face by sweat and she looked care worn. But beneath the wear was a woman of incomparable beauty in any time.

"Mother, oh dearest mother," Dughall said at last. He had a softness in his voice that seemed impossible from such a hard and brooding face. He went to her and knelt down. Dughall rested his head against her stomach and embraced her. I watched as she gently caressed his hair.

"My son, look how you have grown. I do not understand what magick brings you or this angel who has slain my attacker to me, but of both, I am most glad," she said.

It was at that moment that Dughall looked down beside him and finally saw the dead body of the man that had been his mother's night 'companion'. Instead of being pleased that I had taken the jerk out for him, Dughall looked on me with fury.

"How dare you come here and defile my childhood home? You witch!"

"Dughall, mind your tongue," his mother said. "This angel of the future came just in time. That man was set on doing me great harm. I do not think I would be alive if she had not come when she did."

"I know he was going to do you harm, dearest mother. That is why I came back to this time. I came to stop the brute from slaying you mother.

"Oh mother, you have no idea what I have been through. You do not know of my suffering, my death, and the countless years of horrific ennui as I waited. I had to bide my time. All that I have done I did so that I could come back to this time and prevent this jackal from taking your life. But this Brighid's whelp witch from the future has ruined it all. She has ruined my moment, mother!"

"Dughall my sweet, nothing is ruined. Be glad for the help dear son. I am well and unharmed. You can go peacefully back to your time knowing that I am safe."

"Back to my time? Mother, I have no time. Do you not see? I belong here. I always have. You are a part of me, Mother, and I a part of you. And I have waited, mother, oh so long I have waited."

I could swear I saw tears come to his eyes. *Is it possible that Dughall has feelings? Is it possible that he could be human again?*

"Dearest one, do not fret. You can stay. We will figure it out. Do not worry any more dear son." Dughall's mother continued to stroke his hair.

"Yes, mother, and together we will rule this land. Oh, I have dreamed it and planned it for so long and now, all the forces are aligned. Now is the time mother. You will be a slave no more. You will be a queen."

"With the help of the angel, our slavery will end today to be sure. But a queen? Why I have no such sights."

"This child save you? But mother, *I* will free you. And together we will rule, I promise you that. I will make those who have held us suffer as we have suffered. Revenge will be ours!"

She took his head in her hands, one palm on each side of his face and looked long and deep into his eyes.

"You are my son, that is true, but a part of you has surely been lost."

"What are you saying mother? I am your son, as I have always been."

"I did not teach my son to seek revenge and glory."

"But you did, Mother. You always told me that I was exceptional and destined for greatness. You taught me to bide my time until I could prove myself."

"Yes, it is true that I always saw in you a potential for greatness. But I never taught you to seek revenge or to inflict suffering on others. Is that what you thought I wanted for you? My poor son. All these years that is what you thought I wanted for my dear son?"

"Of course mother, to rule over the land. We will have riches and power. And with all that I have learned from the future, we will rule over a vast empire. The entire world will be ours. Do you not want to be a queen mother? To have all that you desire?"

"Dughall, my son, my heart's only desire has been to see you happy. Not pleasure from gold adornments or beautiful women on your arm or power. No, all I have wanted for my son is that he know happiness within himself." She put her hand over his heart as she spoke.

"What are you saying mother? Are you saying that you will not come with me? That you will not help me as I conquer this land then rule by my side?"

"No Dughall, I have no desire to build an empire with you. I am content to receive the help of this angel to escape my captivity then live with my son, young Dughall, in an honest life. That is all I have ever wanted."

Dughall's face looked as crestfallen as a dog that sat, begged, stayed and rolled over then didn't get the promised treat. While still kneeling, he looked away from us both for a moment then slowly rose.

Dughall may have learned a lot of things while in the *Umbra Nihili*, but he apparently didn't learn to close his mind to the sight. In a flash, I knew what he meant to do.

The jeweled dagger that Hindergog had given me was sheathed at my waist. I held the Sword of the Order in my hand, its blade still wet with the blood of the man I'd already killed.

Dughall grabbed the sword from the sword belt of the dead man. It was a fat, well-worn broadsword. It wasn't nearly as elegant of a weapon as the Singing Sword in my hand, but if I gave Dughall an opening, he'd be able to kill me with it.

Dughall must have been stronger than his body looked. He had no problem picking up the large, heavy sword and he was able to hold it with one hand. Dughall wasted no time and lunged at me. I easily parried his attack and stepped to the side. His sword caught only air.

His eyes were dark with anger as he slashed at me. I used my sword defensively and easily blocked his swing.

"I am not your enemy, Dughall. I was only trying to help you."

"You lie. Your so-called Goddess is a spiteful wench. She sent you to shame me."

"No. That's not how it is at all."

He thrust his blade at me again and nearly nicked me, but I stepped backward and his attempt to run me through missed by a few inches. *Close call.*

I had stepped backward as far as I could. My back was against the wall of the tiny room. Dughall's looked changed from anger to amusement. He could see that my back was against the wall.

I chanced a quick look up to see if I could fly over him. The ceiling was too low. If I tried to perform a somersault, I'd end up bashing my head against the ceiling. My only option was to fight and hope that my newfound strength was enough to fend him off.

Dughall came at me again with all the fire and fury that he had saved up and intended to unleash on the man who lie dead on the dirt floor. My arms moved as if on autopilot. I tried my best to be in the flow of things as Madame Wong had taught me. I was alert and aware.

At least I thought that I was. But in a brief moment of inattention, Dughall's heavy sword knocked the Sword of the Order out of my hands. It caught me by surprise and for a second, I thought myself a goner. But then something inside me clicked and I remembered the dagger sheathed at my waist.

I moved to the side, dodged and ducked his attempts to kill me as I fumbled with the sheath at my waist. My hands were shaky as I tried to open the fabric fastener and retrieve the dagger. I kept moving as Dughall continued to swing at me. He landed a solid slice to my left arm and I could feel the warm blood trickling down my forearm and onto my hand. I finally got the clasp open and grabbed the dagger. Panic began to set in as I contemplated how I'd take out a man wielding a long sword with a short dagger.

Size does not matter. Focus. Be one with Akasha.

It was Madame Wong's voice in my head. My months of meditating, of defending myself against the swats from her cane, the countless hours chopping wood. It had all been for that moment.

I took a deep breath and tried my best to ground myself. I allowed the cleansing air to fill me as I focused on being one with the stream.

Be one with Akasha.

I could feel the air molecules move before I saw his blade come at me. My arms moved instinctively as I blocked his blow with the small but strong dagger.

The sight stone on the hilt of the dagger began to glow and it changed from milky white to as clear as mountain water. In an instant, I could see in my mind's eye what Dughall would do next. I knew what angle he'd come at me and I could see where my dagger needed to land.

I thrust upward and knelt at the same time. I heard the whoosh of Dughall's sword catching air as I felt my dagger find purchase in Dughall's gut.

My hand still held the dagger as Dughall fell to his knees. His face was nearly level with mine. His mouth was open with shock as he looked down at the wound that blossomed crimson through his shirt.

"How?" he asked.

I let go of the dagger and he fell over. He lay with his eyes open. I watched as he sucked in his last gasping breath then he breathed no more. His dark, brooding eyes were glassy and hollow.

Before that day, I'd never killed anyone. But there I stood in a tiny room littered with the bodies of two lives I'd taken in one afternoon. My stomach roiled and lurched from the smell of blood, sweat and urine. I was nauseous too from the deed I'd done. Maybe it was right to kill Dughall. I had, after all, defended myself. But I still felt sick that I'd actually taken the life of another human being.

I looked over and Dughall's mother had fallen to her knees. She wept quietly.

I didn't know what to do or say. All I could think to say was, "I'm so sorry. Please forgive me. I didn't want to have to kill your son."

"You do not need forgiveness. You did not kill my son," she said. "My son died many years ago. This thing was a demon."

She crawled across the floor to his dead body and cradled him in her lap. "My poor, dear son." Fresh tears broke out in her eyes and fell to his face. The tears made his stony face glisten in the late morning sun.

I leaned against the wall and slid down. I'd willed myself not to puke, but I didn't have the strength left to fight off the tears that threatened to fall. I felt fat tears slide down my cheeks.

"Why do you weep?" she asked. "He was your enemy. He tried to kill you."

"I don't know. Maybe I'm crying because I should have hated him, but in the end, I felt sorry for him. Maybe it's because I've been away from home for so long. Maybe it's because I don't know if my dad and my friends are out of danger or not. And maybe I'm crying because it seems like I prepared for this forever and now it's over."

She didn't say a word but gave me a brief warm smile. As I sat in that tiny room filled with the stench of two dead men, I could see why Dughall became the madman that he was. His mother was more than just a mom. She had a warmth, compassion and knowing about her that was rare. I could see why he loved her so much. A love that fierce can drive a person to do all kinds of crazy things.

Before long we heard the sound of another person entering the small abode. "Dughall," she said.

It was, in fact, the young Dughall. He was about my age. The young Dughall didn't have the hard-chiseled brooding look about him yet. And his hair wasn't jet black but was instead flecked here and there with red highlights from the sun. His skin was bronzed by the southern Italian sun rather than alabaster white. His eyes were the same dark brown, but the eyes of the young Dughall were more playful and warm, less like two lumps of cold, unforgiving coal. If it wasn't for the fact that I knew how he turned out all grown up, I might have thought he was cute.

Without saying a word between us, Dughall's mother and I settled on a story about the two dead bodies that didn't include a future Dughall coming back in time. The young Dughall had no way of knowing that the large dead man was indeed himself from the future.

Using my sight to guide me, I helped them escape their bondage and set out on a new life. Who knows, maybe it will turn out different for Dughall. He hadn't, after all, had to endure watching his mother die.

I said my goodbyes and prepared myself to go back to the Netherworld. I wanted to spend some more time with the Goddess before I went back to my own time. I still had a lot of questions for her. And like she said, I could jump back into my time whenever and wherever I liked. So why not stay a while longer, really figure some things out?

I looked forward to getting answers and then a long rest. But you know, things don't always work out like you plan.

60 AFTERNOON AT THE HORROR MOVIES

When I was ready to go, I got myself to a quiet spot on top of a hill dotted with cypress and olive groves. It was a beautiful place, and as I closed my eyes to mediate on my return to the Netherworld, I thought maybe I'd like to go back there some time. *Maybe I'll come back and check up on the young Dughall. If he's going wonky again, I'll kick him back to right.*

I concentrated on my breath as Madame Wong taught me but soon doubt crept into my mind. *How do I return to the Netherworld?* After all, the portal I used to enter it was far away from there and in another time. I wasn't near any known vortex of energy.

But I knew that doubt would prevent me from returning not only to the Netherworld but also to my own time. I focused all that I had on the Goddess. My mind held the image of her shimmery blue-green ever changing face. I concentrated on how I felt when I was with her. Soon, the peaceful feeling I'd had in her presence filled me. *Match her frequency.*

When I felt like it was the right time, I opened my eyes. I blinked my eyes open and I was back in my kitchen where I'd first met Brighid. And she was there as well making chocolate chip pancakes.

"I thought you might be hungry," she said.

From somewhere deep inside came long, riotous laughter. The kind where you think you might pee yourself.

"Did I say something amusing, dear one?" she asked.

297

"No, you didn't. I'm sorry it's just this whole situation. I'm still not sure any of it has been real. I may be in my tree house at home right now, asleep after the slap to my head from Muriel, and I'm in a delirium dreaming this whole thing."

"Yes, that is possible I suppose. But you are here with me, whether a dream or not, so you may as well eat." I swung myself onto a stool at the counter and she placed a large plate of steaming pancakes in front of me.

They were just as I liked them. Smothered in butter and dripping with maple syrup.

After I wolfed down about a half-dozen pancakes, I was ready to ask some questions. I had so many questions still inside me. I wanted to ask why are we here? Where did we come from? Where will we go when we die? Is there a God? If so, where did he or she come from?

"Yes, you have many questions."

"I want to know everything."

"I know you do, young one. In time, in time. You already know the answers to many of your questions if you allow the answers to come. Others you will find in time."

"I don't feel like I know anything anymore."

"Good."

"Why is that good?"

"Not knowing is closer to allowing the truth than knowing all."

"So what you're telling me is that you're not going to answer my questions right now."

She didn't say anything but smiled at me.

"Okay, but I have to get an answer to this one last question. Am I now a High Priestess?"

"You have become a warrior and have learned some of the mysteries. But no, Miss Emily, you are not a High Priestess yet. Perhaps someday you will come back to the Netherworld and learn more of the mysteries of Akasha. Then, perhaps, you will become a High Priestess."

"I would like that." I took a big gulp of café au lait to wash down the starchy cakes.

"What now then?"

"You return to your own space and time."

"But when in time do I go?"

"Ah, that is an excellent question. I think that this will help you decide."

In an instant, we were no longer in my kitchen but in the misty, foggy, timeless nowhereness of the Netherworld. And before us was what looked like the portal that I came through the first time. But instead of being a hole, it was more like a movie screen. I could see vague images appear out of the mist.

"Watch Emily at the unfolding of critical events that have happened in your space-time while you have been in the Netherworld."

With a wave of her hand, the picture became clear. It was like I was watching the ghost of a movie. The images were there but with an ethereal shimmer. It was like they were there but not quite.

As ephemeral as they were, the images showed me what had happened. I saw Fanny and Jake go to Dublin. I saw my dad on the plane and then meet up with them. He was no longer Zombie Man.

It was hard to watch without feeling a ripping tide of emotion within me. I thought I was as good as dead to him. I had convinced myself that he didn't care enough to look for me.

I had been so wrong. I could see in the replay of a life that had happened without me that he did care. All he could think of was saving me. And he was helping out Jake and Fanny to boot. Go figure.

As the scenes played out, it felt like they were moving faster and faster until at last I saw my dad, Fanny and Jake holed up in a little building at CERN. Then Dughall's smirky face ran into the portal he created. After that, the images became downright frightening. The more I watched, the more it felt like I was watching it all unfold in real time.

Mere seconds after Dughall ran through the portal, the portal exploded, ripping apart the magnificent giant magnet that had created it. The whole collider was in danger of a cascade of explosions as those particles that were accelerating through it and colliding with each other were backed up in a large packet, much larger than was ever anticipated by the designers of the machine.

The portal that Dughall had created rapidly dissipated itself and became a nonfactor. The only thing to contend with there was the fire that raged due to the explosion. But up the stream from super magnet number two it was a different story.

As an observer of a story that had already unfolded, I watched in horror as the particle beams, now with many times more particles than expected, collided in collector number one. Conspiracy theorists had warned of the possibility of black holes being formed by the LHC, but the scientists had quickly dismissed any concerns. Scientists had said that because the collider smashed extremely small bits of particles, any black holes that formed would be extremely small and would burn themselves out before they became larger than a subatomic particle.

No worries.

Apparently not one of the scientists had anticipated the possibility that some idiot like Dughall would not only be able to successfully infiltrate their security, but use their machine to create an anomaly and the conditions ripe for the formation of a black hole worth worrying about. Time to worry.

I watched in horror as the hole became larger and larger, sucking in the matter of the machine that had created it. Up top, I saw my dad working feverishly with the other scientists to come up with a solution to stop it while Fanny and Jake sat in the corner of the main control room looking on worriedly.

"Come on guys, it's now or never. There has to be a way," he said. "This thing is getting away from us."

"We know Liam, but there just isn't enough energy left in this thing to pulse it again," offered one of the scientists.

"What else can we use, dammit?"

They were all silent for a moment. Even through the vacuum of space and time I swear I could hear their brain cells vibrating with thought.

"What about anti-matter?" offered a tentative voice.

"What? Who said that?" said Liam.

"Me Sir." It was none other than Mr. Ted Schaeffer.

"Anti-matter. Okay, thoughts. Could it work?"

"Well, theoretically it could work," said a scientist. "But the problem is, if we put together all the anti-matter ever produced on the whole planet and were able somehow to get it down there – which we couldn't do without dying because the temperatures down there are still -200° – well, it wouldn't be enough to do diddly."

That was the last anyone heard from Mr. Ted Schaeffer. He melded back into his computer station.

I watched in horror as my dad along with the other scientists worked feverishly for a solution. As they worked, the building began to shake. The electricity went out. There were sirens and bells and ascending alarms.

I could do nothing but stare and cry as I watched the entirety of CERN collapse into a black hole the size of a large town. The black void grew exponentially by the minute. My dad was lost. Fanny and Jake were lost.

No kid should see both of their parents die.

My tears flowed in a torrent down my face. *Lost. All is lost to me. I'm too late.*

"Why the tears, child?"

"I've lost them all," I hiccupped.

"Oh goodness dear one. Lost? You've lost nothing. Do you not remember anything that I have shown you? Anything that you have learned here?"

"You mean, I can stop this from happening?"

"Of course you can. Why else would I show this to you?"

"But hasn't it already happened? I mean, how can I change the future?"

"By changing the past, is that not obvious?

"Goddess, I'm so tired and confused. I don't know anymore what to do."

"You simply step into the stream dear, like you did before. Only this time, you will step into the stream at the place where you can stop these events from unfolding as you have seen."

"But how? Even if somehow I'm able to choose the right moment to step into the stream, how do I stop a runaway black hole?"

"You know the answers to these questions young one. Allow the stream to move through you. Become one with the web of all things. You are, after all, Akasha. Become one with Akasha.

"But before you go, remember well these words I now give you. The torc on your arm and the knowledge you have gained here are not to be used for folly. A Priestess of the Order of Brighid uses her skills and powers for the best interests of all sentient beings, not her own self-purpose. Do you understand?"

"Yes Goddess. It's like what Hindergog told me about the dagger that he gave me." I pulled the dagger from its sheath and held it in front of me.

"Yes, the same as the dagger. And know this too young one, that if you ever use the torc or your powers for your own selfish purpose, there will be consequences for you dear Emily."

I nodded my understanding. "Good, now it is time for you to fulfill your purpose."

As if she had reached into my brain itself, I saw flash before my mind's eye a vision from my memory of the time I was with Madame Wong and first saw the Web of All Things. It was like I was in that time and place again. The Netherworld and the human world, all that I had known or would know, melted away.

Once again I was in the loving bosom of the Web. I was enveloped in the vibrating harmonies of countless strings of the Great Web, all with their own distinct note yet all in harmony with the others.

It was no memory. It was happening again.

I felt myself inexorably drawn a certain way. I don't know even now what guided me or why I went the direction I did in the infinite web.

But direction and guidance drew me to one particular shining orb. One particular note. One particular voice in an endless sea of voices.

It was like touching without touch. Melding together of two entities. In that moment, at that time, I knew once and for all where my mother was.

She wasn't in the kitchen making pancakes. She wasn't in her studio painting. She wasn't in the garden planting geraniums. She wasn't even in a coffin underground.

She was there, in the web. She had been there all along.

I can't describe in words the feeling that I felt in that moment. Joy. Jubilation. Neither one comes close. To know, really know, without any doubt of mind, body or soul. To have, in that moment, not one doubt or fear about anything. To know that I am eternal and that she is eternal and that we are connected always and forever. I wanted nothing more than to stay there feeling that way.

Suddenly the utter bliss of knowingness was interrupted by what felt like a terrible ripping. I heard a large whooshing sound and my innards felt like they would be ripped apart.

Just when I thought I couldn't take the pain anymore, I fell with a thud onto the floor of command central at CERN. It was as if the cosmos upchucked me right where and when I was supposed to be.

"Emily!" said a familiar voice.

"Dad?"

My eyes were still adjusting to the harsh light of the fluorescent modern world. I had become accustomed to the misty fog of the Netherworld. But my skin still had all its senses about it, and I could feel all about me the warm embrace of my dad's big arms. They were real. Solid and real. This was no hologram or ghost image of the past.

"Dad," I said. A river of tears flowed.

"Em," he said. I felt drops from his eyes rain down on top of my head. After a few minutes, he took me by the shoulders looked me in the eyes and said, "Don't ever leave me again!"

"I won't, Dad. At least not until I go to college."

He wasn't a zombie anymore. I had my dad back, at least for now.

I hadn't realized that Jake and Fanny were there too until I felt a tight squeeze around my middle.

"Fanny!"

"It is so good to see you, Em. Oh my gosh, look at your arms girl." Fanny felt my arm muscles. "What were you doing in that place, working out?"

"Something like that," I chuckled.

Jake stood behind Fanny, smiling wide, but there was a tear in his eye. I looked at him, and he looked at me and somehow it felt good but awkward. I'd never felt that way around Jake before. I wondered if he felt it too.

"I'm so glad you're back." He came toward me and Fanny stepped aside and so Jake could hug me. The hug felt awkward too.

"Glad you guys made it back from the Netherworld okay too," I said. Jake and I ended our strange embrace. They looked at me like I'd sprouted a second head.

"What are you talking about? We never went there," said Fanny.

"So when I was rescuing you guys from the Ninjas, you weren't really there." I said it more to myself than anyone else. Their look of puzzlement answered my question. I didn't have time to tell them all about it just then so I said, "It's a long story. I'll tell you about it later."

If Jake wasn't really there, then he didn't know about the electrical feeling that happened when we'd touched hands. *If he doesn't remember us touching hands, then why is he acting all weird?*

That was a puzzle for another day.

61 EMILY MEETS A BLACK HOLE

"Look kiddo, we all want to catch up with each other and Emily I'm dying to hear about all you've seen and been through, but we've got a bit of a situation going on here."

"I know all about it, Dad. That's why I came."

"I don't want you anywhere near here. This thing is growing more unstable by the minute. Sensors and cameras, the ones left anyway, show that it's growing untold powers of ten by the second. We don't have much time, and I want you out of here before this thing, well ... "

"Dad, I know exactly what's going on and what will happen. That's why I'm here now. I can fix this."

"I know that you've been to another dimension – man, I still can't get my head around that. But this is a job for scientists, not mystics."

"It's a job for a Priestess of the Order of Brighid." I unsheathed and pulled out the bejeweled dagger that Hindergog had given me.

"What's that?"

"A gift."

"It's beautiful kiddo, but I don't think that little dagger's going to stop a runaway anomaly."

"This isn't just a dagger. I don't have time to explain now. But this dagger can be anything I want it to be. It can become whatever I ask it to become."

"I'm not even going to argue with you right now about how that's impossible wishful thinking."

"Okay, so don't argue. Just tell me this. That guy over there. Ted Schaeffer. He had an idea about anti-matter."

My dad looked over and found Ted Schaeffer with his head buried in his computer monitor, his fingers once again feverishly entering code like his life depended on it. For a second time, it did.

"Yes, he offered that."

"Well, would it work? I mean if you had enough of the stuff and if someone could get down there and plant the anti-matter in the right way, would it shut the anomaly down?"

"Well, theoretically it could work."

"I don't want could, Dad. I gotta know for sure. Will it work?"

He looked me deep in the eyes as his human computer ran calculations. After about a minute he said, "Yes. If we had enough anti-matter, and it was delivered in the right way, it would destroy the anomaly."

"Okay then. All I need to know is how much and how to deliver it, and we're good to go."

"Wait, you're not thinking of going down there, are you?"

"Of course. You're not thinking I'm just going to stand here with my thumb up my butt and watch as the whole world gets sucked into a black hole, do you?"

"I'm going to ignore your smart tone due to the black hole underneath our feet threatening our planet, but are you crazy? I can't let you go down there. It's instant death."

"I know that you find all this hard to believe. Right now you may think that you're in bed having a terrible dream and that you'll wake up tomorrow, and your neat world full of numbers and equations will be the same as it was before any of this started. But you have to trust me on this one. I have the ability to do this. I'll be fine, Dad."

The look on his face told me that he didn't want to believe me. He wanted to order me to stay. But the look of defeat in his eyes showed that he wouldn't stand in my way.

"Okay then, all I need now from you and your number cruncher geek squad there is a number. Tell me how much anti-matter I need and how to deliver it. And let's get that pronto."

My dad mustered one more look of 'please don't do this' only to be met with my look of 'yeah, right'! Then he was off to huddle with the other Coca Cola-swilling Wile-Coyote-Genius types while they put their brains together to find the answer.

While they ran equations, I watched the video from the remote camera playing the Dughall entering the portal scene over and over again. Out of the corner of my eye I thought I saw something. It looked like someone flying. I rubbed my eyes and looked behind me, but all I saw then were nerds running around like blind rats trying to find a way to stop what Dughall had created.

Within minutes, Dad and the Geek Club gathered around me and delivered the information.

"How are you going to do it?" asked the head scientist dude. He no longer looking strong and in charge but defeated and tired.

"If I told you, you wouldn't believe me. Okay, stand back boys," I said. I tried my best to tune them out and create a sphere of positive energy around me. I closed my eyes and got myself into a deep, standing meditation. The training with Madame Wong was fresh in my mind and helped me get into the state of being that I needed to be in. The alarms, the buzz of the people, the smell of their bodies (long overdue for a bath), the hum of the human world. I left all of it behind.

Through the power of only my breath and the strength of the focus of my mind, I created the resonant frequency with Akasha that Dughall used the LHC to create. Only my resonance didn't create a path of destruction in its wake.

I created a phase shift through space-time the old school way, the way it had been done for millennia and before the creation of particle accelerators. In the control room, they saw my body solid and real. Then, right before their eyes, I started to fade in and out then poof! I was gone. That's what *they* experienced.

For me, it was all silence and the beautiful background hum of the universal resonant frequency of Akasha. I was able to tune my receiver to that station and let it take me wherever and whenever I wanted to be.

I felt an intensely cold draft about me and opened my eyes. There it was. The black hole.

Immediately I envisioned a force field around me. I created a protective cushion of space between myself and the frigid air of the collider.

You may think that you've seen darkness before. The inky blackness of a moonless night sky. Let me tell you, you know nothing of darkness until you've seen a black hole.

It was strangely beautiful. A part of me wanted to linger and watch it. At the very center it was complete and utter dark. No flicker or spark of light in any way. A black so complete that you could almost feel a cold breath coming from it.

All around the center, there was a swirling vortex of matter being sucked in. Colors whirled as objects were pulled apart by the intense gravity of the center, leaving only remnants we perceive as color. The swirling vortex was hypnotic, and for a moment, I felt like I wanted to join it.

But I swear I heard a voice from somewhere outside of me whisper, "The anti-matter." That whisper jerked me back to reality.

The swirling vortex grew by leaps and bounds each second. I didn't have much time before it swallowed me too.

I unsheathed my dagger and commanded it to become the exact quantity of anti-matter the good gentlemen scientists had instructed. Before my eyes, the knife transformed from a beautiful jeweled dagger to a large round container pulsing with electromagnetic energy. It became a Penning trap full of anti-matter.

Doing exactly as Dad had told me, I commanded the trap of anti-matter to enter the black hole. I hoisted it with all my strength down the corridor. I don't have much of an arm, but I guess having the forces of nature on your side helps. The canister flew a straight and true trajectory, end over end, with impressive velocity right into the heart of the black hole.

I watched the black hold suck in the Penning trap. What used to be my gift from Hindergog was lost in the bottomless blackness. Nothing happened. I watched and waited. I don't think I breathed at all. Seconds ticked by as the blackness grew larger and larger and threatened to take me with it.

It didn't work!

I knew that I had to get out of there before I was pulled apart, molecule-by-molecule, by the intense gravity of the anomaly of darkness. But I stood motionless and racked my brain, trying to think of something else I could try. I searched the recesses of my brain for some kernel of wisdom that Madame Wong or the Goddess had given me that I could use to save my world.

As I stood thinking, there was a huge explosion. It was like all the TNT from every Fourth of July fireworks display there ever was went off at the same time.

Safely inside my protective bubble of positive energy, I saw fire whiz by me followed by flying metal and other shrapnel. And at the very heart of it, what was once a core of utter blackness there was a tremendous sphere of glowing light.

At first it was the size of a football field, but it quickly began to dwindle. Soon it was no smaller than a car. It was a small star, birthed before my eyes. What less than a few minutes before had been a swirling vortex of obsidian had become a ball of intense light, no larger than a softball. Perfect light from perfect dark.

Second by second it grew smaller and smaller until finally, in a blink, it disappeared. My small star was gone forever. Where there had once been a black hole, and then an infant star, there was only rubble, debris and the remnants of the most expensive machine ever built by man.

But there was also a faint glimmer amongst the rubble. Something shiny was in that pile of debris. I hovered myself in my protective bubble closer to see what it was.

I used my telekinesis to free the glinting object from the wreckage and I hovered it to me. I held out my hand and the jeweled dagger that Hindergog had given me flew into my outstretched palm. It was tarnished and covered in black soot, but it was intact. You'd never know it had been a container full of anti-matter that just collided with a black hole. I sheathed the dagger and thanked it for a job well done.

Left in the wake of the explosion was a total disaster. The LHC, the work of so many people and so many billions of Euros was gone. Totally gone.

There was a gigantic hole a mile underground full of rubble and ruin, but up top you would never know. Anyone who wasn't there to see it would never believe it. In fact, the vast majority of people would probably never know any of it had happened.

CERN would make up a plausible story about overheating or some other mechanical failure explanation for the complete and total destruction of the most expensive and grand machine ever built by humans. But Jake, Fanny, my Dad and I know the truth.

62 CLICK YOUR HEELS THREE TIMES

"You won't find faith or hope down a telescope,
You won't find heart and soul in the stars,
You can break everything down to chemicals,
But you can't explain a love like ours.
It's the way we feel, yeah, this is real."

From "Science & Faith," The Script (Daniel
O'Donoghue and Mark Sheehan) ©2010

The sun shone through a few puffy clouds as I walked up the sidewalk to a house I had known my whole life. No, that's not quite true. I had lived in the place my whole life, but it wasn't always the same house.

Once it was filled with colorful paintings of flowers and my mom's voice singing and humming. For a while it was a building overflowing with a dull, grey dread.

It is once again a house filled with color and life. But it's not the same house as when my mom was alive. That house is gone, but I now know how to find it if I want. Thing is, these days I don't want to go looking for it anymore.

It would be great to report that after we got back from Europe they stopped calling me 'Freak Girl' and that I became popular and adored. That didn't happen. But I stopped caring about what Greta and her cronies thought. I'd lived through tutelage with Madame Wong and faced down a black hole. Somehow Greta's nasty comments didn't seem to matter after that.

Greta's still here but Muriel is gone. By the time we got back she had packed up her stuff and left. I guess it was okay to be the bully, but when push came to shove, she wasn't willing to hang around if it meant she'd have someone shoving back.

As I walked across the porch today, I didn't care that the boards squeaked. There wasn't any dread or fear at all as I put my hand on the doorknob and turned it.

I walked down the familiar hallway and toward the smell of pancakes, coffee and bacon. I could hear their voices bantering.

"More chocolate chip pancakes?" my dad asked as he flipped another batch.

"I'll take more," said Fanny.

"Figures piggy. You're going to be fat as a house," teased Jake.

"Shut it nub before I take you down."

"Come on guys, give it a rest will you? Can't we enjoy a pleasant Sunday morning together without your bickering?" asked Dad.

"We are enjoying," said Jake.

"Yeah, this is us enjoying," added Fanny. She shoved about three normal forkfuls into her mouth at once.

Dad smiled wide as he worked the pancakes on the griddle. His smile widened as he looked up and saw me standing in the doorway.

"Oh hey, Emily's back with the juice. Thanks, Em," he said with a wink.

"No prob Dad." I handed him the juice. I threw a copy of the *Weekly World News* down on the counter of the breakfast bar in front of Jake and Fanny.

"What's this?" asked Jake.

"I thought you'd all get a kick out of the cover story. Check out the photo on the front. Look like anyone we know?"

Jake and Fanny both stared at the front page, and I soon saw their eyes about to bug out of their heads as they recognized the woman on the cover.

"Holy chiz!" said Fanny.

"I can't believe it," said Jake.

"What?" My dad reached for the paper.

His turn for eyes buggin'. There on the front cover of the *Weekly World News* was a wild-eyed photo of our beloved Aunt Muriel. The headline above the picture read, 'Woman Attacked by Niece Possessed by an Alien'.

My dad threw the paper across the counter, laughed and went back to flipping pancakes. "Oops, these are a bit burnt."

"That's okay, I'll eat them anyway," said Fanny as she held out her plate for more.

"Dad, that's all you're going to say? 'Oops, these are a bit burnt.'"

"What should I say? My sister is crazy. I just wish I had been here – really here – to see it sooner. I'm so sorry," he said as he hugged me.

"I know, Dad. You don't need to keep apologizing." I hugged him back. "Okay, who needs more coffee?" I hovered the coffee pot over to where Jake and Fanny sat.

"Come on, use your hands," said Jake. "You know it freaks me out when you hover things."

"It only freaks you out because you can't do it," I quipped. I ordered the pot to give Jake more coffee.

"I'll take some more." Fanny held out her cup for more.

"Oh no, no more for you." I set the pot back down. None of us wanted to see Fanny on mega-caffeine.

A new typical Sunday with family. Click your heels three times.

Tomorrow is Monday, and I'll leave this house again. I'll walk out the door and try to find a way to be me and yet fit in; be Emily but a part of everything else too. And at the end of the day I'll come home.

ACKNOWLEDGEMENTS

In the beginning, there was just a seed of thought, a vision of a golden torc hovering over rolling green hills. That dream would never have become <u>Emily's House</u> without the love and support of others.

Thank you to Ellen Schneider for creating the Feng Shui Networking Group, and thank you to Ellen for your support in this endeavor. Thank you also to the lovely ladies of the Feng Shui group for your encouragement. None of you laughed when I said I wanted to write novels instead of practice law. I thank you for that.

My deepest gratitude to Deborah. Your support of my dream is appreciated more than you can know.

Thank you Colleen for slugging through an early version. You rock girl! A special thanks to Bridget Magee, one of my biggest cheerleaders. You believed in my project and me when I didn't believe in myself.

Thank you to Claudia McKinney at Phatpuppy Art for the fantastic cover art; to Cheryl Perez at You're Published for cover design; to Jason G. Anderson for formatting for all digital platforms; and to Gary Smailes at BubbleCow for editing.

Thank you to Jill Robinson for creating *Emily's Theme,* original music for the book trailer. Your talent blows me away. Thank you. Thank you to Mark Corneliussen of for your enthusiasm and creativity in creating the book trailer for <u>Emily's House</u>.

Thank you to Sarah for sharing your mom with Emily for half of your life! You are my muse and constant source of inspiration. Thank you for listening to my stories and encouraging me to write them down.

Last but not least, thank you to JRF. It has been said that, 'with love, all things are possible'. You kicked me in the pants and said 'write it already'. I did, and I couldn't have done it without you. Thank you.

ABOUT THE AUTHOR

Natalie is the author of The Akasha Chronicles, a young adult paranormal fantasy trilogy. She was born and raised in Ohio and spent her formative years living on a working farm. Though she practiced law for almost twenty years, she is now retired from the practice of law and spends her days writing stories for young readers.

Natalie finds creative energy and inspiration in the high desert environment surrounding her home in Arizona where she lives with her husband, young daughter, geriatric dog and two young cats. When Natalie isn't writing, eating chocolate or playing with cats, she enjoys traveling, reading, meeting readers at book fairs, chatting on social media, and searching for the best iced coffee in town.

You can connect with Natalie here:

Twitter: @NatalieWright_
Facebook: www.Facebook.com/NatalieWright.Author
Blog: http://www.NatalieWrightsYA.blogspot.com
Website: www.NatalieWright.net
YouTube: http://www.youtube.com/user/WritesKidsBooks
Google +: https://plus.google.com/u/0/101662949356723296903/posts
Goodreads: http://www.goodreads.com/author/show/468945.Natalie_Wright
Pinterest: http://pinterest.com/natwrites/
Wattpad: http://www.wattpad.com/user/NatalieWright_